Trusting Tristan

By
Ceci Giltenan

Trusting Tristan

By
Ceci Giltenan

Copyright 2017 by Lexi Hawthorne/Ceci Giltenan
www.duncurra.com

Cover Design: Duncurra LLC

ISBN: 978-1-949407-02-0

Produced in the USA

Dedication

To my husband, even though words aren't necessary, here they
are:
I love you truly, madly, deeply.

Chapter 1

Cassandra Hastings had grown to love Hidden Gem, the private BDSM club, tucked inconspicuously within Island Treasures, an adults-only resort near St. Petersburg. It was where she'd been introduced to Dominance and submission and had met the club owner, Tristan Cabot. He'd been the one to teach her about the lifestyle, and she wore his training collar. It was intended to be temporary, just until she was experienced enough to handle herself with different Doms in the club. That had been over six months ago. She hadn't asked to remove the training collar. She had believed he would either tell her when he thought she was ready, or discuss a different level of relationship. And, to her delight, they had just begun to do the latter.

In many ways, she felt closer to and more comfortable with him than she had anyone else in her life. So she knew something was wrong the minute Tristan entered the club and strode towards her through the crowd, anger practically rolling off him in waves. She'd never seen him like this.

She'd been waiting for him at the bar, chatting with a friend, an older sub named Tina, and a brief look of concern flashed across Tina's face too.

Tristan stopped in front of them. "Good evening, Cassandra, Tina."

A well-trained and polite sub, Tina lowered her gaze and answered, "Good evening, Master Tristan."

His tone and demeanor drew the attention of other club members. While Cassie was concerned about what had him so upset, she too greeted him as a good submissive should. She lowered her gaze, "Good evening, Sir."

"Tina, please excuse us."

"Yes, Master Tristan." She nodded and walked away, casting a concerned glance at Cassie as she left.

"You have put me in a very bad position, Cassandra."

What? Cassandra was instantly confused. "I'm sorry, Sir. What have I done? Does this have something to do with the condo?"

"No, Cassandra. You lied to me about your interest in this club and have breached confidentiality."

She looked up, completely shocked and unable to school her features. "Excuse me, Sir? I have never uttered a word to anyone about this club."

"You are the editor of a series of novels set in a BDSM club, correct?"

"No. I mean, not yet. I've been contracted to edit such a series."

"Cassandra, how could you do this? How could you betray everyone here like that?"

Betray everyone? How could simply editing a book betray anyone? "I don't understand why you are so angry or why any of this is relevant. I signed a confidentiality agreement with the club. I have not broken that agreement and I never, ever would." The fact that he thought she might nearly shattered her.

"For the moment perhaps, but that is only a technicality. You weren't honest. Trust is the single most important aspect of a D/s relationship, but you hid something from me. And in doing so, you misled everyone here."

"Sir, I told you in our first meeting that I edit books that contain BDSM elements. I told you that those books were part of the reason I became interested in the lifestyle. But I was interested in the lifestyle for myself, Sir. It had nothing to do with my professional life. I did not hide anything from you."

"No? I'll ask you again. Are you, or are you not, the editor for a series of books about a BDSM club?"

"I am, but—"

"There is no but. You are the editor for the series. And did you, or did you not, disclose that to me?"

"There is nothing to disclose."

"Damn it, Cassandra, answer the question. Specifically, did you disclose that you edit books about a BDSM club?"

She realized that he was not prepared to listen to, or accept her explanation. "No."

He glared at her as only an angry Dom can. After several long moments he squared his shoulders. "Your betrayal cannot go unpunished."

"I haven't betrayed anyone."

"You betrayed me by not telling me about your professional interest in being here."

She wanted to say that her interest in the club had never been a professional one, but strictly speaking, that wasn't true. She had been curious about the lifestyle for some time before she came to Hidden Gem. But the thing that finally pushed her to explore was accepting the assignment to edit Scarlett Turner's new series, the setting for which was a BDSM club in Philadelphia.

She made one more attempt to explain. "That's not the way I see it. Let me explain."

"The 'whys' don't matter, and I don't care whether you consider dishonesty a betrayal of trust or not. You are new to this community; you aren't the owner of this club with an obligation to protect the privacy of its members, and you aren't the Dominant in this relationship."

She stood silently. Clearly, nothing she could say would change what he believed.

He stared at her for several long moments. "So this is what you will do. You will submit to a *public* punishment of my choosing, willingly, here and now. Or you will leave and never return."

Public punishment. Cassie hated public punishment. She hated punishment period. Doing a scene was one thing—punishment, especially in front of others, was entirely different. For that reason, she was a very obedient sub and being punished publicly was a soft limit for her. He knew that and this was a negotiation. She could accept it in this situation or leave.

Tristan continued. "If you choose to accept the punishment and reconfirm that you will never disclose anything that occurs within these walls, your slate is wiped clean. If you choose to leave, you will never be welcome back here. Additionally, should there ever be any question that you violated your confidentiality agreement, I will pursue legal action against you."

This entire situation was ridiculous. She was honest to a fault. She would never betray a trust and certainly never reveal confidential information. She thought Tristan knew her better than that, and she was appalled that he'd even suggested it. In that moment she was so crushed and angry she could barely speak. Trust had been broken today, but she wasn't the betrayer. He had publicly called her out. Maybe she should have told him about the project specifically. Maybe then she would have had the opportunity to explain why it wasn't a conflict without the entire club watching and believing that she would betray them. But there was no going back now. In that moment her decision was made. Whatever she thought she had discovered here had just been destroyed. She would leave and never return, but she would do it on *her terms* not his.

"Yes, Master Tristan."

His expression was unreadable. "Very well. If you consent, you will go to that spanking bench," he motioned to one on a raised platform in a highly visible area of the main room, often used for demonstrations, "and remove all of your clothes."

Completely naked? Another thing she didn't like and thus part of the public punishment.

"I will secure you to the bench and place a vibrator against your clit."

She wondered why he'd do that. If she was also experiencing pleasure, she had a higher tolerance for pain.

"I will administer ten strokes with a cane."

Maybe *that* was the reason for the vibrator. A cane, when used for punishment, hurt a lot and was another soft limit.

"I will touch you with my hands in any way I see fit during the punishment. You will count the strokes and when we are done, you will come."

Ah, now she understood. She would be completely exposed in every way—allowed to keep nothing private. Ten strokes of the cane was a drop in the bucket compared to the rest. This was clearly a punishment intended to push her to the absolute edge of her limits.

"Do you understand?"

"Yes, Sir."

"Do you consent to this punishment? Even though it includes several things on your list of soft limits?"

"Yes, Sir, I consent."

"As always, you can use your safewords at any time. The punishment will stop and you can leave."

"I understand, Sir."

"Then go to the bench, remove your clothing and kneel beside it until I am ready."

"Yes, Sir."

She walked calmly to the bench. A small crowd was already beginning to gather. *You can do this, Cassie.* She always preferred wearing sexy, feminine outfits in the club, and tonight had been no different. She wore an absolutely sheer, cream-colored lace tunic. It was meant to be worn over something else, but all she had on underneath was a beautiful dark pink lace bra and matching thong. It didn't conceal much, but it made her feel less exposed somehow. For a moment, she hesitated to remove it. *Just leave, Cassie. It's what you will do in the end anyway.*

No. She had done nothing wrong and she wouldn't leave with everyone in the club thinking she had betrayed them. *Strip, Cassie, it's just lace.* She pulled it over her head, folded it neatly and placed it on the floor beside the bench. The bra and thong were even harder to remove with an audience. *Do this to please your Dom, Cassie.* No, that argument wouldn't work tonight. This wasn't about anyone's pleasure. It was punishment, pure and simple. *All right, then do it so you can leave with your sense of honor intact.*

Her bra came next. Perhaps the hardest thing to remove was her thong. It was just a little lace and elastic, but it was the last bit of her shield. Steeling herself, she hooked her thumbs in the elastic at her hips, sliding it down and stepping out of it. After placing her bra and thong on top of the lace tunic, she knelt beside the bench, head down, hands behind her back and knees slightly spread, as she had been taught.

Normally, kneeling and waiting for Tristan was calming and allowed her to center herself. Today it wasn't.

She stayed in that position for upwards of five minutes before he arrived. He adjusted the bench before stepping in front of her.

"Except for counting, you will not speak until your punishment is over. Stand up."

She obeyed.

"Position yourself on the bench."

This bench had two levels. Two padded surfaces on which to kneel that could be adjusted wider to increase the spread of the legs. And a higher padded surface to support the upper body. It could be tilted downwards, effectively raising one's ass in the air. He had attached a vibrator to an adjustable bracket.

She climbed onto the bench. He fastened restraints around her ankles, knees, waist, shoulders, elbows and wrists. Then he adjusted the bench, spreading her legs wider, lowering her torso and positioning the vibrator against her clit.

He turned the vibrator on low. The gentle buzz was pleasantly stimulating. Then he ran his hands lightly over her body. The soft caress felt very good and allowed her to relax. They had played this way often, and she enjoyed it. Maybe this wouldn't be so bad. He slid his hands down her back to her ass. He took a cheek in each hand, giving them a firm massage.

Then, to her horror, he spread her cheeks apart as if displaying her and said, "Every inch of you is beautiful even if you are shy about sharing it."

Murmurs from the crowd around them reminded her that she was completely exposed in the middle of the club, surrounded by onlookers. Attempting to block everything out, she closed her eyes.

He gave her backside a little swat. "No, you don't. You will not hide anything from us. Not even your lovely eyes."

He increased the speed of the vibrator before sliding a long finger into her, fucking her with it for a few strokes before adding a second finger, filling her. "You like this part, don't you little bird? You are very wet." He pulled his fingers out. "See how wet she is?"

Again the voices around her made her hyper aware of just how intimately exposed she was. She couldn't even close her eyes. *But you can keep your mouth closed.* And she vowed she would.

He stepped away from her. "Well, as pleasant as this is, you have a punishment coming."

He moved closer to her again, touching her lightly with the cane this time. He let it slide down her back to her buttocks and down the backs of her thighs. He tapped it lightly several times across the fleshiest part of her ass. Whack. He brought it down sharply in the same spot.

She bit her lips to keep from crying out.

"Count," he ordered.

"One."

He caressed her gently again with the cane before selecting another spot. Again, he tapped the cane lightly several times before delivering a second hard stroke.

She clenched her teeth. "Two."

He repeated that pattern two more times, landing on a different spot each time.

After she said, "Four," he stepped closer and rubbed her abused backside.

It eased the sting a little but to her dismay, he increased the speed of the vibrator then finger-fucked her again. This time he brought her much closer to orgasm before stepping away and giving her one hard stroke of the cane across the fleshy part of her ass, exactly where he had delivered the first blow.

Her eyes watered and she sucked in a raspy breath. "Five."

Again he caressed her with the cane and tapped several times on a spot before striking it hard.

Six, seven and eight landed on her upper thighs. The pleasure of the insistent buzzing against her clit interspersed with the pain caused by the cane was disorienting. She trembled and tears ran down her face, but she remained silent. Her voice was hers alone and she would hold onto it.

After eight, he stopped again to rub her ass and thighs. "Good girl. You are amazing."

If they had been playing, those words would have filled her heart. But this wasn't play and she didn't want to hear them. She wanted it to be over.

His talented fingers brought her to the edge of orgasm again before he gave her the last two strokes, both hard, and both directly on the crease between her thighs and her ass.

The last one nearly took her breath away. "Ten." *It's over.*

But it wasn't. Tristan massaged her tender backside again, increased the vibrator speed to its highest setting. Then he fucked her with two fingers.

The residual sting left by the cane, the intense sensation caused by the vibrator, and his fingers filling her had her hovering on the edge of orgasm. A little part of her didn't want to give in and she fought it.

Then his low, sexy voice penetrated the fog of bliss. "Come for me now, little bird."

She was powerless to stop it. Her orgasm ripped through her in wave after wave of ecstasy. But she didn't utter a sound. That gave her a sense of power that she had never experienced.

Tristan immediately moved the vibrator away from her sensitive clit. "That was beautiful, little bird. I'm proud of you."

Sounds of approval came from all around her.

Tristan removed the straps holding her to the bench and helped her stand, before putting his arms around her.

Cassie accepted his comfort for a moment as she steadied herself.

"That was absolutely magnificent," he whispered. "When I said don't speak, I didn't expect you to be completely silent." He kissed the top of her head.

She nodded, stepped backwards out of his embrace and swiped at the tears on her cheeks. She didn't want kisses and kind words now. She wanted to go home.

Every piece of equipment in the club had a container of disinfectant wipes nearby. She pulled several out and began wiping down the bench.

Tristan touched her arm. "You don't need to do that, Cassandra. One of the subs on duty will. Come with me and we'll talk."

She pulled away from him. "I do need to do it, Sir."

Tristan frowned but let her finish. "It's done now, little bird. Come with me."

She shook her head and moved to where her clothes still lay neatly folded. She had her thong on and was fastening her bra before he stepped in and picked up the lace tunic.

"I didn't tell you to dress, Cassie."

"No, Sir, you didn't. But it has been a long day and a very long week. I need to go home and get some rest." She strove to sound unaffected.

He put his hand around her waist, guiding her towards one of the more private areas provided for aftercare. "Not before we talk."

Again, she pulled away from him. It took supreme effort to remain calm. She had ceased to be submissive the moment she decided to accept the punishment. However, she respected the space they were in and the rules that applied. She would not embarrass herself or him by doing anything less. Her voice was soft and controlled. "Perhaps we do need to talk, but not now. Not in here. May I please have my dress, Sir?"

"No. Cassandra, this isn't the way it works as long as you are wearing that collar. Come with me now."

Chapter 2

Eight months earlier

Cassie stared at her computer screen after reading a message from Scarlett Turner.

> Why don't you just give it a try? I know you're interested and you might really like it. One thing's for sure—you'll never be able to understand it if you don't see what it's all about.

Scarlett was an author whose books Cassie had been editing for the last three months. Currently, she was working on the third in what was to be a seven book series loosely inspired by the musical Seven Brides for Seven Brothers, *Seven Subs for Seven Saunders*. The Saunders were all brothers or cousins, they all lived on the family ranch, and each of them embraced the BDSM lifestyle to some degree.

However, the message from Scarlett wasn't about any of her books. At least, not specifically. For several weeks now, Cassie had asked Scarlett a lot of questions about the lifestyle. Her questions had ostensibly been to understand it all better so she could edit more effectively. But with this one message, Scarlett had cut through Cassie's façade.

Something about the lifestyle appealed to Cassie. She wasn't sure what it was or why it intrigued her so, but when she read Scarlett's stories, they awakened a longing she'd never felt before.

Maybe it was just the insanely hot sex. Cassie had dated off and on through college and she wasn't a virgin, but she had never experienced anything remotely close to what Scarlett described in her books. And she hadn't had sex at all in the last two years. *That's what I get for living in God's waiting room.*

Three years ago, right after she completed college she returned to the Tampa area to take care of her only living relative, her grandmother, who had rapidly advancing Alzheimer's disease. She tried to date some that first year, but she didn't have friends in the area and meeting men her own age wasn't terribly easy. She did finally meet someone she liked through an online dating service. But before they could develop much of a relationship, her grandmother's condition deteriorated to the point that leaving her for even short periods became impossible. Even with professional, live-in caregivers, her grandmother often became extremely agitated when Cassie wasn't there. It sometimes took hours to calm her down afterwards. Stewart was a nice guy, but eventually things with her grandma just became too difficult.

It had been just over a year since her grandmother had passed away. After a few months Cassie had tried to start dating again, but it was no easier than it had been before. She didn't have the challenges posed by caring for an elderly grandmother, but meeting people was no less difficult. She had inherited her grandmother's estate and still lived in her house. Her neighbors were mostly retired couples.

Oh, and there was a new app that had become popular. Meeting men came down to swiping left or swiping right and Cassie had tried it, but so far hadn't met anyone she actually wanted to make a date with in person.

Now she read the words over and over again. *Why don't you just give it a try?*

"Because I don't have the first clue about how to try it," she said to the screen.

> Scarlett, you make it sound so simple. It isn't exactly like trying on a pair of shoes. I can't just go down to the BDSM store and order up a Dom in my size.

Cassie chuckled at the mental image that conjured.

No, you can't *order up a Dom in your size*. But you could tap into the local BDSM community and go to some public events. At the very least you might meet a few nice people.

Cassie laughed.

Tap into the local BDSM community? You clearly have mistaken me for someone else. I'm a hopeless introvert. I could no more just show up alone at a public BDSM community event than I could sunbathe naked in my front yard.

Scarlett's reply came almost immediately.

Well of course you wouldn't sunbathe in the nude in your front yard—it's illegal in most places and I suspect you are a rigid rule-follower. But wouldn't you sunbathe nude if you could?

Cassie snorted. "Uh, no."

I don't really see myself sunbathing nude anywhere.

Given all the kinky things Scarlett's characters did, her answer didn't surprise Cassie.

You're kidding right? Being nude on the beach or in the water is one of life's great thrills. I can't imagine passing up the opportunity. You really wouldn't go to a nude beach? Not even with a bunch of your friends?

Cassie thought about it. Would she? *Not likely.*

Maybe, but the question is purely hypothetical because I have no such friends.

Wow that sounded pathetic. But Scarlett responded before Cassie could clarify.

> No offence, Cassie, but how old are you and why don't you have any friends?

Good questions.

> I am twenty-six and I don't have friends in the Tampa area because, even though this was technically my home from about the age of seven, I went away for high school and college. Then after college, I needed to take care of my grandmother. It was a twenty-four/seven job for the last year of her life. I still live in her house and most of my neighbors are retired.

Cassie had added "I don't get out much" to the end of that message but then deleted it. She sounded more and more pathetic as this conversation went on.

> You live in Tampa, Florida?

Cassie frowned.

> Well, just north of Tampa, yes. Haven't I told you that before?

Scarlett answered.

> I knew you lived in Florida, but I didn't know you lived near Tampa. One of the best BDSM clubs on the east coast, outside of New York, is somewhere near St. Petersburg. Its existence is well known, but everything else about it is kept very hush-hush. Even its location is a secret. You have to know someone in it or have some other connection to be considered for membership.

> I have a friend from college who is also an author. She writes under the name Mona Moore. As it turns out, her virtual assistant is a member of the club. If

the only thing holding you back is not knowing
anyone in the community, I'm sure I could get you
her contact information. She'll tell you anything you
want to know about the lifestyle. Maybe she could
even arrange a visit to the club for you.

Visit a BDSM club? Cassie typed "No, thank you", but
deleted it before she hit send. All Scarlett was offering to do
was introduce her to a friend. That was one tiny step towards
not becoming a reclusive cat-lady. It didn't have to be anything
more than that.

Okay. I'd like that. Just meeting someone closer to
my own age would be nice.

Scarlett sent her a winky face emoji.

How do you know she's not eighty?

Cassie laughed.

I don't. I just assumed that if she was a "virtual"
anything she'd have to be under forty.

Scarlett sent her a laughing emoji.

Well that's probably a safe assumption, but I've
never met her so I can't say for sure. On the other
hand, if she is eighty, she's probably a pretty hip
eighty if she plays regularly in a BDSM club. So if you
want to meet her, give me your phone number. I'll
pass it on and suggest she call you. Maybe the two
of you can meet for coffee or something.

Cassie did give Scarlett her phone number and Julia
Barnes, Mona Moore's virtual assistant, called the next
afternoon. They made arrangements to meet at a restaurant in
Clearwater for lunch on Saturday.

"You can't miss me," said Julia, "I have mermaid hair."

"What's mermaid hair?" asked Cassie.

Julia just laughed. "You'll know it when you see it."

She had been right. As Cassie waited outside the restaurant, she saw a woman walking towards her who had sandy blond hair styled in a pixie cut. But instead of lighter blond highlights that other women might have, she had streaks that were pink, purple, blue and green. *Mermaid hair.*

"Julia?" Cassie asked.

Julia grinned and pointed to her head. "Yup, and now you know what mermaid hair is."

Cassie laughed. "I couldn't imagine, but the description works."

Julia opened the door to the restaurant. "Come on. This is one of my favorite places."

Julia was—well, there was no other word for it—*effervescent.* She was cute and bubbly. She was about Cassie's height, had slightly almond-shaped blue eyes and an adorable button nose. She wore a light green floaty skirt, a lacy white sleeveless blouse and strappy sandals. Altogether, with the pixie cut and multi-colored hair, she had a sweet, elfish look.

Cassie wore white capris and a conservative blue and white-striped polo. Next to Julia, Cassie felt like one of her retired neighbors. As soon as they entered the restaurant Cassie could understand why Julia liked it. It suited her style. Instead of the classic matching dining tables and chairs one would expect to see, there was an eclectic mix of tables surrounded by armchairs, as well as groupings of sofas, chairs and coffee tables.

"This place is great," said Julia. "They make their own bread and it's to die for. It doesn't really matter what you have on it. They could probably put a shit sandwich on the menu and not only would it sell, it would be delicious. I told Max that. He's the owner. I said I'd give him a blow job if he'd put it on the menu for just one day."

Cassie's mouth fell open. "He didn't."

Julia laughed. "The fucker did. But not the way I meant it. He added *shit on a shingle*—creamed chipped beef on their toasted brioche bread."

"Did you...you know?"

"Give him a blow job? Hell no; he cheated. Besides, it's one of his bestsellers now. *He* owes *me*."

Once they placed their order at the counter, Cassie followed as Julia made her way to two overstuffed chintz chairs on either side of a small table.

When they were seated, Julia flashed her a brilliant smile and with no attempt to lower her voice said, "So, you're interested in the BDSM lifestyle."

Several people at nearby tables glanced their direction. Cassie felt a hot blush rise in her cheeks.

"There's nothing to be ashamed of, Cassie. What consenting adults choose to enjoy together is really no one's business."

Cassie nodded. "I agree, but that's a good reason to be a little discreet, don't you think?"

Julia leaned in and lowered her voice. "Discreet is not announcing to the restaurant that I was a naughty sub last night and my punishment is to wear a butt plug all day."

"Are you serious?"

Julia laughed. "Of course I am. But don't worry, it's not really a punishment. I love anal play and it keeps me deliciously turned on all day."

Cassie should have been appalled but she found it oddly arousing.

It was fair to say Julia was not like anyone Cassie had ever met. They chatted over lunch and Julia answered all of Cassie's questions in her disarmingly forthright manner. To her surprise, after a little while, Cassie no longer felt embarrassed. And that had apparently been Julia's goal.

By the time lunch was over, Julia asked, "Do you remember the bet I told you about when we first got here?"

"The one about a blow job for a shit sandwich on the menu?"

Julia grinned. "Yeah, that's the one. Do you realize you couldn't say 'blow job' aloud when I told you about it?"

Cassie smiled. "I guess that's true. But we've talked about all kinds of other things since then."

"Like butt plugs," said Julia matter-of-factly.

Cassie chuckled. "Yes, like butt plugs."

Julia shrugged. "That's kind of what the lifestyle is like. Until you're exposed to it, you see it as foreign and forbidden. But as you learn more, meet new people and maybe experience a little of it, you realize it's just another way to have fun and perhaps even find fulfillment."

Those words stuck with Cassie and over the next few weeks, every time she found herself thinking about the possibilities, the words "find fulfillment" came back to her.

Chapter 3

Meeting Julia had been the best thing that had happened to Cassie in years. Julia had instantly made it her mission to reawaken Cassie's social life.

The day after they had met for lunch, Julia called. "Hey, Cass, do you want to go to a club with me on Thursday night?"

"Uh...I don't think I'm quite ready for that."

"Ready for what?"

"Well, you know...I'm interested in the lifestyle but I'm not ready to jump into it just yet."

Julia laughed. "Well, duh, Cass. Of course, you aren't. But I wasn't asking you to go to a BDSM club. I do enjoy other things too. The Drunken Pelican is having a salsa night and I thought it might be fun."

Cassie was glad Julia couldn't see how embarrassed she was. "God, I'm sorry Julia. That was pretty stupid of me. Um...I don't know anything about salsa dancing."

"Don't worry. There'll be any number of cute Latin men who will jump at the chance to teach you. Come on, it'll be a blast."

"Okay. It does sound interesting. I'd love to."

And that's how it started. Except for the occasional special event, the BDSM club Julia went to was only open on Friday and Saturday nights. She found all sorts of great things to do at other times. Cassie soon learned that Julia was a wicked flirt, but she knew how to draw lines.

"Don't get me wrong, Cass, I love to have a good time at a night club, but I'm not interested in more. I prefer my sex with a big dollop of kink, and for that you have to know and trust someone implicitly or be in a really safe environment, like a well-monitored club."

"So you don't have sex outside the club?"

"Well, I've been to some private parties, but really only ones given by people in the club and using club rules."

"So only in public?"

"Well it's not exactly *public*. Everyone in the club goes through a screening process. It's really a fairly close-knit community. And in the club there are lots of different places to play. Some are less public than others. Still, like I said, it takes a huge amount of trust to play in private and I won't do that until I meet the perfect Dom for me."

"What is the *perfect Dom*?"

Julia tilted her head to one side and seemed to seriously consider the question for a few moments. "The perfect Dom is the one who makes me want to be the perfect sub. He is someone to whom I can relinquish all control and know, without a doubt, that if I submit to him, he will give me precisely what I need...what I crave...even if I don't know exactly what that is myself."

"Wow." Were there really people out there like that?

Julia grinned. "I know, right?"

"The idea of giving up all control is scary, though."

"It should be. That's why trust is so important. You can only give up control to the degree you trust someone. But when you absolutely do and you can finally let go of it all, it's a freeing experience."

"I can see how it would be." Not only that, Cassie longed for it. She had been independent and in control of everything for most of her adult life. Eventually, she was also responsible for her grandmother and all her affairs too. The idea of letting someone else take control, even just for a little while, was tempting.

"You want it, Cassie. I know you do. We've spent a lot of time together over the last month but every time this subject comes up...well, I can tell the lifestyle appeals to you. Why don't you just bite the bullet and try it."

Good question. What did she have to lose? "You're right. The way you describe things is enticing. I am interested, and I'd like to try it. But I don't know how and it is a little scary." And that was an understatement.

"Well, the 'how' is easy. I can arrange for you to come as a guest to my club. You will have to submit all the paperwork required for membership."

"Even just for a visit?"

"Yeah. There are rigid privacy and non-disclosure agreements. Frankly, I'm an open book. I don't care who knows what I like or what they think of me for liking it. But understandably, there are people who like to keep their private life private. Therefore, the owner is a real stickler about confidentiality. He wants the club to be the ultimate secure environment on all levels, so that anyone who plays there can relax, be themselves and enjoy the lifestyle that they find fulfilling. But just like the relationship between a Dom and a sub that can only happen with trust. The members have to have confidence that everyone who enters the club is there for the same reason. The only real way to do this is to treat a visitor as a potential member."

"Wow." That was a little unnerving. The idea of taking a peek at the lifestyle while not actually divulging anything about herself was one thing. Essentially applying for membership was something else.

"Your safety is important too, so there's also an extensive list of sexual activities that you must review to determine soft and hard limits and a questionnaire about past experiences. That's to help identify things that might trigger bad reactions. They'll also do a background check and you have to have a physical to be cleared medically."

"My doctor has to know?"

Julia laughed. "Well, the forms don't say 'deviant sex maniac application' on them. They're just generic physical evaluation forms like the ones for certain kinds of jobs. But testing for sexually transmitted diseases is required. If asking your doctor for that would make you die of embarrassment or you don't have a doctor, the club has a list of several physicians who are members. You can make an appointment with one of them if you want."

"And that's it?" As if it wasn't overwhelming enough.

"After the paperwork is done, you have to meet with the club owner. He'll go over all the rules and regulations, show you around and then debrief with you."

"Debrief?"

"Yeah. You'll just talk about what you experienced and how it made you feel and stuff. After that, he decides whether you are tentatively eligible to join. Then you can come as a guest for a month."

"What happens after that?" Cassie shocked herself with that question. Why did it matter what happened after the first month? She wasn't really planning to actually become a member…

"It depends on whether you want to join or not."

"Let's assume I do." *Where, in hell, did that come from?*

"Well, the owner meets with you again to discuss the financial stuff. I should warn you, joining as a regular member is really expensive. Most country club fees pale in comparison. However, there are working members. It costs a lot less, but you have to volunteer a certain amount of time working at the club. I'm a working member. We do things like man the front desk, wipe down equipment after it's been used, tend bar, act as monitors, help clean up at the end of the night, do laundry, you name it."

"So if you have the money to be a regular member, or are willing to be a working member, what happens?" She was all in now, she needed to know.

"The owner discusses all potential members with some of the senior members of the club. Although now and then they turn someone down at this point, usually poor candidates are weeded out with all of the background checking or the trial period. So they usually offer one of the two forms of full membership or if they aren't completely sure, they offer a probationary period."

"That's all a little daunting."

"Yes, but it's what makes playing at the club safe. Everyone there knows that every single person who goes through the doors has been very well vetted."

"I guess so."

"So do you want to do it? Do you want to apply as a guest?"

Did she? Something about it called to her, she wouldn't have probed this deeply if it hadn't. And if she were going to try it, this was the safest possible way. "Yes, I do."

Chapter 4

It took nearly a month to complete all the paperwork, including all of the medical testing, and to be cleared by the club's owner for an initial visit.

By far, the hardest form to complete was the list of limits. It was thirty-three pages long and included every sex act Cassie was aware of and many she'd never even imagined. For every single item, she had to indicate whether she had done it or had it done to her. If she had done it or had it done to her, she had to rate how much she enjoyed it on a scale of one to five. If she had never tried it she had to indicate if she was curious about it or if it was a soft or hard limit. A soft limit might be explored after discussion and negotiation but a hard limit was not negotiable.

When she had completed it, she realized she had done almost nothing on the list. She was curious about a few things and a few others were soft limits, but the vast majority of the acts listed were hard limits. She figured this would probably make her ineligible to even visit, but Julia assured her otherwise.

"That list is huge because it's meant to cover as much as possible. Most people have a lot of hard limits and most new submissives have a big list of soft limits because they just don't know how things will go yet. You'll look at your limits again after you've had more experience."

Until everything was completed and approved, Cassie didn't even know the name of the club or where it was located. But finally Julia informed her that she had been approved and her first meeting with the club owner was scheduled for Friday evening.

At last, Cassie was going to get a glimpse of the world she'd only read about and she was as excited as she was nervous. Julia gave her directions to the club and arranged to meet her in the parking lot fifteen minutes before the appointment with the owner.

A string of little barrier islands stretch from Clearwater to St. Petersburg, connecting to the mainland or other islands by bridges. To her surprise, the directions led her to one of these islands, the entirety of which was an elite, adults-only resort called Island Treasures. It was a completely private island and no one could even drive onto it without first passing through security.

She stopped at the gate and rolled down her window, not sure of what to say to gain entrance. But the guard just asked her name, checked a list and then waved her through. She followed Julia's remaining directions and found the parking lot where they were to meet. Cassie had arrived nearly fifteen minutes before the time she was supposed to meet Julia and, of course, Julia wasn't there yet. Cassie wasn't sure what else to do, so she parked and rolled down the windows to wait. The evening was unusually warm for March and after about ten minutes, she couldn't stand sitting in the car any longer. She rolled up the windows, got out of the car and leaned against the hood to wait. Julia should be here any minute.

Before long her attention was drawn to a tiny anole lizard on a nearby palm tree and she walked closer. It had to have been newly hatched because it wasn't more than an inch long. She marveled at the miniscule little creature. She put her hand out and it crawled onto her fingertip.

She held it up to her face. "You are very cute."

A deep, rich male voice from behind startled her. "Can I help you?"

She spun around and was momentarily awed. The owner of that voice was nothing short of gorgeous. He was tall, had dark brown hair and deep blue eyes. Strong broad shoulders filled out a white linen shirt that was open at the neck and tucked into black dress pants.

"I…I…I'm sorry. What did you ask?"

He smiled, causing the corners of his eyes to crinkle. "I asked if I could help you. You've been standing here for a while, inspecting that lizard."

"Oh. No, thank you. I don't think so. I was just waiting for a friend. I'm supposed to meet her here, but I tend to be early to a fault. This little guy caught my eye." Almost absently she moved her finger toward the tree, returning the anole to where she found him.

"So it isn't time for her to be here yet?"

Cassie's brow furrowed and she glanced at her watch. "Ah, well, I guess she's a few minutes late too."

"On an evening like this, most people would wait in their air-conditioned car."

Cassie nodded. "I suppose so. But sitting in a car, just letting it run, burns gas and isn't particularly good for the planet. It's cooled down a lot now that the sun has set."

He smiled again. "That's very green of you. I like that."

"I figure every little bit helps."

"I'm sure it does. Tell me, why are you waiting for this friend?"

Cassie wasn't sure how much to tell him. After all, just because the club was on the resort grounds didn't mean that everyone there knew about it. She settled for generalities. "We have a meeting with an acquaintance of hers." Cassie glanced at her watch again and frowned. "If she doesn't get here soon, we're going to be late. I hate being late."

"Why?"

"Why do I hate being late?"

"Yes. Is it a job interview or something really important?"

"Not exactly. But if I make an appointment with someone, for anything, really, even just a cup of coffee, they have made time for me. I think it's disrespectful to make them wait."

"That's admirable, but it's a rather old-fashioned value that seems to be ignored these days."

She shrugged. "I guess it was just how I was raised."

"I see. Would you like to come inside?"

"Do you work here? At the resort, I mean?"

"Yes. I'm a member of Island Treasures' management team." He gestured toward the building. "It's much cooler and you can see the parking lot from my office."

Management team? Then he surely knew the owner of the club. Maybe Cassie could be on time for the meeting and make an apology for Julia. Still, she had read the club rules carefully. Mentioning anything specific about the club to a stranger was a violation of privacy rules. Maybe this guy wasn't associated with the resort at all. She had no way of knowing.

"Thank you very much for the kind offer, but I told my friend I'd meet her here in this parking lot. I don't want her to worry if she doesn't see me."

"Very well. Suit yourself. But if you change your mind, there's a door at the end of that building." He motioned to the one nearest them. "Tell the person on the desk that Tristan said to send you up."

"Thank you. I'm sure she'll be here in a few minutes."

It was more than a few minutes. Julia showed up several minutes after the time they were supposed to have met with the club owner. "I'm sorry, Cass, I didn't count on traffic being as bad as it was."

"We're late."

"I know, but who can predict traffic jams?"

Uh, everyone who lives in the greater Tampa-St. Pete area between September and May and goes out on a Friday evening. "Well, let's not make him wait longer. Where are we going?"

"It's just over here. We go in that end door there. The BDSM club is called Hidden Gem. Cute huh?"

Cassie's brow furrowed as Julia led her to the door Tristan had told her to go in. He hadn't lied. He said he was part of the management team, he must be associated with the club.

There was a small reception desk just inside at which sat a well-dressed, slender blond man.

"Julia, you're late. This must be Cassandra. I'm Denny, I work the desk here sometimes."

He held out his hand and Cassie took it. "Yes, I'm Cassie Hastings. It's nice to meet you."

Julia frowned. "All I get is 'Julia, you're late?' Yeah, it's great to see you too. I had a good week, how about you? How's your cat?"

He rolled his eyes and laughed. "I had a great week and you are only getting later. What do you want to make a big bad Dom angrier for?"

"I was stuck in traffic. Who can predict that?"

Denny shook his head. "Literally everyone but you. Go on, take her up before the boss implodes."

Cassie frowned. This wasn't starting well and she hated that. Part of her wanted to flee, but that would only make things worse so she followed Julia through a door that led to an elevator lobby and the door to a stairwell.

Julia pushed the elevator call button.

"Come on, Julia, we're late. Let's just take the stairs."

She shrugged. "Okay."

They went up the stairs to the second floor and then down a short hall. Julia knocked on the door and opened it when a deep voice called, "Enter."

Cassie realized before she stepped into the room that the voice belonged to the man she'd met earlier—Tristan.

Chapter 5

Tristan looked up as the two women entered his office. He had assumed the woman he'd seen waiting in the parking lot was Cassandra Hastings. When he'd first noticed her, he was puzzled by why she chose to stand out in the heat instead of remaining in her car with the air-conditioning on. He'd intended to ask her in this interview but as time passed, Julia hadn't arrived and the woman still stood outside. His curiosity had gotten the better of him.

It had only taken a few moments of conversation to confirm his suspicions. And just a few more minutes to learn that she was born to be submissive. She was thoughtful and polite. She showed respect to him—a complete stranger—as they talked, but also as the person with whom she had an appointment. She placed her concern for the environment over her own comfort and she demonstrated loyalty to a friend. The first reason she'd given for having to wait was that she had arrived very early, even though their meeting time had already passed. And she hadn't wanted to come inside for fear Julia would worry about her if she wasn't there waiting.

Of course that last bit could have been an excuse to avoid the unknown. She was in a strange place and knew nothing about him.

Now, she stood in front of him, appearing nervous, embarrassed and perhaps a little afraid. All appropriate emotions under the circumstances and none of which Julia seemed to be feeling.

"Good evening, Master Tristan," Julia said brightly.

"Good evening, Julia."

"This is Cassie, the friend I told you about."

He stared at Julia, raising one eyebrow.

Finally reading his displeasure, her pupils widened for a moment and she dropped her gaze. "Uh, Cassandra Hastings, that is."

"Thank you, Julia. I believe our meeting was scheduled to start eight minutes ago."

"Yes, Sir. I'm sorry. Cassie was here but I got stuck in traffic."

"Traffic? Was there some major accident?"

"No, Sir. Just heavy traffic."

"Julia, there's always heavy traffic at this time of day. You've lived here long enough to know that. And if you'd planned for the traffic, you wouldn't have been late."

"I'm sorry, Sir."

"*I'm sorry* isn't enough. You have shown disregard for your friend and disrespect for my time. You will submit to a punishment of my choosing later this evening."

Julia bowed her head, but Tristan didn't miss the hint of a smile on her lips.

"Yes, Sir."

Julia liked punishment and tended to be a bratty sub to get it. Some Doms liked that, but he didn't. He would happily have done a punishment scene with her if she had negotiated it, but he would not allow her to manipulate him. She wouldn't enjoy this punishment. "I believe you are working as a server for the first two hours this evening. Is that correct?"

"Yes, Sir."

"Then you can go now and get ready to start work. I'd like to chat with Miss Hastings alone."

"Yes, Sir. I'll see you later, Cass," she said as she turned to leave.

"Oh, one more thing, Miss Barnes."

"Yes, Sir?"

"You are not allowed to play with anyone tonight without my permission."

"Yes, Sir." She frowned and left the office, closing the door behind her.

Miss Cassandra Hastings' gaze followed her friend as she left the room, but she said nothing. Tristan rose from his chair and came around the desk, offering her his hand. "I'm Tristan Cabot and I'm glad to see you didn't perish in the heat while you waited for her."

She took his hand and as she shook it, looked him in the eye. "It's very nice to meet you. I do appreciate your concern. If a little heat would do me in, I'm living in the wrong place."

Tristan found it interesting that she hadn't used the word "but" in the exchange. Many people would have said "I do appreciate your concern, but…" not realizing that the word "but" minimizes the effect of what comes before it. It's like saying, "I appreciate it, but I didn't need it, so I didn't really appreciate it all that much." Again it showed respect and genuine gratitude. He was impressed.

Not only was she well-spoken, she was perfectly poised. If this were a job interview, she would have instantly made a good impression. Although she wasn't dressed for a job interview, she wasn't dressed as a typical sub-out-for-a-night-at-a-BDSM-club either. Her skirt was black and very short, but not skin tight or made of leather. It flared, like a skater's skirt. Her long, shapely legs were bare and instead of stilettos she wore the most delicate pair of jeweled flat sandals he had ever seen. Her toenails were perfectly pedicured and polished with the same deep shade of red as her lace top. Through the lace, he could just barely see a hint of a red bra covering full, lush breasts. Her light brown hair was piled in a loose bun, exposing the long slender column of her neck.

In a word, she was exquisite.

"Please, come sit with me on the couch so we can chat."

She nodded. "Certainly."

She crossed to the couch and sat gracefully, ankles crossed, hands folded. Also atypical for a young woman her age. According to her paperwork, she was twenty-six.

"Cassandra, tell me a little about yourself."

"There isn't much to tell. I live just north of Tampa and I work as a freelance editor."

"What sort of things do you edit?"

"Nearly anything I'm offered, but mostly romance novels."

"Romance? What kind?"

"Pretty much all kinds. Historical, contemporary, new adult, young adult, paranormal, erotic."

"Have you edited books that feature BDSM elements?"

"Yes."

"So you are familiar with the lifestyle?"

She smiled. "I'm familiar with what I've read. But that doesn't mean what I've read is accurate."

"Fair point. Is that why you're here? What you read interested you?" That was sometimes a problem. There was both good and bad BDSM romance out there and thus there were many misconceptions.

"Yes. I finally got the courage to send an email to one of the authors whose books I edit in order to find out more. I wanted to know how accurate her portrayal was. You must realize, most romance readers want the fairy tale. They want a perfect hero who sweeps a woman off her feet. Everyone knows, or they should know, no one in real life is perfect. Romance novels are fiction and good relationships take a huge amount of work. Still, I wondered how much reality varied from her fiction."

"And what did she tell you?"

Cassandra laughed, the sound sweet and musical. "I think she must be in a particularly wonderful relationship. She would have me believe her life perfectly imitates art."

"You don't believe her?"

"Actually, I do believe she loves her life and her partner and that it comes pretty close to perfect. But I'm not convinced all such relationships are perfect. Still, it made me want to know more. She told me she had an author friend whose virtual assistant lived down here and was in the lifestyle."

"Julia?"

She gave him a cheeky grin. "You don't miss much, do you?"

"Ah, Cassandra, it isn't nice to tease a Dom." Still, he couldn't help but smile. There was a sweetness about her that was enticing, even in her moment of sarcasm.

She gave a nod, a smile still lighting her face. "Point taken. I apologize. Yes, Julia is her friend's virtual assistant. We met and had a chat over lunch. It was fun. We hit it off and I don't really have many friends down here, so she sort of took me on."

"Took you on?"

She laughed again. "She thought I didn't get out enough, and in fairness, she was right. So she has done everything possible to pry me from my lair. She's dragged me to all kinds of fun things that I'd have never gone to alone."

He smiled. "Like what?"

"Like the Magical Beasts, Beings, Bands and Beer Festival. People went in all kinds of crazy costumes. There were lots of local bands playing throughout the day and stands selling everything from handmade jewelry and candles to turkey legs. Not to mention a huge variety of craft beers…and dragons. Lots and lots of dragons."

He watched her as she chatted. She was completely adorable. Utterly feminine and graceful, but at the same time she had a youthful energy and innocence that was incredibly desirable. "So at what point did you decide you wanted to visit Hidden Gem?"

"After she had fielded about a million questions about the lifestyle, Julia suggested I try it. She said a club was the safest way to experience it because of rules and monitors and such. So here I am."

"Tell me, what is it about the lifestyle that appeals to you?"

She cocked her head to one side, appearing to consider her answer. "That's a bit complicated. I'm not sure I completely understand it myself, but I'll try to explain. I guess...well...I'm self-sufficient. I rely on no one. I have no one to rely on."

"Not even your family?"

"I don't have a family. I was raised by my grandmother. My great-uncle helped her out financially but he didn't live nearby. I adored grandma, but being raised by a grandmother is different. She was sixty-four when I went to live with her and seventy when I became a teenager. She recognized her limitations. Even good teenagers are not easy to raise, and her health was declining. She sent me to a boarding school when I was fourteen."

Tristan frowned.

She shook her head. "Oh, don't get me wrong, I actually loved it and I received a stellar education, but one definitely learns to be independent in a boarding school."

Raised by a grandmother and sent to boarding school. That certainly explained her formal, refined manners. He wondered why she had been raised by her grandmother, but since she had offered no explanation, he decided not to ask.

"Do you still live with your grandmother?"

She dropped her head and looked away for a moment. "No. As it turns out, my grandmother was in the very early stages of Alzheimer's when she sent me away to school. I didn't realize it. I would have done things differently if I had. After prep school I went to Boston College. My great-uncle lived in Boston. In my second year, he moved down here. He said it was because he couldn't stand the cold anymore, but it was really because grandma couldn't live alone anymore."

She paused and shook her head. "I think the stress was too much for him. He had a fatal heart-attack right after I graduated from college. So I returned here to take care of her. She passed away a little over a year ago."

That story tore at Tristan's heart. Although still poised and in control, he saw deep sorrow in her eyes. "I'm sorry, Cassandra."

"Thank you. I loved them both very much and I still miss them."

"I'm sure you do. The loss of a loved one is never easy. It would appear that your grandmother did a very good job raising you. You seem to be a strong, independent woman."

She nodded. "I believe I am and I'm proud of that. But when I read and edit books about dominance and submission, I…well, I wonder what it would be like to not have to be the one in control all the time—to simply give myself over to someone and trust that they'll take care of me."

"You've never done that? All of your relationships have been vanilla? You've never dipped your toe in the water at all?" He knew this was true based on the way she had filled out her list of limits, but he wanted to hear her answer.

She shook her head. "No."

"Did you ever suggest to anyone that you might like to try a little kink?"

She smiled and a warm blush spread from her neck to her hairline. "No. I think women in general worry about the opinions of others. I know I do. When I'm with a man, I worry about what he thinks of me. Is he having to work too hard? Am I making him feel good? Am I doing the right things? Then there is always the fear that if I asked for something…well…a little kinky, he'll be shocked and think I'm a tramp."

He smiled at the old-fashioned word, but even as she said it, the color in her cheeks deepened. He wondered if she knew exactly how close she had come to the heart of the matter. "And why do you think this would be different if you were submitting to a Dom?"

"Because I wouldn't have to think about it. If the books are even partially true, a good Dom would be focusing his full attention on me alone. I wouldn't have to worry about what he thought of my response. I believe there'd be a tremendous freedom in that. We would be doing exactly what we'd both agreed upon and wanted to do, and he would be getting the response he desired from me."

"And what if you didn't like something that you tried, or the response he wanted made you uncomfortable?"

"I'd tell him. And if it was a deal breaker, if neither of us were willing to adapt, I wouldn't play with him again. Isn't that the way it is in all relationships? You go out a few times to see if you're compatible, and things move on or they don't?"

"Yes, I suppose it is." He considered her for a moment. "So what concerns you about the lifestyle?" After reading her limits list, he expected he knew the answer.

She blushed even deeper than before. "I'm a little uncomfortable about the notion of public play. I don't like the idea of being exposed. It scares me a little."

He was right, but he tried to keep from smiling. This lovely woman, who had come here tonight to experience a BDSM club environment was *shy*. "Does it scare you more than, say, a spanking or a flogging?"

"Yes."

"Why?"

"There's a safeword. If something hurt too much physically or it was going farther than I wanted it to, a single word would stop everything. But being exposed is rather necessary in a club environment." She smiled. "And yet, that's exactly why a club seems to be a better way to explore the lifestyle."

"I see, and you are right on both counts. A club environment does come with a degree of exposure, but it is also the safest way for someone new to the lifestyle to play."

"So you understand my dilemma."

"I do, but I don't think it is insurmountable. Cassandra, based on everything you've said, I think there is a side of you that yearns to release control. And yet, because you have never experienced it, you can't possibly imagine the kind of trust that develops between a Dom and a sub. So the idea of giving up that control leaves you feeling vulnerable, naked, exposed. I am certain that with time, in a safe environment and under the control of the right Dominant, you can move beyond that."

She smiled and nodded, but he knew she didn't quite believe him.

"You don't believe me?"

"I want to believe you. Really I do. And you're right, I've never experienced the kind of trust you describe. So the part of me that has trouble believing you is rooted in inexperience, not doubt."

He chuckled. "That was an incredibly beautiful way to honestly say you don't believe me and yet not question my sincerity."

She looked away, a shy smile on her face and the blush rising again in her cheeks. He couldn't remember ever meeting a woman he found more desirable and yet she had never even dipped a toe into his world.

"And it was insightful as well," he continued. "The only way to understand the nuances of trust and power exchange, and to begin to understand this lifestyle, is to experience it. I know you have read all of the rules and you understand the basic behavior expected of submissives inside this club. Do you have any questions?"

"I don't have any questions right now. I have read the rules and I think I understand them."

"Frankly I don't expect you'll have any difficulty at all. Most of the rules are based in mutual respect and you seem to be well grounded in that. I'll just remind you of a few things that might not come naturally to you. Although you may certainly watch scenes, at all other times generally keep your eyes slightly downcast, especially in the presence of a Dominant. In fact, don't make eye contact with any Dom or Domme unless told to do so. Remember to address Dominants as Sir or Miss, or their name preceded by Master or Mistress. So Master Tristan or Mistress Diana and so forth. You never address a Dom simply as Master or Mistress without their name, unless you have been collared by that person."

She nodded. "Okay...uh...Sir."

He smiled, a little surprised by how much he liked hearing "Sir" from her lips. "You catch on quickly. Just for the record, within the confines of the club, the rules apply absolutely. Failure to follow them will earn a punishment. They are also customarily observed within the building or grounds, but that is not a requirement. Unless someone is in a formal D/s relationship and follow stricter power exchange rules, outside of the club environment I personally don't consider anyone Dominant or submissive."

She appeared to visibly relax at that. "Thank you for explaining that. It helps a lot, actually."

"I'm glad." He stood and held a hand out to her. "So, now that you are prepared, Cassandra, allow me to show you the club. After you've seen some of the BDSM lifestyle in practice, I hope it will help you understand things even more fully."

Chapter 6

The walk through the club had left Cassie feeling just as conflicted. Much of what she saw, she found very stimulating and erotic. However, when she imagined herself enjoying the same things, the fact that it was all done in view of other people bothered her.

Afterwards, when she *debriefed* with Tristan, in addition to talking about what appealed to her and what didn't, he had addressed the issue head on.

"As you saw, there are very open areas and much less open areas in the club. But you are right, no place is completely private and that is as it's meant to be. So, if you want to try the lifestyle in this environment, you will need to come to grips with that."

"I understand. I'm just not sure I can."

"I, on the other hand, am completely sure you can."

She frowned. "How can you be so certain?"

"Because I've watched you this evening. You are naturally submissive. You have all the qualities. You are kind and respectful. You put the needs of others first. You blossom under praise. In short, you are a people pleaser. And as such, under the guidance of a strong Dom, with whom you develop trust, you will be able to work through your shyness."

She smiled at him but said nothing. She didn't think she'd ever be comfortable exposing anything intimate to strangers.

He laughed. "I think this is a case of you wanting to believe me but not quite being able to. How was it you described it earlier?"

She felt herself blush. "I think I said, the part of me that has trouble believing you is rooted in inexperience, not doubt."

"Exactly. So I am going to suggest you get a taste of the trust that can develop between a Dom and a sub and see if we can poke some holes in your doubt."

"How would I do that?"

"Come back tomorrow night and do a scene with me. We will discuss the specific details when you get here, but I promise you, it will be very light. No nudity and no sexual contact other than kissing."

She wanted to experience this. She knew if she didn't at least try, if she let her innate shyness spook her, she would always wonder what she'd missed. "Okay. I'll do a scene with you tomorrow."

"Excellent. Now, allow me to walk you to your car."

"You needn't bother. I've taken up enough of your time tonight."

"That was the wrong answer, Cassandra. As a Dom, if I ask to do something with you, it's because I want to do it. Don't second guess it and worry that you are putting me out. It will please me most if you just do it. So, let's try again. Allow me to walk you to your car."

She smiled. "Certainly, Sir. Thank you."

He grinned and took her arm. "Much better."

When they reached the parking lot, Cassie was surprised to see Julia waiting there, looking none too happy.

"Julia, what's the matter? Are you having car trouble or something? Do you want me to call Triple-A?"

Tristan shook his head. "There is nothing wrong with her car. If there had been, we'd have arranged for any assistance she needed in the club. Miss Barnes, would you like to tell Cassandra why you are out here or shall I."

"It's part of my punishment."

Cassie was confused. "You're punishment? I thought...I mean this is a BDSM club."

"You thought she'd get a spanking?" asked Tristan.

"Well...yes."

"As it turns out, so did she. But that isn't the way it works. What was your punishment, Miss Barnes?"

"I had to wait out here with Master Adam, at least twice as long as you waited for me, Cassie."

Until then Cassie hadn't noticed the tall man in black leathers who leaned casually against the side of the building.

"And I have to apologize to you. I'm sorry, Cassie. I know you were nervous about tonight. I'm sure having to wait for me and ultimately being late for your appointment made things worse."

Cassie shook her head. "It's okay, Julia. I really do appreciate everything you've done for me. I know it was just poor planning."

"Is that true, Miss Barnes? Was it poor planning?" asked Tristan.

"No, Sir. Honestly, Cassie, I knew you wouldn't get in trouble and I didn't think about how anxious you would be. I thought it would be fun to get a spanking from Master Tristan and I thought being late would earn one."

"But a sub who behaves badly earns an unpleasant punishment and you enjoy spanking too much for it to ever be a *punishment* I would mete out. You understand that now, don't you Julia?"

"Yes, Master Tristan."

"So, waiting out here, admitting the truth and apologizing was her punishment for being inconsiderate towards you, Cassandra. Miss Barnes, what was your punishment for making me wait and trying to manipulate me into spanking you?"

Julia hung her head, looking so truly miserable it made Cassie's heart ache a little for her.

"Everyone I played with tonight brought me to the edge but I wasn't allowed to have an orgasm."

Cassie tried not to react but could scarcely believe what she'd heard.

"Waiting isn't pleasant, and neither is being manipulated, is it, Julia?" asked Tristan.

"No, Sir."

"So, if you want to do a spanking scene with me or any Dom, what do you need to do?"

"I need to ask and negotiate it."

Tristan smiled at her. "That's right. I hope you've learned that now."

"I have, Sir."

"Good girl." He caressed her cheek. "I know it's been a frustrating evening. I'll lift the ban on your orgasms tomorrow."

"Thank you, Sir."

The whole evening had given Cassie a lot to think about. In the club, she had seen a variety of scenes between consenting adults, many of which were enticingly erotic. But learning about Julia's punishment unsettled her. She wasn't sure how she felt about it.

Eventually she decided to set aside her discomfort over the whole concept of punishment until she learned a little more. She had agreed to do a public scene with Tristan tomorrow and she needed to focus on that first.

~ * ~

When Cassie arrived the next evening, Julia was waiting for her.

Cassie hugged her. "You didn't have to do this."

Julia laughed, "No, I didn't. But I wanted to."

"Thanks. I really do appreciate it. If possible I'm more nervous tonight than I was last night."

"Why?"

"I agreed to do a scene with Tris—I mean, with Master Tristan."

"You're kidding."

"No. I told you the whole idea of playing in public bothers me. He wanted to do a mild scene with me, no nudity or sex, to let me see how it feels."

"Wow. No nudity or sex. It doesn't sound too challenging."

"And by that you mean boring?"

"Not at all, sweetie. Nothing Master Tristan does is boring. I just mean it shouldn't be too stressful for you. I can't wait to see what he does."

They went into the club and Julia introduced her to Diana, a very tall, beautiful woman who was working the desk.

"Mistress Diana is a Domme and one of the Club Monitors here. But she's also a really good teacher. If you have any questions or need advice, she's great."

"That's nice of you to say, Julia," said Mistress Diana.

Julia shrugged. "It's true." She put a hand to the side of her mouth, as if conveying a secret, and said in a stage whisper, "But it's also true that she's wicked with a crop, so don't piss her off."

Diana laughed. "Follow your own advice girl or I'll see that your ass is warmed tonight."

"Yes, Mistress Diana," Julia said with a cheeky grin.

Julia showed Cassie around the locker room. It had all the amenities of a plush spa and the lockers were equipped with changeable number locks, like those on hotel safes.

"Sometimes scenes are very physical and you want a shower before you go home. Then too, most of the time people change into their club wear here—at least most subs do. Driving around town in sexy lingerie or with your tits hanging out can be tricky. You lock your purse and street clothes in a locker so you can just have fun in the club without worrying about where you put your stuff."

Cassie had worn a red cotton knit dress that fit snugly to her waist before flaring out. She'd shortened the skirt quite a bit, and she'd left her hair down, hoping to make the look more club appropriate. She frowned when Julia mentioned street clothes. "I didn't bring anything to change into. I don't really have anything but ordinary clothes. I was going to wear this."

"Don't worry. Honestly, I wouldn't have thought of that dress as particularly sexy if I'd seen it on a hanger, but on you, it's hot. How would you feel about taking your bra off though?"

Cassie frowned. "Would that make me look less frumpy?"

Julia laughed. "You don't look frumpy. But as far as sex appeal goes, nothing has quite the same impact as blissfully free tatas." She leaned in conspiratorially. "It makes Doms want to bind them up."

Cassie smiled. "I guess I can do that without dying of embarrassment." So she removed her bra and put it in the locker with her purse.

There were already lots of people in the club and a variety of scenes underway when they left the locker room. Tristan had been standing at the bar. Cassie had learned they didn't serve alcohol, but they had or could arrange for practically any other beverage one could imagine.

As soon as he saw them, he smiled and crossed the room.

"Good evening, Julia, Cassandra. You both look lovely tonight."

"Good evening, Sir, thank you," they both answered in unison, causing Julia to giggle.

"Julia, I know last evening was not particularly pleasant for you. Tonight Master Adam would like to do a scene with you that I suspect you will find much more fulfilling."

Julia looked delighted. "Really? Thank you, Sir."

"You're welcome. He's waiting for you at the bar. Go present yourself."

"Yes, Master Tristan." She hurried off towards the bar.

After Julia had left, Tristan said, "I'm glad you came back."

"Did you think I might not...Sir?"

He smiled. "I certainly hoped you would. Still, you experienced many aspects of our world last night. It can be overwhelming."

She nodded. "Yes, Sir. It can. But I don't want to spend my life wondering, what if."

"I'm glad to hear that. Then, are you ready for our scene?"

"I think so. What do I need to do?"

He pointed toward one side of the club. "Do you see the raised platform, with a stool on it, over there?"

"Yes, Sir."

"We sometimes use that area for demonstrations. It isn't in the middle of the room but it isn't private either. All I want you to do is sit on the stool and hold onto it."

"What are you going to do, Sir?"

"I'm going to kiss you. You will remain fully clothed. As tempting as they are, I won't touch your breasts or anything below your waist. But there may be people who gather to watch. If there are, I will introduce you."

"You're just going to kiss me?"

"Yes. Are you comfortable with that?"

It wasn't at all what she'd expected, but it seemed simple enough. "Yes, Sir. I am."

He smiled broadly. "Good, then let's go."

He took her hand, led her to the platform and helped her situate herself on the stool. "Remember, hold onto the stool and don't let go. Also, even though I know this seems like a very light scene, you know the club's safewords?"

"Yes, Sir. 'Yellow' if I am approaching my limit and 'red' if I want everything to stop."

"Good girl."

He turned away from her for a moment. Until then she hadn't noticed that several people had gathered around the platform.

"Good evening, friends. This beautiful young woman is Cassandra. She is very new to the lifestyle and is hoping to learn more about it as our visitor over the next few weeks."

His introduction was met with murmurs of welcome.

"Tonight, she is going to help me with a simple demonstration. I am going to show you how to properly kiss a woman."

There were a few chuckles from the crowd and Cassie had the vague sense she was missing something.

He turned back towards her. "Cassandra, focus only on me. Do you understand?"

"Yes, Sir."

"Good." He gave her a warm smile before moving to stand behind her.

For a moment everything was still. She glanced around at the gathering crowd and stiffened.

"Only on me," he repeated as if he knew the moment her focus had shifted. He took her hair in his right hand, holding it to one side, exposing her neck. He kissed the back of her neck once. Only his lips touched her but even at that simple touch, desire rose within her.

Then he kissed her again, sliding his lips up her neck before placing a soft kiss behind her ear.

She shivered and smiled.

He gave a low throaty chuckle and his kisses became harder. He moved back down her neck to her shoulder. Finally touching her with more than his lips, he gripped both shoulders with his hands, massaging lightly before he pushed the neckline of her dress out of his way, exposing her left shoulder and kissing it.

She became instantly nervous and although she didn't let go of the edge of the stool, she turned her face towards him, pulling away slightly.

He kissed her cheek and her temple before whispering in her ear, "Cassandra, I understand your fear and your limits. Can you give me your trust?"

Could she? She wanted to. She nodded.

"I need to hear the words, little bird. Do you trust me?"

"Yes, Sir. I trust you."

That simple reminder and acknowledgement allowed her to relax.

He kissed her cheek again, before turning his focus back to her neck and shoulders. He nipped lightly at her neck then ran his tongue from her neck to her shoulder, sending another wave of delightful shivers running through her. She felt him smile against her neck before he kissed it again. Then he trailed his tongue up to her ear, this time sucking gently on her earlobe.

The sensations were amazing. She had never experienced anything like this before, and he was only kissing her.

Soon, his kisses became hungrier and more demanding, his hands pushing down slightly on her shoulders. It was nearly overwhelming.

As if sensing her sudden insecurity, as he kissed her he slid his left hand under her arm and around her waist, embracing her even as he continued to hold her right shoulder firmly with his other hand. The sensation of physical support infused her with a feeling of deep serenity. She didn't have to worry. He was there and he would take care of her.

As his kisses became more intense, he threaded the fingers of his right hand into her hair closing his fist around it and pulling slightly to move her head where he wished. She was completely in his control and she realized that was exactly where she wanted to be.

He moved around her left side to stand in front of her. With his right hand still fisted in her hair he tilted her head back, kissing up the column of her throat to her lips.

She was lost in the sensation of his lips on hers. She let go of the stool with her left hand and raised it to caress his cheek.

He turned his head slightly and nipped at the side of her hand causing her to gasp. "Where should this soft hand be, little bird?"

She frowned. *Where should it be?*

He chuckled. "I'm glad you are enjoying this. What did I ask of you before we started?"

Her eyes flew open and she gripped the side of the stool again. "I'm sorry, Sir. I forgot."

"Don't worry. You'll learn to remember soon enough."

He started kissing her once more. Her neck, her shoulders, her throat, her cheeks, her eyelids and finally her lips again. She opened to him, allowing his tongue to plunder her mouth. She leaned towards him when he pulled away, only to feel the tug of his hand in her hair. He was in control. This was on his terms and she relaxed completely, closing her eyes again and simply allowing him to kiss her as he desired.

Finally, his kisses gentled again. He let go of her hair and caressed her cheek with his right hand. His left hand massaged her right shoulder lightly as his lips moved from her mouth to her cheek, then her temple and the top of her head. He stroked her hair lightly before breaking contact and stepping away.

She opened her eyes, and looked up at him, feeling dazed. The look of approval on his face suffused her with almost as much warmth as his kisses had.

"You were amazing, Cassandra."

He leaned down and took both of her hands in his, loosening her grip on the edge of the stool. "Come with me now."

He pulled her to her feet and putting an arm around her, walked with her to a quiet area, shielded by a beautifully painted screen.

She was still in a sensual fog as he sat on a sofa and pulled her down onto his lap. She snuggled against his chest, content to rest there for a while.

She wasn't sure how long they sat there like that, but eventually her head cleared and she realized she was sitting on the lap of a man who she barely knew, who had just kissed her into a stupor…*in public*. She gasped and pushed away from him trying to sit up. "I—I—I'm sorry," she stammered.

Chapter 7

Tristan let Cassie sit up, but held her firmly on his lap with one hand while stroking her back with the other. This was exactly what he had expected. Reality had just come crashing in on her and he needed to help her assimilate. "That was one of the most beautiful scenes I have ever experienced. Why would you apologize?"

"I-I-I don't know. I just..."

"Yesterday evening, when we first talked, you said that if the books you read were even partially true, a good Dom would be focusing his full attention on you and you wouldn't have to worry about anything. You said you would be doing exactly what you'd both agreed upon and wanted to do, and the Dom would be getting the response he desired from you. Did you mean what you said?"

"Yes, Sir."

"And did we do that? Did we enter into a scene, agreeing in advance about what would happen?"

"Yes, Sir."

"Did you enjoy it?"

She blushed hotly. "Yes."

"*Yes, Sir,*" he reminded her, "and I enjoyed it too. Why would that embarrass you?"

"It was...I was...I mean..."

"What do you mean, Cassandra?"

"There were people watching, Sir."

"But you agreed to that."

"Yes, but I thought you were just going to kiss me, Sir."

"I did just kiss you."

She frowned. "I know, but it was so...so...intimate."

He refrained from chuckling. There was a delicious innocence about her that he found intriguing. "Kissing is an intimate activity."

"I guess so, but I've never been kissed like that."

"Then you've never been properly kissed."

"Perhaps, but if I'd known it was going to be like that, I might not have wanted to do it in front of people, Sir."

"You had a safeword. At any time did you want to stop the scene?"

"No, Sir."

"Why?"

She smiled. "Because I liked what you were doing."

He knew admitting that hadn't been easy for someone as shy as she was. He stroked her cheek, tucking a lock of hair behind her ear."I could tell. I liked what I was doing too. And more than that, I liked how you were responding. Like I said, it was stunning. Did you feel burning embarrassment in the moment?"

"No, Sir. I...I forgot they were there, but—"

"—but they were. I know that. Cassandra, for the moment, I am acting as your Dom. You agreed to trust me. Your needs are my highest priority. I know that you need to feel safe. I know that you worry about what people think. Therefore I would never have kissed you like that in front of anyone who would be judgmental in any way. So while you felt as if you were in the public eye, you really weren't. You were surrounded by like-minded people. Friends whose only reason for watching was because it was a thrilling, beautiful scene. Any member of this club who saw it and didn't find it exciting would have moved on to something else." Actually, by the size of the crowd that had formed by the time the scene ended, it would seem most people who saw it happening, stopped to watch in awe.

She began to relax a little and he gently coaxed her back down until she was cuddled against him once more. After a moment, she frowned again.

He had to know why. "What was that?"

"What, Sir?"

"The thought which brought a frown to your face."

"It was no—"

"Don't dare tell me it was nothing. That would be a lie for which I would have to punish you."

"It was only…well, I was wondering why you didn't want me to touch you?"

He smiled and gave her a little squeeze. "It isn't that I didn't want you to touch me. You are touching me now. Do you remember your answer when I asked why the lifestyle appealed to you?"

"You mean about giving up control and trusting someone to take care of me?"

"Yes. I believe you said women worry about what their partner is thinking or if he's having to work too hard to please her. You also said women worry about whether they're doing the right things or not. Giving over control means not having to think about any of that. If you only have to do what I ask you to do, there is nothing for you to be concerned about. So I asked you to hold onto the edge of the stool. The fact is, had I not made that stipulation, there is nothing you could have done that would have disappointed me. But your thoughts would have been focused more on what you were *doing* rather than what you were *feeling*. And I just wanted you to feel."

She appeared to think about that for a few moments. "Wow."

He chuckled. "Right?"

She smiled. "Thank you, Sir."

"You're welcome. Thank you."

She frowned. "For what?"

He kissed the top of her head. "For giving me your trust and for submitting to me so beautifully. By doing that, I received *exactly* what I wanted."

"Then, you're welcome, Sir."

He probably shouldn't push her anymore. She had responded so well up to this point. Even the ease with which she addressed him as "Sir" was impressive. But somehow he knew she needed to take this next step. "Now, I'm going to ask you to do one more thing that might feel a little difficult at first. But you've given me your trust once tonight and I'd like it again."

"What do you want me to do, Sir?"

"I'd like for you to simply agree to do it without first knowing what it is."

She took in a deep breath and let it out slowly. "Okay. I'll do it."

He was floored. The request was intended to push her a little. To help her better understand the meaning of trust, but he didn't think she'd agree. He kissed her head again. "You amaze me. Thank you. What I would like for you to do is walk through the club with me for the rest of the night. Simply stay at my side. Perhaps watch a few scenes."

What he was actually asking her to do was face some of the people who had watched them and by the momentary look of alarm on her face, she knew it.

But she took a deep breath and said, "Whatever you wish, Sir."

He beamed at her. "The perfect answer."

For the rest of the evening, she did as he had asked and stayed at his side while he guided her through the club. As it grew later, he marveled at how smoothly she had slipped into the submissive role. When someone complemented them on the scene, she blushed profusely but did not become flustered. If a reply from her was required, it was always polite and gracious.

She also responded to his commands, as simple as most of them were, immediately and perfectly. At one point in the evening, he joined some friends who had gathered at one of several groupings of chairs and sofas. The music was lower in this part of the club and it was intended to be a place for conversation. Subs occasionally sat beside their Dom/mes, or on their laps, but more often subs knelt at their feet.

As they reached the area, Tristan said, "Cassandra, it would please me if you knelt beside me."

She simply said, "Yes, Sir," and sank gracefully to her knees. Every dominant within sight openly admired her. Tristan couldn't help but feel proud, even though he'd done almost no training with her so far.

At the end of the evening, he asked her to join him in his office after retrieving her things from the locker room.

He looked up from his desk when she knocked on the open door. "Come in, Cassandra. Please sit down." He motioned towards a chair and rounded the desk to sit in a chair beside her.

She sat primly, with her hands folded in her lap—her old-fashioned manners showing again. But her brow was furrowed and she bit her bottom lip.

He frowned. "What's bothering you?"

She looked up at him. "Bothering me? I'm just wondering what I did to upset you, Sir."

Tristan was flabbergasted. "You didn't upset me. What on earth gave you that idea?"

She cocked her head to one side. "Julia said she'd never heard of anyone being called to your office after a night at the club. She asked what I'd done, but I can't think of anything."

Tristan had trouble suppressing a laugh. "That's because you haven't done anything wrong. Trust me, Cassandra, if you do something for which you need reprimanded, I will tell you immediately and if a punishment is required, it will be given then and there."

She nodded, looking relieved.

"On the contrary, you behaved as a perfect sub tonight. It's as if you have been doing it for years."

She blushed. "Thank you, Sir."

"How did you feel, staying at my side as a submissive all evening?"

Her blush deepened but a small smile played at her lips. "I liked it."

"What did you like about it?"

"Honestly, I don't mean for this to sound clichéd, like every book I've ever read, but after a few minutes, after I got used to it, I felt...peaceful. I knew I was pleasing you because I was doing exactly what you asked of me. And I liked that."

"Were you still embarrassed by having done a public scene?"

"At first, yes. But you weren't. And nobody else was. Eventually, it didn't seem like such a big deal."

That was exactly what Tristan had hoped for. "How did you feel when I asked you to kneel?"

She smiled. "Comfortable. Safe. I felt as if I belonged."

He took one of her hands in his. "Cassandra, it seems as if you have been seeking something for a long time and I think this may be it. You adapted perfectly to the role and by your own admission it gave you peace. Do you want to come back here? Do you want to experience more of the lifestyle?"

She met his gaze. "I do. I want it more than I thought possible."

He smiled at her. "Then come back next weekend. I'd like to try another scene with you. One that will push your limits just a little. Are you game to try?"

She smiled broadly and nodded. "Yes, Sir. I am."

"Good girl. Then I am going to make one demand of you. Do not pleasure yourself or allow anyone else to do so this week."

She stared wide-eyed at him. "Excuse me?"

"You heard me. You are not allowed to climax. For the next seven days, your orgasms belong to me. Can you do that?"

She frowned. "Yes, of course, I can. But why?"

He chuckled. "I will let that pass because we are not in the club. When we are playing together, never ask me why I've given you a command. But seeing as we aren't in the club, and because it will further your education, I will tell you. For the next week, when hot, erotic thoughts come into your head and you feel the desire for release you will think of me. You will remember that for the time being, your orgasms are mine, not yours. I want that sweet sexual tension to build throughout the week and I want to be the one on your mind when it does."

She nodded, a slow smile spreading across her face. "Okay, Sir."

"Excellent. Then allow me to walk you to your car."

He walked to the parking lot with her. He had a strong urge to enfold her in his arms and give her a goodnight kiss that would leave her breathless and needy, but he restrained himself. He didn't want to send the wrong message.

As he watched her drive away, he regretted that decision. She was the most delightful woman he had met in ages. He thought he enjoyed well-trained, seasoned subs. Much to his surprise, he found both Cassie's naiveté and her natural inclination to submissiveness intensely attractive.

Chapter 8

On Saturday night, Cassie had been so confident about the desire to push her limits, she had easily agreed not to pleasure herself. After all, she didn't do that very often anyway. But even that night, after she was home and in bed, the memories of everything that she had seen and done at the club bombarded her senses. She wanted to let go of the tension that had built over the evening by pleasuring herself to orgasm, but she didn't give in.

As the week passed, to her dismay she learned things that are forbidden become a million times more enticing. Every mildly sensual scene that she read as she worked ignited her desire. Even just reading about a kiss reminded her of the mind-numbing way in which Tristan had kissed her. The more erotic scenes practically overwhelmed her. She yearned for the climax she had promised not to give herself.

By Wednesday, it felt as if sexual release was absolutely the only thing on her mind. As she got ready for bed that night she stared at her reflection in the bathroom mirror. "Why are you doing this to yourself? After all, you are a grown woman, the *master of your domain*. Stop this foolishness."

But she couldn't. A part of her, a surprisingly strong part of her, wanted to do this. She wanted to prove that she could. But more importantly, she wanted to please him. She imagined what it would feel like to tell him she had failed.

Failed? What the hell's the matter with you? He's practically a stranger. You don't owe him anything. You don't even have to tell him.

That was all true. Still, it didn't change the fact that, for reasons she didn't completely understand, she wanted to follow his command.

At last, Friday evening had arrived. Finding something to wear had been an ordeal. Although her friends in college insisted she had the figure for it, she had never been comfortable wearing tight, form-fitting clothes. She had always preferred dresses with princess lines, or flared skirts, believing they accentuated her figure in a more subtle way. And while she hadn't been opposed to wearing short skirts in college, for the last few years, her clothing choices had become more conservative.

However, buried in her closet, she'd found a short navy blue skirt. It had a silky underskirt with a sheer overlay. It was floaty and feminine—so much so that shortly after she had purchased it she realized a light breeze could lift it, exposing much more than she intended. Which was probably why it had ended up in the back of her closet. She had paired it with a white, silk and lace camisole that she usually wore under a suit jacket.

Shoes were another problem. Hers tended to be casual and comfortable. High heels were a hard limit for her. She had laughed when she had first seen them on the extensive list of limits, but on her first night she had realized why they'd been included. Most of the subs she had seen in the club wore heels, some extremely high. A few subs were barefooted and a few others wore gladiator type sandals that laced up the leg. She finally decided on a delicate pair of sandals that laced across her feet and tied around her ankles.

Now she stood once more before her bathroom mirror questioning both her wisdom and her sanity. For a week, she had willingly denied herself a very simple pleasure. Now she was dressed in the sexiest clothes she owned, preparing to go to a BDSM club where she had agreed to do a scene intended to *push her limits*, with a very experienced Dom. The same Dom who had been on her mind all week and who was responsible for her current state of heightened arousal.

Well, stupid or crazy, she intended to follow through with this. She silenced the voice of caution that usually guided her actions and went to her car.

When she arrived at the club, Julia once again waited for her in the parking lot.

"You didn't have to wait for me, Jules."

"I've only been here a few minutes, and I wanted to." She winked. "But after this weekend, you are on your own."

Cassie laughed. "Deal."

Once inside, Julia introduced her to Tina, the older woman who was working the desk and Cyndi, another sub who was checking in.

Tina smiled warmly. "Cassie, it is good to see you back this week and lovely to officially meet you. I saw the scene you did with Master Tristan last week, hon, and nearly melted. It was…well, it was beautiful."

Cassie felt the blush rise in her cheeks. But after having walked through the club with Tristan last Saturday and heard the same sentiment expressed in a multitude of ways, she wasn't as embarrassed as she might have been otherwise.

Cyndi bobbed her head exuberantly. "It was one of the hottest things I've ever seen happen between two fully clothed people. Your authors couldn't make that shit up, Julia."

"Yeah, I heard about it, but now I'm really sorry I didn't see it," said Julia. "Still, I was getting a little heat myself back in the alcoves with Master Adam." She grinned. "I had been a very naughty secretary. But as much fun as that was, it sounds like I missed an incredible scene."

"You did," said Cyndi. "Just thinking about it, I'm all hot and bothered. I've got to go find a big, bad Dom to play with now. I have to work later. See ya." She left through the door to the women's locker room.

"Way to go Cassie," said Julia. "You are already becoming a legend."

Cassie's blush deepened at that exaggeration. "Thank you, but I didn't do anything. It was all Master Tristan."

Tina looked shocked. "Oh, sweet girl, you are clearly new to all this. Master Tristan is a skilled Dominant, I would have expected nothing less from him. But it was your response that was beautiful. I know you were scared, but you trusted him and let him take control. And by doing that, the two of you ended up some place magical." She sighed.

Many people had complemented them on the scene last week, but no one had said it quite the way Tina had. She'd made it clear that simply the act of submission was beautiful and Cassie hadn't quite absorbed that yet. "I hadn't thought of it that way."

Tina grinned. "Then you should start thinking of it that way. Have you ever watched one of those reality shows where people are given something that they really need? You know like enough money to go to college or to get out of debt?"

"Yes."

"And do you sometimes cry knowing what a gift they've been given?"

Cassie smiled. "Yes."

"Why?"

Cassie cocked her head to one side. "Why? Doesn't nearly everyone cry at those shows?"

"Yes, but *why*?"

"I don't know exactly…I guess…I guess it's amazing to see someone give such a wonderful gift and know that the person getting it not only needed it, they really truly valued it."

Tina smiled and nodded. "Exactly. And when you give someone your trust and submission, it's the same thing. At least it is in this community. We see it as an incredibly wonderful gift and when the Dom in question really truly values it, it is amazingly beautiful to witness."

Cassie was floored. She really hadn't thought of it like that. In the moment it was the most sensual, delightful kiss she had ever received. She assumed all of the compliments had been about Tristan's skill and really hadn't believed she'd played any role.

Tina patted her arm. "I'm glad to see you understand a little more now. Look for it tonight when you watch other scenes."

"I will. Thank you, Tina."

"Don't mention it. Now, the two of you should get on into the club. I know Master Tristan is waiting for you, Cassie."

Once in the locker room, Cassie put her purse and sweater in a locker.

Julia pulled off the T-shirt dress she was wearing. Underneath, she wore a bustier that pushed her breasts up but didn't cover them and a matching thong. She exchanged her flip-flops for six-inch stilettos.

When she was finished changing she looked at Cassie and frowned. "Come on, Cass, at least ditch the bra."

Truthfully, the bra concealed more than the cami did but she couldn't quite bring herself to go into the club wearing just a bra. So she took it off and put in the locker.

"Oooh, much better. You have gorgeous breasts, show them off."

Julia grabbed her arm and pulled her towards the door to the club.

Just as Tina had said, Tristan appeared to have been waiting, watching the locker room door. He strode toward them looking dangerously handsome in black jeans and a tailored black dress shirt with the sleeved rolled up. "Good evening, Cassandra, Julia. You both look lovely tonight."

"Thank you, Sir," said Cassie.

"Thank you, Master Tristan," said Julia, giving a little shimmy that caused her boobs to bounce. "I suggested Julia lose the bra. Free the tatas, that's what I always say."

Tristan smiled. "Yes, I'm aware of that. I believe Master Jude and Master Kent have something planned for you and your lovely tatas, Julia. You won't want to keep them waiting."

"No, Sir," said Julia. "May I be excused?"

"Certainly. Have a good evening."

"Thank you, Master Tristan," she said as she hurried off.

Tristan turned his attention to Cassie. He reached out and pushed a lock of hair behind her ear. "You really are exquisite."

Her cheeks warmed. "Thank you. I don't actually have club clothes, just ordinary stuff."

"Well you manage to make the ordinary, extraordinary. Tell me, did Julia tell you to leave the bra behind last Saturday?"

Cassie nodded, knowing her cheeks burned even hotter with embarrassment.

"Let me hear your voice, Cassandra."

"Yes, Sir."

"Were you comfortable with that?"

She shook her head. "Not at first, but after a while I felt pretty overdressed and was glad I wasn't wearing it."

"And tonight?"

"This cami doesn't cover much…"

"That isn't what I asked. Are you comfortable not wearing a bra tonight."

She glanced around. Compared to most people there, she was dressed like a nun. And truth be told, the silky fabric of the cami felt good against her nipples. "I wasn't when I took it off in the locker room, but I am now. I like the way it feels."

He smiled broadly. "Good. I'm sure Julia is trying to push you a little and that's okay. But I don't want you doing something that makes you very uncomfortable just because she suggests it."

"I won't, Sir. Thank you."

He gave her a broad grin, his eyes twinkling mischievously. "I, on the other hand, reserve the right to push you from your comfort zone a bit harder."

She smiled. "I have no doubt, Sir."

He chuckled and held out a hand. "Your panties please."

Her eyes went wide. "M—my panties?"

"Yes, Cassandra. Your skirt is long enough to cover that delicious backside thus we are not encroaching upon any of your limits. Remove your panties and put them in my hand. Don't make me ask again."

She swallowed hard. There is no way on earth she would ever have imagined removing her panties—in public—and then giving them to the man who had asked for them. And yet, that is exactly what she did. Almost without hesitation, she slipped them off and handed them to him.

He smiled approvingly. "Good girl." He put them in the pocket of his jeans. "One more thing, last week I gave you an order. Did you follow it?"

She gave a tiny huff of frustration. "Yes, Sir."

He chuckled. "Harder to follow that you thought it would be? Are you feeling a little needy tonight?"

A little needy? The sights, sounds and smells of the club had only increased the desire that burned within her. She felt like a quivering mass of sexual yearning. "Yes, Sir."

He leaned close to her ear. "Thank you for suppressing whatever sarcastic comment might have been on the tip of your tongue. I'm impressed."

She smiled, suddenly very glad that she had held her tongue. She liked his praise.

"Last week you also agreed to do another scene with me tonight. Are you still up for it?"

"Yes, Sir," she answered without hesitation before adding, "but we will negotiate it, won't we, Sir?"

He smiled with what appeared to be pride. "We certainly will. Good girl. Now, come with me."

He took her hand and led her to the back of the club. The front half of the club was completely open with equipment for scenes set up in the center and along some of the walls. The back half of the club was divided into alcoves, each decorated with a different theme, the ubiquitous medieval dungeon, a doctor's office, a lush harem, a Victorian bedroom complete with a four-poster bed, the captain's cabin of a pirate ship, a prison cell, an executive's office, a futuristic space ship, and several others. They all had useful equipment worked into the décor. While there was an air of privacy to them, and they didn't always draw a crowd of observers, what went on inside them was visible from the outside. Several Club Monitors were stationed nearby and Cassie had learned the previous week that these skilled Dom/mes kept a close watch on the scenes playing out in the more secluded rooms.

He took her to an alcove that was decorated exactly as the "play rooms" she had read about, black and red with lots of leather. In the middle of the room was a spanking bench. Butterflies took flight in her stomach. This looked like it was about to get very real.

As if sensing her trepidation, Tristan's hand tightened on hers. "You have nothing to be afraid of. Look at me."

Cassie did. If only to keep from staring at the spanking bench in terror.

"Cassandra, I know your soft and hard limits. I know this is all new to you. Do you trust me to stay aware of these things at all times?"

"Y-yes, Sir."

He smiled. "I would have preferred a little more confidence, but for the moment, I'll take that. So this is what I'm proposing. You will get onto the spanking bench, wearing the clothes you are wearing. Notice the back of the bench, where your bottom will be, is facing the back wall. No one but me will be able to see your gorgeous backside, or anything else that isn't already exposed. I will secure your thighs and your waist to the bench, for your safety—so you don't fall off. I will secure your wrists as well, but not snugly. You will be able to pull your hands out if you need to. Do you understand all of this?"

She nodded.

"I need to hear the words, little bird."

"Yes, Sir."

"Good. After you are in position, I will give you a sensual spanking. Do you know what that is?"

"Yes, Sir, I think so. It's meant to be enjoyable."

"Exactly. The pain is mild and intended to stimulate the release of endorphins, which actually enhance your pleasure. To that end, I will only spank you with my hand and I will also touch you in any way I see fit. Do you understand?"

She nodded. "Yes, Sir."

"Good. Now the most important part, you are not allowed to come, until I tell you to."

Her eyes snapped to his. "Come? Here?" Her voice squeaked.

He chuckled. "Yes. Here. You have gone a full week without climaxing, surely you deserve to come tonight?"

Another blush burned her cheeks. "Yes, but…"

"But what? Has anything I described encroached on your hard limits?"

"No, Sir."

"Have I agreed to shield you from public nudity? A soft limit?"

"Yes, Sir."

"If we were in complete solitude, is this something you would want?"

"Yes, Sir." *Dear God,* she wasn't sure she had ever wanted anything more.

"Then you will do this for me because tonight I am your Dom and it is what I want. I want to see your ass turn pink from my spanking, hear you moan with pleasure and watch you come. Do you consent?"

She took a deep breath. "Yes, Sir. I do."

He gave her a brilliant smile that warmed her to her toes. "Excellent. Then come here to the spanking bench.

She glanced toward the open wall as she walked to the bench. There were people outside, but no one seemed to be specifically watching. She climbed on the bench and, as he'd said he would, he fastened a strap around her waist and one around each thigh. The position of the straps caused her legs to be spread, opening her to him.

After fastening the last one, his hand slid up her inner thigh, under her skirt, to her pussy. One finger slipped inside and circled her clit. After a week of denial, that was almost enough to make her come.

"You are very wet, Cassandra." He removed his finger and stepped in front of her. He held up the finger he'd touched her with. It glistened with her moisture. "You see how wet you are? You are ready for this."

He put his finger into his mouth, sucking her wetness from it. "Ah, my precious little bird, you taste every bit as delicious as I thought you would. Someday, perhaps you'll let me feast on your lusciousness. But today I'll satisfy myself with a taste or two."

Her eyes went wide, completely stunned.

He put one of her hands in a padded leather restraint. "Tug your hand out of that, just so you know you can."

She pulled and twisted a little. Her hand slid out as if the restraint were just a snug bangle. He did the same on the other side. Then he crouched down, so he was looking her directly in the eye. "What are your safewords?"

"Yellow and red, Sir."

"Good girl. I expect you to use them if you need to."

He stood back up and ran his hand from the back of her head, down her back. "This is your first real experience with bondage and pain. We are both learning what's good for you. If something becomes too intense you must tell me. Do you understand?"

She nodded.

He gave her a stinging slap on her ass. "Answer me." His tone of voice had changed, holding a note of menace.

"Y-yes, Sir. I understand. I'll tell you if it becomes too intense." Even so, she feared that the sudden change in his demeanor accompanied by the slightly painful swat was right on the edge of too intense already.

"Good girl." His tone was still steely, but had lost its menace.

His hand reached under her skirt and massaged the place where he had just spanked her. The sting had already passed, leaving a pleasant tingling sensation in its wake. She tensed, expecting another swat but to her surprise, his fingers slid between her legs again. Touching her, massaging her, exploring her most private parts. First he tapped lightly on the head of her clit several times, then he circled it. The pressure felt good, but it was not nearly enough.

After playing with her, building her need to fever pitch, without warning, he removed his hand. He spanked the fleshy part of her left cheek and rubbed it a little before doing the same to her right one. It didn't hurt, not like the first swat had, but it left her skin tingling. He continued doing that, covering her entire backside and upper thighs with the light spanking. Before long, the blows became a little harder. The sting lasted a little longer but the tingling that immediately followed became more intense too. Finally he landed one harder blow right in the center at the spot where her cheeks met her thighs.

Her eyes watered and she sucked in a breath. Before she could react, he was rubbing lightly over the area he had spanked and it felt divine. Just as she was sinking into that delightful sensation, his fingers found her clit again, tapping and circling in a maddening rhythm that took her to the edge but no farther.

She moaned and tried to push against his hand, willing him to increase the pressure.

He tsked at her, removing his hand altogether. "That's a naughty girl." He spanked her once, the burning pain lasting a moment longer than all the others. "I will give you what I want you to have, when I want you to have it. Do you understand me?"

"Yes, Sir," she moaned. She had yearned for release all week and here she was, on the edge and he forced her to stay there.

He started spanking her again. She knew the blows were harder than those first few, but the sensation was indescribable. It hurt a little but the feeling that remained just after the blow was worth the small discomfort. It felt as if every nerve ending on her ass and thighs was awake and singing. The light brush of his fingers across the sensitive skin had become almost as stimulating as touching her clit.

He gave her two more hard swats on the crease of her thighs and she realized she was on the edge of orgasm. She had to pant to hold it back.

His touch softened again, gently stroking her sensitive backside as he whispered. "Good girl. You are remarkable."

Just when she'd gotten it under control, his fingers found her clit again, tapping and circling. Then he slipped a finger from his other hand, into her and she fought desperately for control until he whispered, "Come for me now, little bird."

She cried out, overcome with the most powerful, earth-shattering orgasm she had ever experienced. Her body felt electrified as wave after wave of ecstasy swept over her. He didn't take his hands from her until the last shudder had passed.

She was vaguely aware of him removing the restraints that had held her on the bench. She tried to stand up, but he scooped her in his arms and carried her to the same screened quiet area he had taken her to last weekend. He pulled a blanket over her and she contented herself to snuggle into his embrace.

Chapter 9

Tristan simply could not believe what had just happened. He had pushed her little by little, starting gently and then building. She had responded to every touch, appearing to delight in the growing sensations to such a degree that he didn't stop. Hell, when he'd expected her to finally say "yellow", she nearly came. And when she did climax, it was with absolute abandon.

She had submitted to him and given him her trust so completely she shattered into a million pieces. Women like Cassandra, shy and always in control, didn't do that easily. He had never seen anything like it and it left him so hard, he ached.

But he had to put all thoughts of himself aside for the moment. She had trusted him and he wouldn't let her down now. He just held her close as she returned to earth. When she did finally realize where she was again, just like the last time, she sat up straight in his lap.

Her hand flew to her face. "Oh, dear God. I can't believe…I mean I just…oh, God…how could I just…"

He stroked her back. "Shh, Cassandra. Hush now. That was spectacular. You were absolutely breathtaking."

"But, I've never…I mean…that was…oh, dear God, I'm so embarrassed."

He put a hand under her chin, turning her face towards him as he pulled her hands away from her face with the other hand. "Tell me what has you so upset."

"I've never done that before."

"You've never had an orgasm?"

"Yes, I've had an orgasm, just never one like that. *I yelled.*" Her tone of voice suggested that she thought what she'd done was terrible.

"Cassandra, I know you saw both men and women yell and moan in the grips of orgasm last week."

"Yes, but *I* don't do that." She covered her face with her hands again.

He forced himself not to laugh. It would be the totally wrong response, but her innocence gave him joy. "Cassandra, my little bird, clearly no one has ever adequately pleased you. That is exactly the reaction I wanted from you and it thrills me that you came so intensely." Again, he pulled her hands away from her face and kissed each palm. "You are like no woman I've ever played with. You gave me precisely what I sought and for that I am grateful beyond words."

"Really, Sir?"

"Really." He coaxed her down against his chest again. He could practically hear her thoughts whirring and he wanted them to stop. "Cassandra, will you let me do it again?"

"What? Spank me?"

He chuckled. "No, little bird. Your ass may be somewhat tender as it is. Let me make you come again. Here. On my lap."

"Are you serious?"

"Very serious." Even as he said it, one hand slipped under the blanket and stroked her thigh. "No one can see you. Let me please you again."

"I...I..."

"It was a long week wasn't it?"

She smiled. "Yes, it was, *Sir*."

"Then remember that I am your Dom, relax, and let me do this."

"Yes, Sir." She rested her head against his shoulder and he slipped his fingers into her warm, wet pussy again.

This time he didn't tease. He applied pressure and set a rhythm intended to make her build instantly. "Try not to move and remember, don't come until I tell you to."

He smiled at the little groan that escaped her lips.

Within minutes, she was panting and trembling with the effort it took not to move.

"Come for me now," he whispered.

Her body instantly shuddered and pulsed as she came in his arms. A soft moan escaped her lips. When the spasms had passed, he cupped her pussy with his hand, squeezing lightly, keeping indirect pressure on her clit.

"One more time?" he whispered.

"I don't think I—"

"When you're here, with me, it's not your job to think. Just feel. You've been a very good girl. Do you want to come one more time?"

Her eyes went wide, but she nodded. "Yes, Sir."

So he began again, this time circling her clit with his thumb briefly before putting two fingers inside her. She threw her head back and panted trying once again to hold back the orgasm threatening to devour her.

As soon as the word "Come" passed his lips, she shattered again. Then she curled into his embrace like a sleepy kitten for several long minutes. He would have been content to sit with her like this for the rest of the night if need be, but soon enough she began to emerge from her post orgasmic haze.

"That was…that was…" She lifted her head and looked into his eyes. "Honestly, there isn't a word for it."

He chuckled. "I have to agree. I enjoyed every single moment of it."

She looked confused. "You enjoyed it? But, you didn't…I mean…I didn't—"

He put a finger to her lips. "Cassandra, I have already told you. We did precisely what I wanted to do and I got exactly what I desired out of it—your submission. I have to tell you, it took my breath away."

"Well, thank you, Sir. I…like I said, there are no words."

"No words are needed. Your response told me everything."

She smiled shyly and blushed. After everything that he had just done to her, she could still blush and for some reason that delighted him.

"Are you feeling up to rejoining the world?"

"Yes, Sir."

He helped her stand. "Are you okay?"

"I think so. I don't think I could run if my life depended on it, but I'm okay."

He would have had her stay with him as he made the rounds of the club, just like she had last week, but she was clearly spent. She needed rest and hydration but he still needed to check on things. "I'm going to take you to the place where many of the single subs hang out. We'll get you something to drink. You need to take it easy for a little while."

"Yes, Sir. Can I have my panties back first?"

He grinned. "No."

"But, Sir, I'm…sticky." Again, she blushed profusely.

"And I quite like that about you." He put his hand in the small of her back and guided her to one of the seating areas on the edges of the club. It was an area that had come to be called the "Sub Lounge", because single subs frequently congregated there. Once there, he motioned for Tina to join them.

Tina had years of experience as a sub. She and her husband had been charter members of Hidden Gem. Her husband had died of cancer a few years ago. Tina didn't play with anyone anymore, although there were older Doms who would have loved the opportunity, she said she wasn't ready for that. Still this is where her friends were, it felt more like home than any place else. So she came most weekends, eventually falling into a motherly role with the club's subs, giving them advice or a shoulder to cry on when they needed it. She also had no qualms about kicking someone's ass if it were necessary—figuratively that is. The gentle woman wouldn't hurt a fly. But she didn't like bratty behavior and made no bones about it. Tina would keep an eye on Cassandra for him.

"Good evening, Tina. How are you tonight?"

"Very well, Master Tristan, thank you. And you, Sir?"

"Couldn't be better. I was just wondering if you could do a favor for me."

"Of course, Sir. Just name it."

"Cassandra has had an eventful evening. I'd like for her to relax and replenish for a while. Can I leave her in your hands while I attend to some business?"

A slow smile spread across Tina's face. "Of course, Sir. I'd be happy to help. Cassie, honey, what flavor sports drink do you like."

Cassie wrinkled her nose. "Water is fine. I don't really like sports drinks."

Tristan was about to step in to say Cassie needed more than just water but Tina was on top of it.

Her brows drew together slightly. "Do you like peaches, hon?"

"I love them."

"Well, Mistress Elaine is working the bar tonight and she makes an amazing peach smoothie. How about you try one?"

Tristan nodded approvingly. Elaine's smoothie would include both electrolytes and some protein. It was just what Cassie needed.

"That sounds great. Thanks. But I can get it myself."

Tristan frowned. "Cassandra, I have instructed Tina to look after you. You aren't going to make it hard for her to obey me are you?"

She smiled, shaking her head slightly. "No, Sir. I won't."

"Then be a good girl, sit down and let Tina bring you a smoothie."

"Yes, Sir. Thank you, Tina. I appreciate it."

"No problem at all. I'll be right back."

Tristan smiled. "Excellent. You are in good hands, Cassandra."

He left to make rounds of the club. As he'd intended, fewer people saw the spanking scene with Cassie, but those who did were as impressed with her as he'd been. Two of his best friends, Diana and Adam were among them.

"She's a natural submissive," said Diana. "Either that, or the two of you have some sort of deep, cosmic connection."

"I don't believe in *deep, cosmic connections*," said Tristan.

"You don't have to believe in them for one to exist, but either way, I've never seen any sub respond so perfectly."

He couldn't deny that.

"It would be interesting to see how she does with a different Dom," said Adam.

Tristan frowned. He didn't like the idea of her playing with another Dom. He had never reacted to a new sub this way. Even though he had no hold over her, he didn't want anyone else to have her either. "I'm not sure she's ready yet. Her aversion to public play makes it difficult. I wouldn't want her hurt."

Diana said, "There are plenty of skilled Doms here who would consider her needs."

Fuck. They had been friends for years and Diana had a well-tuned bullshit meter. "There are, it's just that…"

"Do you intend to collar her?" she asked.

"Damn, Diana, how'd you get there? She's a newbie and I've only known her a week."

Diana shrugged. "I got there, Tristan, because you seem to be oddly possessive of a *newbie who you've only known a week*. Normally you pick someone to train a new sub after your first interview."

And there it was, she had drilled to the core of the issue. Tristan shot Adam a look, hoping for a little back up, but knowing he was as astute as Diana.

Adam shook his head. "Sorry, buddy, I have to take Diana's side in this. Cassandra needs to be someone's responsibility. Either she is yours or she isn't. You must make that plain to everyone. Especially her."

Tristan frowned. "She's not mine. But she's different and it's too soon to pick a Dom for her even just to train with."

The statement was met with arched eyebrows, but no further comment.

The words, *she's not mine*, haunted Tristan the rest of the evening, but he told himself a reasonable person didn't collar a sub after one week and he wasn't in the habit of taking on trainees. He had too many other responsibilities. He'd find someone to work with her soon.

It took about an hour, but after he had checked in with all of the Club Monitors, he made his way back to the Sub Lounge. As a number of scenes had been completed, there were more subs relaxing there than when he'd left Cassie. However, as he approached, he realized she was not among them.

He found Tina. "Where did Cassie go?"

"Julia joined her about fifteen minutes after you left. They chatted for a while and then left together about ten minutes ago."

"You let her leave?"

"Master Tristan, she drank her smoothie and then a bottle of water. She was strong and steady and seemed to have recovered. I had no reason to insist she stay."

"But I hadn't given her permission to leave."

"I'm sorry, Sir. You didn't tell me that. Funny, she was so sweet. She doesn't seem at all like the sort to openly defy an order."

He shook his head in frustration. "She isn't. I didn't tell her not to leave. I didn't think I had to. I'd assumed she'd stay until I returned." But he'd had no reason to assume that. She was not his sub. She was only bound by the house rules unless she agreed to others with a particular Dom.

Tina said, "It would seem she's somewhat inexperienced. I suspect it pays to be extremely clear with her."

"Tina, that was a lovely way to tell me I fucked up."

She smiled coyly. "Master Tristan, I would never presume to tell you any such thing. She seems to have everything it takes to be a good submissive. I think it might be easy to forget she's also new to all of this. But she and Julia both said they'd be back tomorrow."

Tina was right. He'd made a mistake, but all things considered, it was an easy one to make. It wasn't the end of the world. He would make things clearer to Cassie tomorrow. He leaned forward and kissed the older woman's cheek. "You are priceless, Tina."

"Thank you, Sir."

He'd talk to Cassie again tomorrow. Better yet, he'd call her in a little while to make certain she made it home safely.

He went to his office and pulled her file. He frowned when he saw she had a Lutz address. She had said she lived just north of Tampa and technically she did, but it was at least an hour's drive from the club. He didn't want to risk calling her while she was driving, so he waited about an hour. That should have given her plenty of time to get home.

When the hour was up, he called, but there was no answer.

He didn't leave a message, but called again in fifteen minutes.

Still no answer.

He waited fifteen more minutes and tried again and still, the call went to voicemail. He would have preferred to speak to her, but it looked like he'd have to leave a message. "Cassandra, this is Tristan. I'd intended to see you again before the evening was over. I didn't realize how far from the club you lived and I'd like to know you made it home okay. Please give me a call as soon as you get this message." He left her his cellphone number.

It was almost closing time and he needed to go back to the club, but cellphones were forbidden because of the privacy risk they posed. He certainly wouldn't break his own rule. He went to the lobby and Cyndi, a chatty elementary school teacher and sub who was a working member of the club was at the desk.

"Hi, Master Tristan. It's been a great night, don't you think? I had a blast as always."

"I'm glad to hear it. Cyndi, I have to go back to the club, but I'm expecting a call on my cell."

"Okay, I'll take it for you, Sir."

"If it rings, don't answer it. Just send someone to get me. I'll call the person back."

"That's okay, Sir. I can answer it and just tell them you'll be with them in a minute. That way you won't have to call them back."

He adopted his most severe Dom voice. "Cyndi, you are not in your classroom and thus you are not the one in charge. I have given you your instructions. If you do not follow them, I will punish you and I promise you won't enjoy it."

"Yes, Sir." Her tone was a little petulant but he ignored it. Being surrounded by second graders all day had to take a toll on a person.

He returned to the floor until closing, but asked Sean Casey, another good friend and club monitor, to see that everything was taken care of before locking up. He went back to the front desk to get his phone from Cyndi.

She smiled and handed it to him. "Not a single call, Sir."

"Thank you, Cyndi."

"I hope everything's okay."

"It's fine. Good night."

He sprinted up the stairs to his office, double checked Cassie's number and called her again, still only reaching her voicemail. It was after two now. She had left shortly after eleven. She should have been long home and returned his call by now. He left another message. "Cassandra, I'm worried about you. It's after two and you haven't returned my call. No matter what time it is, please call me as soon as you get this so I know you're okay."

He usually stayed in his suite at the resort on Friday nights but he wasn't anxious to leave his office. If something had happened to Cassie, and she didn't get his message, the only number she had on which to reach him was the club number.

And yet, he had to be honest with himself. If something had happened to her, it isn't likely he'd be the first person she would call. They'd only known each other a week—even though it felt much longer, like the kind of *deep, cosmic connection* in which he did not believe. Finally, exhaustion won out and he made his way to his suite.

He didn't sleep well and woke up earlier than usual for a Saturday morning. Although his cellphone had been on the nightstand, with the ringer set to high, he checked it anyway to see if he'd missed a call.

Nothing.

Now he was angry. How could she ignore his messages and let him worry like this? He dialed her number, not caring how early it was and like all the other times, it went to voicemail. "Cassandra Hastings, you may think this is amusing, but I do not. You experienced a very intense scene last night and then left without giving me the opportunity to make certain you had recovered. Obviously, I have called several times and left you two messages letting you know that I am worried and you have ignored them. Call me as soon as you get this. Otherwise, I expect to see you in my office this evening before you go to the club."

Part of him, a very large, angry part of him, wanted to drive to her address to see if she was there. However, that was a violation of her privacy and he wouldn't give in to that desire, no matter how much he wanted to. But, by God, she'd better have a good explanation for this behavior or he'd show her the difference between a sensual spanking and punishment.

Chapter 10

Cassie hadn't been sure what all was in Mistress Elaine's smoothie, and she hadn't realized exactly how wiped-out the scene had left her until she felt the energy from the smoothie picking her up.

"Yeah, girl, for vanilla sex you can just roll over and go to sleep. But a BDSM scene is strenuous on so many levels, mentally, physically, and emotionally," said Julia, "you've got to actively take steps to recoup."

They chatted for a while, and Cassie drank a bottle of water on top of the smoothie. After that, she no longer felt shattered—just a normal degree of tired. She yawned. "I have a long drive. I think I should hit the road before my energy flags again."

"Damn, that's right. What is it from here, an hour?" asked Julia.

"Just a little more than an hour."

"Hey, I'm not sure that's a good idea. This was your first real scene, you've got to be dragging. How about you follow me home? I live much closer, near Pinellas Park. You can spend the night and we can go shopping tomorrow for some other outfits for the club. Then, if you're up to it, you can drive home tomorrow night."

Normally Cassie wouldn't want to put someone out by being a surprise overnight guest, but she was really tired. "Okay. That sounds like a plan."

It still took twenty-five minutes to get to Julia's place, but that was significantly better than an hour plus. Her apartment seemed nice, but Cassie paid very little attention to it. She was more concerned with sleep than anything else.

They slept in until late morning, then got ready to go out for brunch and shopping. That's when Julia realized she didn't have anything decent to wear. As long as she wore her bra under it, the silk cami would be okay. The skirt was a bit of a mess. Even if she cleaned it up enough to be presentable, there was no way she was going out in public with nothing underneath it on a breezy day.

Julia laughed hysterically when Cassie—wearing her cami with a towel around her waist—explained the problem. "Kept a souvenir did he? That's a good sign."

"He didn't *keep a souvenir*. He just forgot to give them back. We didn't see him again before we left."

"Believe what you want to. I think Master Tristan likes you."

"Oh, stop. Can I just borrow something to wear please?"

"Of course you can." She tossed her a pair of cute denim shorts. "Although I'm tempted to make you go commando so all day long you can be reminded who has your undies in his pocket."

"Well, if you want me to go with you, you better loan me some *undies*, because I have no intention of going shopping commando."

"Then it's granny panties for you."

Cassie laughed. "I don't care."

Shopping with Julia was a blast and while their tastes varied considerably, they both managed to find some great things.

Their first stop was a lingerie store.

Cassie was looking at a beautiful cream-colored bra and thong set, trimmed with pink ribbons and pearls.

"Cassie, pearls and pink ribbons aren't exactly a common look at the club."

"Maybe not. Still, I've been thinking a lot about this. I know black leather, latex and chrome are the norm, but I feel out of place in that stuff. I think that's one of the reasons I'm nervous. Exposing myself like that doesn't feel like me. But these things are beautiful. I'd feel pretty in them and I think maybe I'd have more confidence and be a little more comfortable."

Julia gave her a puzzled look. "You know, that makes an odd kind of sense. You go right ahead and do what works for you, girl."

Shopping for fancy undergarments reminded Cassie of something her grandmother used to say and she smiled at the memory.

"What's funny?" asked Julia.

"I just remembered, my grandma always warned me never to wear matching underwear sets."

"Why not?" asked Julia. "Don't tell me she thought you'd go to hell or something."

"Oh no, nothing like that. She figured I'd live longer."

Julia looked skeptical. "Okay…why?"

Cassie grinned. "She watched a lot of crime shows and she said every time they showed a murdered woman, her bra and panties matched."

Julia snorted. "You're kidding."

"I'm not. But she was. Before she got really ill she was pretty funny."

In the end Cassie went home with four new bras, matching thongs, a beautiful lace trimmed, pink slip dress that she could never wear in public but would work for the club, and a sheer lace tunic that Julia had insisted she buy.

"If you aren't comfortable showing off your incredible assets, you can wear it over some of that gorgeous lingerie and feel a little more covered. And I'll get to watch every man in the club drool."

They finished the shopping trip with dinner at a nice seafood restaurant.

The club was open from eight until two and unlike other nightclubs, people normally began arriving pretty close to eight. But tonight Julia had to work the front desk from ten until midnight.

"There's more work to do on the eight to ten shift because you have to check everyone in, but when you're done you still have the whole evening. At least working ten to midnight there's still a little time to play afterwards. The last shift sucks for a sub because it's really hard to play and then have to go to work although some people do it. We'll aim to get there at nine-thirty. I can introduce you to a few more people before I have to be on the desk."

But Denny called at eight-thirty begging Julia to take over early for him. "Apparently Mistress Elaine said she'd do a scene with him tonight and he's so excited he can't focus on anything."

"How early does he want you there?"

Julia laughed. "Five minutes ago."

Cassie grinned. "I'll be ready in a minute."

"No worries. You were going to take your car right? I'll head out now, just come when you're ready. You are going to look great in that new dress."

Cassie ended up putting on the ribbon and pearl edged bra and thong but wearing the shorts and cami over them to drive to the club.

She arrived about fifteen minutes after Julia had.

Julia frowned at her. "You are not wearing those shorts in the club. What happened to the dress?"

"Nothing. It's in my bag. I'll change here. I just kept imagining being pulled over by a policeman or breaking down on the side of the road in that dress and couldn't bring myself to wear it in the car."

"Well, if the cop was a guy, that dress could get you out of any ticket, but go change now. If Master Tristan isn't already in the club, find Tina. She'll look after you."

There was no one in the locker room. She quickly changed out of the shorts and cami and into the slip dress. It was delicate and very feminine. She felt beautiful in it. She still wore the laced sandals she had the previous night, but they worked with the outfit. She took a deep breath and for the first time, stepped into the club alone.

She glanced around, but didn't see Tristan anywhere. It was disappointing but he hadn't asked her to do another scene with him tonight and so they'd made no plans to meet. Without Julia or Tristan, Cassie suddenly felt very alone and out of place. Her initial instinct was to head back to the locker room but Julia had said to find Tina. Still, if she didn't find the older sub in a few minutes, she'd go back.

She looked around the main club area a little but when she didn't see Tina, she made her way to the Sub Lounge. Unfortunately, Tina wasn't there either, nor was anyone she had met before. She stood there for a moment, not sure what to do and hoping maybe either Tina or Tristan would show up.

From somewhere behind her, a man with a Boston accent said, "Girl, I've never seen you here before." It didn't register that he might be talking to her.

In the next moment she heard his voice again, sounding extremely irritated. "Are you ignoring me, girl?"

She turned to look at him. Tall, sandy-haired and powerfully built, the man was perhaps in his late thirties.

"No. I was looking for someone. I didn't realize you were speaking to me."

"Well, do you realize it now?"

She frowned. "Yes, of course I do."

He scowled at her. "And do you realize *where you are?*"

"What?"

His tone shifted to icy steel. "You'd better kneel and present yourself now girl and see if you can remember the correct way to address a Dom."

Oh shit, oh shit, oh shit. Focused only on finding Tina, she had forgotten she was in a BDSM club where rules applied. "I…uh…I'm sorry, Sir…I…"

"I said kneel and present," he commanded.

She sank to her knees.

"*Present*," he said, sounding even more irritated.

She looked up at him. "I don't understand…Sir."

"Do you belong to someone?"

"Ah, now, that's a good question, Jim," came Mistress Diana's voice from behind Cassie.

The man Diana had addressed as Jim looked past Cassie. "What the hell does that mean?"

"Cassandra, sweetheart, what Master Jim is asking you to do is kneel upright, your knees about shoulder width apart, your hands clasped on your forearms behind your back and your head down. I suspect you haven't learned that yet."

Cassie tried to do what Mistress Diana had described, but she felt herself trembling. She had completely messed this up.

"You've been away for few weeks, Jim, this is Cassandra Hastings. Normally, she is rather sweet and very respectful, but she is extremely new to the lifestyle and she seems to be a little lost tonight."

He put a hand out and stroked the side of Cassie's head. "Calm yourself, girl. Relax now. Put your hands on your thighs."

Cassie sank back down onto her heels and rested her hands on her thighs, embarrassed, confused and a little afraid of what was happening.

"As to the question of whether she belongs to someone," Diana continued, "technically she doesn't."

"What the fuck has gotten into Tristan? She could get hurt alone."

"I don't think he realizes she's here alone. She was supposed to go straight to his office this evening."

Cassie gasped and frowned, ready to deny that, but bit her tongue. She shouldn't speak until asked to.

The Dom named Jim took a step closer to her, assuming almost a protective stance. "By her reaction, she clearly didn't know that."

"Cassandra, didn't Denny tell you to go to Master Tristan's office when you arrived?"

"No, Mistress Diana. Denny wasn't on the desk when I arrived."

"Who was?"

"Denny called and asked if Julia would relieve him early, Miss. I was at her apartment but wasn't quite ready to leave and we were driving separately anyway. She was on the desk when I arrived."

"You were at her apartment? Did you go there last night? Were you with her all day?"

Cassie wasn't sure why that mattered, but she didn't openly question the Domme. "Yes, Mistress Diana. I was really tired last night and I live over an hour away. Julia invited me to stay with her so I didn't have to make the long drive."

"That was a very good idea. Last night was probably a little intense for you. But did you not check your cell phone today?"

"My cell phone? No, Miss. I own a cell phone, but I just have it for emergencies. I never get calls on it. I don't give the number out."

"So the number we have here isn't your cell phone?"

"No, Miss. It's my home phone."

"*Holy crap on a cracker*," said Diana.

"What the hell's the matter?" asked Master Jim.

Diana didn't answer him directly. "Cassandra, we need to go upstairs and see Master Tristan right now."

"Stand up, girl." Jim put his hand out to Cassie to help her up. "I'm going with you, Diana. He needs to explain to me how he let this girl go with no protection. If she needs training,

I'll take the gig. She does seem to be a sweet little thing, but she shouldn't be here alone until she learns more."

"Look, Jim. There's been a huge misunderstanding. He didn't intend for her to be here alone and he's going to be furious when he learns she ended up here because Denny didn't ensure that she got his message."

"I'm going anyway."

"Suit yourself."

Cassie didn't completely understand what was going on. Diana headed to a door Cassie hadn't noticed before. Master Jim put a hand in the small of her back and urged her to follow. The door led to an emergency exit and a stairwell. The stairwell was a back entrance to the second floor where Tristan's office was located.

Diana knocked and entered. "Tristan, good news. I just ran into Cassandra in the club and she's fine."

He looked up from his desk and glared at Cassie. She took an involuntary step backwards into the solid bulk of Master Jim.

Diana shook her head. "Tristan, before you explode, Cassandra made the sound decision to go home with Julia last night so she didn't have to drive so far while she was tired. And the number you have for her is her home phone, not a cell. She hasn't been home since yesterday and couldn't possibly have gotten your messages."

"And how is it you learned all of this. She was supposed to come straight to my office."

"Well that would be Denny's fault. He apparently asked Julia to take over early for him, but didn't give her the message for Cassandra."

A look of horror crossed Tristan's face. "So if Julia's on the desk, Cassandra went to the club *alone*?"

"Yeah," said Jim sounding disgusted.

"What happened? Cassandra, are you okay?"

"Yes, Sir," she answered.

"But she nearly ran afoul of me," said Master Jim. "I asked her some questions and didn't care for her answers. Diana stepped in and I realized we had a lost lamb. How could you let that happen?"

"Christ almighty, Jim, I didn't mean for it to happen. She left last night before we could talk. I left messages that she clearly didn't get. Denny needs to be caned for his role in this."

"I'll gladly take care of that," said Diana. "I'll get right on it." She excused herself and left.

Jim said, "Look, Tristan, if you're too busy to give Cassandra the attention she needs, I'll do it. I haven't trained a baby sub in quite a while."

"Thank you, Jim. I appreciate the offer. I'll take care of Cassandra for the moment."

"See that you do. I'll see you later downstairs." He too left.

Cassie just stood there while all this was going on, trying to piece everything together. Apparently Tristan had tried to reach her to tell her not to go to the club. She wasn't sure what she'd done wrong, but he was upset and she was ashamed. To her dismay, tears spilled down her cheeks.

"Cassandra, what's the matter? Why are you crying? Did Master Jim hurt you?"

"N-no…Sir. I don't know what I did, but I didn't mean to make you mad. I'll just get my purse and go home."

"Please, don't cry. I'm not mad. Well, I am mad, but not at you. Come, sit down with me and let's talk."

"I'm sorry I didn't get your messages."

He guided her towards a chair, but sat on it himself and pulled her down onto his lap. "It's not your fault. You haven't done anything wrong. Normally, a sub asks for her Dom's permission before she leaves the club but that isn't a club rule, and I'm not technically your Dom. So I understand why you left with Julia last night. But had you told me first, we would have made plans for today. Your decision not to drive home was a very good one. When I realized you were gone and I learned exactly how far away you lived, I was worried about you and wanted to make certain you arrived home safely."

He kissed her temple.

"I assumed I was calling a cellphone. When you still hadn't called me back this morning, I was furious and I intended to address it with you. On top of that, we needed to sort some things out and so I wanted to see you before you went to the club. I left a message for you at the front desk with Denny. But I understand now that you weren't ignoring me, you just didn't get the messages."

"Then you aren't banning me from the club, Sir?"

"*Banning you*? No, Cassandra, I'm not banning you. But as you may have gathered by your encounter with Master Jim, you are not even close to being ready to play in the club alone."

"I didn't intend to play alone, Sir. I had only been there for a couple minutes and was looking for you or Tina. I was just about to go back to the desk when I met Master Jim."

"Let me amend that statement. You are not prepared to even be alone in the club yet. Normally, a sub as new as you are is assigned a Dom to oversee her training. He helps make sure she learns the basics and that she gains enough experience not to get into trouble."

"Master Jim asked me if I belonged to someone, Sir. I wasn't sure what he meant."

"Well, that's what he meant. I should have assigned someone. As the club owner, I have a lot of responsibilities that require my attention. If I had assigned you to a Dom, he would not have left you alone at all last night, and therefore you would not have left the club without a clear plan for today. I'm sorry. I never train new subs for this very reason."

"I...I'm sorry too, Sir." And she was. She liked Tristan and thought they had a connection. She was disappointed that he wouldn't be the one to train her.

He lifted her chin with his index finger to look into her eyes. "But there's a growing trust between us that I think is important. I don't want to put you into another Dom's hands yet. So even though I don't normally do this, if you are agreeable, I will take responsibility for your training for the time being."

So, he didn't train new subs, but he was going to train her. "I don't want to be a bother, Sir."

"You are certainly not a bother. But the fact remains I may have to attend to club matters from time to time while you are here. So I would like to give you this." He pulled a slender leather collar from his pocket. Hanging from it was a silver disc engraved with TC.

"A collar?"

"A *training* collar, with my initials. It is simply a symbol to everyone in the club that you are under my supervision. No other Dom should touch you or even speak to you without my permission and vice versa. I will work with you during your trial period to teach you more about the lifestyle. Should you decide to join the club, I'll continue to train you until I think you are able to manage on your own."

"I understand, Sir." Even though she was sitting on his lap, this was a professional relationship. He was the teacher and she was the student. Part of her wanted more, but she could handle this. Understanding the boundaries was very important to her.

He smiled. "Good. Wear this whenever you are here." He put the collar around her neck, fastening it snugly. Then he turned it so the disc was in front.

"Now, we need to discuss a few new rules. Unless there is some sort of life threatening emergency, you will not leave this club without my permission."

"Yes, Sir."

"When you leave the club, if you aren't going home, or you are going to be away from home, you will tell me where you will be."

"Yes, Sir."

"I don't share. As your training progresses," he paused briefly, frowning. "As your training progresses, I may allow you to play with other Doms. But while you are in training with me, you will not maintain a sexual relationship with anyone outside the club."

She snorted. "Not a problem, Sir. There is no one else."

He grinned at her. "You will also not snort, roll your eyes or make any other derisive sound or action in response to anything I say."

She smiled. "I understand, Sir, and I will do my best."

"I need a 'yes, Sir'."

"And I would like to give it to you, but I am unfailingly honest. I'm not sure I can completely stop those things, but I promise to give it my all."

He smiled and chuckled. "Unfailingly honest?"

"To a fault, Sir."

"Well, I like that, so I guess *giving it your all* will have to do for now."

"Thank you, Sir."

"And, I have one last rule. If for some reason we have not made plans to meet in the club, you will come here to my office first."

"Yes, Sir."

"Good girl. Now, there is something I need to clarify. There are all sorts of D/s relationships. Power exchanges come in all shapes and sizes. Our D/s relationship is limited to the club. I am not your fulltime Dom. Other than letting me know where you will be, and not snorting at me," he raised one eyebrow, "as with the standard club rules, these rules only apply here. Also within the club you should continue to address me as Master Tristan, never simply as Master."

"Yes, Sir." She understood him fully. He was clarifying again that this was a professional relationship, and no more.

"Now, let's go to the club."

"May I ask you a question before we do, Sir?"

"Of course."

"Last weekend, I told you I knew a little about BDSM from books I had edited. But those books have only contained certain elements."

"Essentially some of the kink but not the full lifestyle."

"Exactly, Sir. It would seem there are basic things that I really don't understand. At one point Master Jim told me to 'kneel and present'. I didn't know what he meant."

"I'm sorry about that. I've said before, submissiveness seems to come so very naturally to you and I have forgotten to teach you some basics. When a submissive presents herself she kneels upright, knees about shoulder width apart, head down and forearms clasped behind her back."

"Yes, Sir. Mistress Diana told me what to do. You've said several times now that I seem to be naturally submissive, and I agree. I like the way it feels…at least here. I think one reason though is that I don't like to make mistakes and I try not to make the same one twice." She gave a small chuckle. "Maybe that's why I'm a good editor. But it is easier for me to avoid mistakes, and to please you and others if I know what is expected of me. The rules you've just outlined help a lot. Thank you. Still, I've seen things in the club, behaviors between Dominants and submissives that I don't understand. I don't want to make more mistakes out of ignorance."

He smiled at her. "That's clear, Cassandra, and I promise that I'll tell you what I expect before you have the chance to fail. Still, it will help you to understand the dynamics between others. Tonight we won't do a scene. Instead, I think it would be a good idea to learn more about different kinds of D/s relationships, and the various protocols practiced. You could find a variety of online sources that talk about rules and protocols, but the fact is, while most people in the lifestyle understand certain basics about protocol, the Dominant partner tailors a protocol to meet his or her needs and desires. It'll be easier to understand this by seeing it in practice. We'll walk through the club tonight and I'll explain some of these as we go. Then we can discuss any questions you have afterward."

That walk through the club was an eye-opener. Cassie really had thought BDSM was pretty much limited to sexual practices and bedroom preferences. And for some people it was. But for others it was much more. There were couples who lived in a 24/7, Master/slave relationship.

She liked the feeling of peace she had when she was here with Tristan. She liked being able to leave worries and insecurities at the door. But she could never imagine giving up all control of her life.

And then there were the many and varied protocols. He explained that nominally there were four levels of protocol: none, low, medium and high. "But again, those terms mean different things to different groups or individuals. The basic protocol practiced within the boundaries of this club would be described as a medium protocol, but individuals can agree to follow stricter rituals."

She saw a couple who, Tristan explained, practiced *high protocol* nearly all of the time they were together, the only exception being when they were in the presence of people who were not in the lifestyle. Communication between them was very formal and the submissive partner never spoke in first person. When her Dominant gave her a bottle of water she didn't respond with a simple, "Thank you, Sir." Instead, she said, "This slave thanks her master for the kindness he shows her."

It actually made Cassie feel somewhat uncomfortable, but she schooled her features. This was between them and it was consensual. She had no right to judge.

She also saw a submissive who was being spanked as a punishment. After each blow he said, "Thank you, Master, for your loving correction."

That, too, gave Cassie an uneasy feeling but she made every effort to maintain a neutral expression.

At the end of the evening, they returned to his office to discuss things.

Tristan asked, "Do you understand a bit more about aspects of the lifestyle that are not specific to the kink?"

"Yes, Sir, I think I do. I really had no idea about the relationship dynamics." She frowned.

"Something's bothering you."

"A few things are, Sir."

"Tell me what they are."

She hesitated for a moment, wanting to be sure she could make her thoughts as clear as possible. "I like the feeling of submission, when I'm here, Sir. But I don't think I'd like it all of the time. As much as I have enjoyed what we've done and I like the idea of perhaps doing more, I'm not sure I belong in the lifestyle."

He shook his head. "Don't jump to conclusions. There are a lot of people like you. They like the kink and they like to explore either the submissive or the dominant side of their personality, but not as a steady diet. They leave the real world at the door and pick it up again when they go."

"So that's okay, Sir?"

A smile softened his features. "Not only is it okay, it's pretty common. I own the club and I am not interested in having a 24/7 submissive. I'm sexually dominant, but outside of the club or the bedroom, I don't need more. I wanted to create a place where people who enjoy the kink, can do so in a safe environment with other like-minded, consenting adults. The degree to which each person embraces the lifestyle outside of the club is their choice. However, the important thing to remember is that everyone who plays here does so of their own volition. Our members enter into the power exchanges that best meet their needs and while we all may not understand it, we accept it. I know several things made you uncomfortable tonight and I was very proud that you gave no overt sign of that."

She smiled. "If I didn't give a sign of it, Sir, how did you know?"

He chuckled. "I said you didn't give an *overt* sign. You didn't raise an eyebrow, wrinkle your nose, frown or do anything else that could be easily read as scorn. But occasionally you looked down or took a step closer to me or even moved slightly behind me. For example, I know, high protocol was something that bothered you."

He had certainly read that correctly. "Yes, Sir. For me, I think speaking in third person about myself would feel…dehumanizing."

"I like that you didn't make an overarching statement about it *being* dehumanizing but rather expressed it as your own feeling. That shows respect and I appreciate it. Honestly, I personally do not care for that level of ritual either and have never asked it of a submissive. Still, there are submissives who love it, and there are certainly Doms who want it. It is all part of the headspace where they need to be."

She considered this for a moment. "I guess if we all liked the same thing there'd only be one flavor of ice cream, Sir. Goat cheese beet swirl doesn't appeal to me, but evidently there are people who enjoy it."

"Are you serious?"

She laughed. "My right hand to God, Sir. Apparently you can get it somewhere in Denver. I went to college with a girl who loved it."

He chuckled. "Well, ice cream flavors aside, there are as many tastes as there are people in the lifestyle. The fact is Marisol is a CEO in the healthcare field. She has one of the most stressful, high intensity jobs I can imagine. Following high protocol when she is with Master Allen is what it takes for her to leave all of that behind."

"I can understand that. At the same time, I don't think it would be right for me."

"It probably wouldn't and it's good to learn these things." He gave her a quizzical look. "Something else seemed to bother you quite a bit this evening. It was when Tyler was administering a punishment to Greg. Until now, I was under the impression that spanking interested you."

She frowned. It was true. She had always found spanking extremely erotic. The spanking he gave her last night had been amazing. "It wasn't the spanking, per se, that disturbed me, Sir. I think it's the whole idea of punishment. It's one thing if both parties choose to engage in something that they both find stimulating in some way. Even if a sub chooses to endure something within a scene that is more painful than she might like, she has chosen to do it to please her Dom. She gets his praise and admiration as well as the satisfaction of meeting his needs. But everyone makes mistakes, Sir, even Doms. It seems only submissives get punished like that. Hearing Greg say 'Thank you, Master, for your loving correction,' did upset me, Sir."

"Cassandra, punishment and reward is a rather fundamental concept in a D/s relationship. It is something agreed upon at the outset. As a submissive, you have agreed to follow the rules of this club. As my trainee, you have agreed to follow several additional rules. If I came into the club this Friday night and found you weren't wearing your collar and were curled up in the lap of another Dom, you would have broken several rules you agreed to follow. In this community you would have earned a punishment—a serious punishment." His voice and demeanor had become stern.

She frowned. "That's a rather over the top example, Sir, and I can't imagine doing it, but if it happened you would have every right to be angry."

"And to punish you."

"I suppose. But if someone so blatantly flaunted the rules, I can only imagine that there was something underneath the surface driving the behavior, Sir."

"But in this kind of relationship, there shouldn't be. A Dom and a sub have to maintain clear, honest communication. If they didn't, and it reached the point where one displayed that kind of passive-aggressive behavior, either the relationship needs to end, or they need to do some serious work. The first step of which might be an intense discussion and then punishment."

"But why, Sir?"

He frowned. "Cassandra, my mother and father were divorced when I was a young teenager. My mom used to complain that when they argued my dad brought up each and every thing she had ever done wrong. Christ, you can see it in politics today. One side of the aisle points fingers and says 'you've done this and this and this' to which the other side answers 'yeah, well you've done that and that and that'. And they bring up the same transgressions over and over again, accomplishing nothing. That doesn't occur in a good D/s relationship. If something happens, it's discussed, a punishment is decided upon and accepted, and then it's over. The slate is clean."

She simply couldn't get her head around this. "But it's one-sided, Sir. This evening you admitted to making a mistake by not clearly assigning me to a Dom. You simply apologized. Denny, on the other hand was going to be punished for failing to see I received a message—that by your own admission wouldn't have been necessary if you had assigned me to someone or told me that you would train me, Sir."

"Cassandra, outside of our world that would seem very unfair. But, by definition, this lifestyle is not egalitarian. Submissives choose to give up power to Dominants and part of that is manifested in the way we handle faults. By accepting the rules of the club, and with my training collar, my rules as well, you have agreed to these norms. The fact is you also failed to follow several rules earlier this evening. You did not address Master Jim appropriately when he first spoke to you, and then when he tried to remind you that you might have forgotten your club manners, you gave him a very flippant answer. You were not punished for that because all parties realized that you were new, and in over your head. And that was my fault. I apologized for my role and your lapses were forgiven. I also have made certain that you will not be put in that position again. That said, if you ever fail to address a Dom appropriately again, you will be punished."

"I understand, Sir."

He stared at her as if trying to read her. "But you don't like it."

"Not particularly, Sir."

"And that is as it should be. It will please me if I never have to punish you."

"Me too."

He chuckled. "I think you will be a very good submissive, Cassandra."

Chapter 11

It had been over five months since Tristan had given Cassie his training collar and as he'd expected, she had continued to blossom in the environment. In spite of her aversion to punishment, or perhaps because of it, she seemed to thrive by following the rules. When her trial period had ended, she had elected to join the club outright, not as a working member. The only people who did that were usually extremely affluent or employed in very high-income careers. She didn't seem to be either.

She lived in a nice area, where well-to-do retirees often had winter homes. But it wasn't where the truly wealthy usually lived. And he knew she stayed busy as a freelance editor, but he couldn't imagine that was a million-dollar career. However, other than the fact that she was able to write the sizable check for membership, her finances were none of his business, and when they were together at the club, they didn't talk about such mundane things.

Her growth as a submissive had been nothing short of spectacular. He had pushed her limits a little further every week and she'd accepted and embraced it. She had only used a safeword once and it had been during a scene where he'd blindfolded her. When they'd talked about it afterwards, he realized she needed to be able to see him, even if it was only an occasional glimpse in her peripheral vision. She read his body language and could sense his approval. Without that, she felt alone and lost.

That had been a profound revelation for him. It was a Dom's prime responsibility to remain focused on his sub. A good Dom learned to read his sub's subtlest reaction. It's how limits could be pushed without going too far and bring them both the most pleasure. And, certainly, good subs needed to read a Dom's signals too. But until he met Cassie, he'd grossly underestimated how important that skill was. Her ability to read him so well gave him immense pleasure. Maybe he'd never valued this intimacy because he'd never experienced it. Now he couldn't imagine not sharing that kind of connection with a sub.

She had come far in other areas as well. Total nudity in very open areas of the club was still outside of her comfort zone, but she had come a long way. She also hadn't agreed to have sex in the club but had absolutely no problem with pleasing him in any other ways and was particularly talented at it. She would stroke him or kneel and take him in her mouth anytime he wished.

It was the deep level of trust building between them that he found most rewarding. She responded to every command immediately and without question. She had an innate understanding of the delicate balance of power exchange and gave him her submission completely and willingly. On top of all of that, she was graceful and poised and made very few mistakes. He was exceptionally pleased with her.

There were Doms who liked bratty subs, but he wasn't one of them. He was both proud and a little in awe of her abilities. Simply put, she was now perfectly capable of playing in the club on her own. She still had plenty to learn, but the environment was safe enough and she was competent enough to begin playing with others, if she wished. Even so, he didn't want her to. He wanted her for himself.

That too was a revelation. But perhaps the most shocking epiphany was that her skills as a sub and the D/s relationship developing between them wasn't enough. He wanted more from her. He wanted everything. Even when she reached the point where she could completely let go of her inhibitions in the club, he knew that still wouldn't be enough. It had become clear to him the club was a carefully partitioned part of her life and he'd never have all of her within its confines. He no longer wanted just Cassandra Hasting's submission.

Tonight, he sat holding her in his lap after the most exposed and intense scene they'd ever done. He had flogged her, in the dungeon alcove, while she'd been bound to the St. Andrew's cross. She wore only a thong, but had been facing the wall and thus felt less exposed. He'd placed a remote control vibrator in her, increasing the power of the vibrations as he increased the intensity of the flogging. By the end she was trembling and fighting back her orgasm, but she didn't beg. She remained silent, knowing he'd give her what she longed for when he was ready. Finally, he stepped close, pressing his body against hers and wrapping his arms around her. He stroked her dripping pussy and whispered, "Come for me, little bird." She cried out and convulsed in ecstasy.

The entire scene had been magnificent. She had given her all, but holding her like this, he wanted something else. He wanted her under him, his cock thrusting into her wet heat and ultimately finding that blissful release with her. He wanted to make love to her and then keep her in his arms all night.

In that instant, he realized he had fallen for her. He loved her and he had never felt like this about anyone. He could ask her to be his sub. Not just as a trainee but collar her as a sign of a deeper commitment between them. But that didn't truly capture what he wanted either. The relationship between a Dom and a sub was deeply intimate and could be closer in many ways that some married couples, but love wasn't necessarily a part of it. The thing he wanted more than anything, more even than her submission, was her heart.

Unfortunately, he had placed a huge hurdle in his own way. When a Dom agrees to train a sub with whom he has no previous relationship, it is important to maintain some emotional distance. Otherwise, as the trust between them deepens it's easy for a new sub to mistake those feelings for romantic love. Serious heartache is best avoided by making boundaries completely clear from the start. Not wanting to hurt Cassandra in any way, Tristan had diligently done that. And for her part, she understood and respected those limits. He was the one who had slipped.

As she began to rouse from her post orgasmic fog, he planted gentle kisses over her face.

She closed her eyes and tilted her head back. "Mmm. I like that, Sir."

"My sweet little bird, you are delicious." *And I want to take you home with me*, was on the tip of his tongue. But the Dom in him slammed on the brakes. In her current state of mind, he was certain Cassandra would do anything he asked. It wasn't fair to discuss a change in their relationship now. They needed to be on even footing, neutral ground. He should make a date with her, outside of the club. Brunch tomorrow would be good.

"Tell me, Cassandra, what do you have planned for tomorrow?"

She yawned. "I usually have nothing planned on Sundays, Sir. I just relax. But this is going to be a crazy week. I have a deadline on Wednesday, plus my house goes on the market Monday, so I have to make sure it is spotless. And you know I'm presenting at that conference most of next week. If I'm going to be able to come to the club this coming weekend, I have to spend some time finishing up my slides for that."

She had told him about the conference and that she wouldn't be at the club two weekends from now, but he'd forgotten. Her house going on the market was news. "You're selling your house?"

"Yes, Sir. It's way bigger than I need. I have a lawn service, a pool service and a housekeeper to help take care of it, but I just don't need that much house. I think I told you it belonged to my great-uncle and my grandmother. Initially I didn't want to sell it because of that. But now I just feel incredibly alone there. The fact that the entire neighborhood is made up of elderly retirees sort of adds to the solitude. Besides, I spend two nights a week here now and it's over an hour's drive one way. I've been thinking I'd move a little closer. Maybe into a condo near the beach. I love the beach."

He frowned. "Why haven't you mentioned this before now?"

"Well, it hasn't really come up, Sir, and I'd only been toying with the idea. But earlier this week I met with a realtor who loved the house. She said unlike other parts of the country, late summer and early fall are the best times to sell in my area. It's when people from up north who are looking for winter homes are interested in buying."

"Cassandra, no one puts their house on the market overnight. You'll get a better price if you do some work to spruce it up. Even just painting can be a huge improvement. I can see that you get help."

"But I've already done that work, Sir. I started when grandma died. Obviously, there were a lot of her things that I needed to clean out and get rid of. I took the opportunity to update a lot then. I completely redid the master bedroom and bathroom. I had the flooring replaced throughout, I had the house repainted inside and out and I remodeled the kitchen. I had to replace the air conditioning three years ago and the roof is only about eight years old. The real estate agent said the house is ready for the market."

He was both surprised and impressed by all of this. He really only knew her as a submissive, which emphasized the fact that they needed more time together to get better acquainted with each other. Time away from the club. Unfortunately, he wasn't going to be able to start tomorrow as he'd hoped. But perhaps there was another way. In addition to Island Treasures and Hidden Gem, he owned a number of properties in the area. Including several beachfront condominium complexes. "So, you've put your house on the market, but you haven't found another place to live yet?"

"Not yet, Sir. As soon as I make my deadline and am ready for the conference, I'll start looking. My agent thinks there will be plenty of time."

"Cassandra, I own quite a few nice beachfront properties."

"You do, Sir? I had no idea."

"Among others I have a large condominium complex on Redington Beach which isn't far from here. Off the top of my head, I don't know if there are any on the market at the moment, but I can look into it. I'd love to take you to look at available properties that might interest you whether I own them or not. How about a week from tomorrow?"

"That sounds like fun and I'd really appreciate your help, but I should probably wait until I get back from the conference. I'll be too distracted until then. Would two weeks from tomorrow be okay with you?

Two weeks before he could take her on a date? He guessed it would have to do. "Two weeks from tomorrow is fine."

This was perfect. He would begin to see her occasionally outside of their club roles and let things progress from there.

Chapter 12

Cassie's week hadn't gone as smoothly as she'd hoped. Her house had been shown four times on Monday and Tuesday. She hadn't expected things to pick up that fast. Each time she dutifully packed up her laptop and went to a coffee shop. By Wednesday, she told her agent that she needed the full work day to meet her deadline. It would take at least several uninterrupted hours at a time to finish the edit. Her agent agreed not to show it that day. The showings started again on Thursday, but it was a little easier to work on her presentation in small chunks.

On Friday, she was ready for an evening at the club. And she didn't want to have to drive home in the wee hours of the morning, only to be up, dressed and ready for potential house hunters bright and early on Saturday morning. Julia was always open to having Cassie spend the night at her place on Fridays. Cassie rarely took her up on it, not wanting to abuse her friend's hospitality. But that afternoon, Cassie had called to ask if she could stay with her tonight.

Late that afternoon, she put away her laptop, packed a bag, put fresh flowers on the table in the entry hall and left. Her house looked as perfectly groomed as a model home.

She did a little shopping and then met Julia for dinner before going to Hidden Gem. It had been a fun afternoon, but when they were finally on the way to the club, all Cassie wanted to do was leave her hectic week behind and be with Tristan. She loved the time she spent with him. He had made it clear from the start that being her Dom was not the same as being her boyfriend. Intellectually, she had accepted that and she observed the boundaries he established. She knew that at some point he would ask her to give him back his training collar and that would be that. She had learned a long time ago how to compartmentalize things to protect herself, so Hidden Gem became one area of her life that was carefully walled off from the rest.

And yet a little part of her heart had ignored all of the sensible warnings her brain gave her. She had never met anyone like Tristan and she cherished every moment they spent together. Occasionally, she allowed herself to imagine what life with him would be like if they were a couple. If he loved her. It usually happened when she was curled up on his lap after a scene, receiving aftercare. And in those vulnerable moments, she believed she loved him.

It often took several hours for her sensible side to regain control. Occasionally, that didn't happen until after she had shed a few tears into her pillow at home. Each time she did it, she vowed to talk with Tristan about ending her training. Loving people, giving them her friendship and, God forbid, her heart, hadn't worked too well in the past. Even though she didn't really want to end her training with him, she knew it was what needed to happen to make sure she didn't wind up with a broken heart. And yet, invariably, the next time she saw him, she told herself she wasn't ready for it to end yet. She still needed him and, clearly, he believed that or he would have stopped her training.

Tonight, when she arrived at the club, he had left a box for her at the front desk with a note.

When you arrive, put this on and come straight to the harem alcove.

Cassie opened the box in the locker room and pulled out a harem-girl outfit.

"Oh. My. God. That's gorgeous," said Julia.

Cassie smiled. It was dazzling, but it was clearly aimed at pushing her limits. "It is beautiful, but…"

"But nothing. Put it on."

"I don't think—"

"Stop right there," Julia interrupted. "Thinking is not part of this. Your Dom wants you to wear that and it will look amazing on you. How can you *not* put it on?"

It would be really easy not to put it on, but Julia was right. Tristan wanted her to wear this, so she would try to do it. "Okay, I'll put it on."

The top was a heavily beaded, peacock-blue satin, shelf bra that exposed her nipples. There was a headpiece, a gold band from which several sheer veils hung. The veil in the front came just to the top of the bra. It would shield her breasts a tiny bit.

The bottom was even more scandalous. It had a wide waistband that came to a point in the front and was made of the same beaded satin. It was designed to sit low on her hips. Set into the waistband were multiple strips of ultra-sheer fabric in varying shades of blue, creating a beautiful skirt. But even when she stood still her pussy and ass could be seen faintly through the fabric. When she walked, both the veil from the headpiece and the strips of fabric of the skirt floated as she moved, revealing unhindered glimpses of her most private parts.

The times before, when she had consented to be nude or nearly so during a scene, they had been in one of the less public areas when she removed her clothing. She'd had at least the illusion of partial privacy. Now he was asking her to walk through the club, revealing more of herself than she ever had.

But the costume was amazing and she felt beautiful in it.

"God, that's stunning," said Julia. "So now are you going to do it? Are you going to walk through the public areas with all of your gorgeous assets showing?"

This was a hard step to take, but it was for her Dom. She wanted to see the look on his face and hear his praise when he saw her in the costume. "Yes. I'm going to do it."

"Well, it's about time. You go, girl. But if you are going to do it, do it right. Take your sandals off and go barefoot. Step out of this room as a slave girl."

"You know, I think I will." Cassie tossed her shoes in the locker, shut it, took a deep breath and walked into the club.

She kept her head down and her hands folded as she walked slowly and steadily through the club to the alcoves. She couldn't see anyone's face, but she heard murmurs of approval from all around her that buoyed her confidence. This was not nearly as hard as she had believed it would be. Why had she resisted it so?

Of all of the alcoves, the harem room gave the greatest illusion of solitude. Sheer lengths of fabric hung around the walls as well as over the opening. Like her skirt, the curtains over the door gave the suggestion of privacy but it was still possible to see and monitor everything happening within. When she reached her goal, she pushed the hangings aside and stepped into the room. Tranquil spa music filled the space, masking some of the noise from the club. Tristan waited for her, lounging against pillows on the low bed in the center of the room. Silently, she knelt and presented herself.

He rose from the bed and crossed the room to her. "Beautifully done, little bird. Look up at me."

She raised her eyes to meet his and received the reward she knew she would. The look on his face was one of pure awe and admiration.

"You are breathtaking, Cassandra. Absolutely exquisite."

"I'm glad I please you, Sir."

He put a hand out to her. "Stand and join me on the bed."

She put her hand in his and followed.

He took his place again on the bed, patting the spot beside him. "Kneel here beside me and we'll negotiate this scene.

"Yes, Sir."

"Cassandra, one of the things on your list of soft limits was sexual intercourse in a public area."

She swallowed hard. "Yes, Sir."

"We have done a variety of extraordinary scenes together. In many of them I have brought you to orgasm and you have done the same for me. But I would like to do more. I would like to bring you to the edge of bliss and feel the power of your climax from inside you. I want to make love to you. This," he motioned to the room around them, "is the most privacy I can give you within the confines of this club. Would you reconsider your soft limit and allow me to make love to you here"

Being nearly fully exposed in the open areas of the club had been much simpler than she had imagined. She felt a little silly that she had avoided it for so long. And the fact was, she had wanted to feel him inside her too. He hadn't said he wanted to fuck her. He wanted to *make love* to her. In this of all places, everyone knew the difference between the two. Maybe she could do this. "Yes, Sir. I would like for you to make love to me."

The smile that lit his face touched her heart. She wanted to do this for him.

"Okay, this is how the scene will go. While we are in this room, you are my slave and I am your Master. You will do whatever I tell you to do and engage in whatever sexual activity I find pleasing. Except for the soft limit we have already agreed to explore, your limits will be respected and you have safewords. Do you consent?"

"Yes, Sir, I do."

"Well, then, my pretty slave, while your outfit is exceedingly beautiful, I want you to take your top off so that I may enjoy your beautiful breasts."

"Yes, Master Tristan." She immediately removed the bra that covered nothing anyway.

To Cassie's surprise, the scene started more as a heady, overwhelming seduction, than a BDSM scene. Tristan kissed and caressed her everywhere.

When she began to respond, exploring his body with her lips and hands, he grabbed her wrists. "No, slave. I want you feeling, not thinking." He enclosed her wrists in two padded leather cuffs attached to the head of the bed by short silky ropes and continued his sensual exploration. He planted kisses down her body, stopping briefly to let his tongue explore her navel.

She giggled and squirmed.

"Be still, slave, or there will be consequences."

She concentrated on remaining as still as possible as he continued his journey, finally reaching her clit. First, he flicked it with his tongue, then he sucked on it. Before she knew it, she was writhing against him.

He stopped. "I told you there would be consequences." His voice was stern. With one arm he lifted her legs up and over her body, exposing her bare bottom. He gave her ten stinging swats on her ass. Then he fastened padded leather cuffs to her ankles and attached them to ropes connected to each corner of the foot of the bed. She was bound, spread eagled and open to him.

He returned his attention to her clit, licking and sucking until she was on the edge of orgasm but he never added enough pressure to send her over.

He kept her there on the edge for what seemed like hours.

It was where she wanted to spend the rest of her life, but at the same time it wasn't. She reached a point where all she wanted was release. "Please, Master Tristan, please let me come."

"No," he said firmly. "You will not come until I tell you to or I will give you a hard spanking and I might decide never to let you come. Also, you will not ask me again. I will allow you that release only when it pleases me."

"Yes, Master Tristan. I'm sorry, Sir."

"You are a good slave. Tonight we're going to find out how long you can hover on the edge and embrace it."

And he did.

With hands, tongue and vibrator he kept her on the precipice. She forgot where she was. She nearly forgot who she was. She existed as a tingling mass of sensation.

When she was certain she could take no more, he stopped. He took a moment to release her ankles, sheath himself in a condom and kneel between her legs. She wanted this. She wanted him to make love to her. She arched to meet him, trying with everything in her not to come on his first stroke. He buried himself in her and it felt so good. He filled her, completed her. She had fantasized about this. He withdrew and thrust into her again. She was ready to come. She just needed to hear his voice, telling her to.

Then her attention was drawn away. The sheer curtains hanging over the opening to the alcove fluttered as someone walked past. The sound of laughter from somewhere outside penetrated the background music.

She wasn't with him alone in a tranquil paradise. For all its appearance of privacy, the harem room was in the club.

Tristan stopped, holding perfectly still. "Where are you, little bird?"

"I…I…I'm sorry, Sir. I was distracted for a moment." She tried to block out everything else in order to focus again on Tristan and the wonderful sensations he elicited.

His brow furrowed, and he started to move again within her.

But as much as Cassie wanted this, it didn't feel right. This level of intimacy was a sharing of souls…it shouldn't happen here. And instantly, the moment was gone. She had slipped back from the edge. She was having sex in a public place and that thought consumed her.

He stopped again. "Cassandra, look at me."

She did and the look of concern in his eyes was her undoing. Tears spilled down her cheeks. "I'm sorry, Sir. I'm so sorry. The curtains moved…and the noises…I lost my focus…it doesn't feel right." A sob escaped her lips. "I'm so sorry."

"Shh, shh, little bird, don't. It's okay." He unbuckled the cuffs holding her wrists, and pulled the satin sheets up, covering both of their bodies. Then he wrapped his arms around her, holding her close and tight.

She tried her best not to cry. She had failed. It had nothing to do with him.

"I'm so sorry, Sir," she whispered again."

"Cassandra, it's my fault."

She shook her head. "No, no, it isn't. It was me. I—"

He put a finger to her lips. "Don't argue with me." It was his Dom voice and she stopped instantly. "I had hoped that by creating as private a place as possible, you would be able to get past this limit. But it is still too soon. You have done so beautifully. You are no longer the girl who blushed profusely in our first scene when I was only kissing you. You are embracing this lifestyle and have come so far. This was my fault. The scene was about what I wanted and not what was best for you."

"I wanted this too."

"Perhaps. But not here. Not yet. I'm sorry."

Cassie wouldn't argue with him. He'd commanded her not to. But this was something she had to address. Until tonight, she had thought it was just shyness, but now she wasn't sure. She needed time to process things. "Sir, I think…I think…well, being more exposed than usual in this costume wasn't as uncomfortable as I thought it would be. And I think if I became even more used to it, maybe this would be easier too."

"Cassandra, sometimes you surprise me. You are very in-tune with the edges of your limits and even how to push them. I think you are right. You were able to walk through the club tonight in that very revealing costume. How did you do it?"

"It's simply lovely and I felt beautiful in it."

He kissed her temple. "Beautiful doesn't begin to describe how you look."

"Thank you, Sir. On top of feeling pretty, I wanted to please you and I wanted to see your expression when you saw me. The only way to do that was to walk through the club."

"Perhaps that's the work we need to do first then. It will please me if you spend the rest of the evening wearing that costume, in the open area of the club, at my side. That way I can admire you to my heart's content and see the looks of awe and envy on the face of every Dom in the club. Can you do this for me?"

"Yes, Sir. I can."

"As always, you have safewords if it becomes too much."

"I understand Sir, but I'm sure I'll be fine."

"And tomorrow night, we will do more of the same. Except you will wear only the skirt and the headpiece. Your beautiful breasts will be completely available for me to see, and touch. Do you agree?"

She took a deep breath. She could do this. "Yes, Sir."

As it turned out, wearing the beautiful costume through the club the rest of the night really hadn't been terribly difficult. She wasn't sure it would be quite as easy tomorrow night, without the top on, but she was going to try.

Chapter 13

All day on Saturday, Tristan had had trouble shaking the sense of failure resulting from the scene in the harem alcove. He had pushed too hard. The previous weekend he had been content to begin building a relationship with Cassie outside of the club. But as the week had progressed, the idea had occurred to him that maybe he could get her past her shyness in gradual steps and the more intimate setting of the harem alcove could be the first one. He couldn't shake the feeling that there was something more at play here than a reluctance to expose herself.

Once she arrived at the club that evening, wearing the costume without the top this time, he was not sure what to expect. He watched her carefully for signs of distress. But after a few shy blushes when he'd complemented her on how lovely she looked, she seemed very comfortable. When things had gone well for several hours he decided to push her a little more.

"Take the headpiece off, Cassandra, and give it to me." The veils attached to it provided a sheer covering to her breasts as long as she wasn't moving.

Her pupils dilated momentarily, but as always she didn't hesitate to follow the order. And as she had earlier in the evening, initially she blushed prettily but after a few minutes appeared at ease.

At the end of the night, Tristan led Cassie to one of the quiet areas reserved for aftercare. He sat in a big comfortable chair, pulled her down onto his lap and put a blanket around her shoulders, just as he would have after an intense scene.

She looked a little confused. "I'm okay tonight, Sir. We didn't do a scene. I don't need aftercare."

He gave her backside one sharp smack. "I am the one who decides what you need. Is that clear?"

She rubbed the stinging cheek. "Yes, Sir."

"And for your information, this entire evening was a scene. One that I know pushed your limits."

"It's getting easier, Sir. I know it's what you want."

"I do want it, and I was very proud of you this evening. But I realized we have never actually talked about why being naked bothers you. At first, I thought it was because you were shy. We have done some intense scenes in which you have been much more exposed than you were tonight. But once you are in a scene it goes away, only to return the next time you enter the club. I do think your natural inclination is to be shy, but there's something more than bashfulness at play here. It doesn't seem like being around others who are nude bothers you and most shy people are equally uncomfortable in that situation."

"Honestly, Sir, I have wrestled with this. You're right, the idea of nudity in general doesn't bother me. It isn't that I think it's wrong. Frankly, I worry that people might think I'm being judgmental because I don't wish to be naked, but I swear I am not. Quite the opposite. I see completely naked subs walking through the club as they would a crowded public street. They are confident and completely unabashed. It doesn't matter what their age or body type is. I really, really admire them and I'd love to be that way."

"But you can be that way. This is a judgment-free zone."

"I know, Sir. It isn't that I fear what people might think. I think part of it is just a reluctance to expose myself. I tend to be a very private person. But I also think I don't exactly know how to be undressed."

"You don't know how? Little bird, I don't understand."

She sighed. "The thing is, I lived with dress codes for most of my life, Sir. I went to private schools and wore uniforms from the age of five. Then in boarding school, it wasn't just uniforms, there were certain rules for how we dressed for everything you could think of. One wears a certain kind of outfit for chapel, another for tea with an advisor, another for a house dinner, another for a dinner with the headmaster, and so on. There were even dress codes that applied if we were just going into the nearby town to shop or see a movie. I am confident that I can dress appropriately for any imaginable occasion."

He smiled. "I remember what you wore your first night here. A cute, short black skirt, a red lace top that just showed a hint of a matching red bra underneath and jeweled sandals."

"Julia said to wear something sexy, Sir."

"Well you hit the mark—beautiful and incredibly sexy."

"I didn't really look like the other subs, Sir."

"No. And you still don't. But your outfits not only suit your personality, they are without a doubt extremely erotic. You turn heads. It's fair to say you do know how to dress, I'll give you that."

"So, it's like I said, Sir, I don't know how to be *undressed*. I feel like a fish out of water. I think that's why I'm comfortable in this outfit. It feels right for the situation but I'm still dressed."

"I guess I understand that, but you can be nearly nude in a scene."

"Well, yes…it's part of the scene, Sir. I'm doing it to please you, and because it is necessary for the scene. It's almost as if a scene has its own dress code. Once I know what it is, and I'm in the scene, I'm okay with it."

"What if the dress code in the club was that all subs had to be naked?"

She frowned. "I guess I would follow it then, Sir."

He looked momentarily stunned. "Well, I'll be damned. Cassandra, I knew you were a people pleaser and a rule follower, but I didn't know how deeply rooted that was. It's just like you said, your issue isn't with being nude, it's with not having rules about what to wear. I do think being shy is a small part of it but when given a rule, it overrides your bashful nature. Last night and tonight I gave you a rule—a dress code."

"I suppose that's true, Sir."

"We'll have to explore this all a bit more over the next few weeks. If you would like to be confident and unabashed in just your skin, I think we can get there. Tonight, I was very proud of you."

"Thank you, Sir."

"That explains a lot. And it leads me to a harder question." A much harder question indeed because he dreaded hearing the answer. "I set the scene up yesterday based on my assumption that your inhibitions were all related to shyness so I attempted to make things feel private. But we have done other scenes—in the relative privacy of the alcoves—in which you have shown beautiful abandon. You have come spectacularly where people could see you. And you have sucked me dry with people watching."

He paused. He was growing to love this incredible woman. Her answer to this next question could quite possibly break his heart. And yet, he couldn't leave it unasked. "Cassandra, if privacy was the only issue, it should have been more comfortable yesterday. Since it wasn't, I think there is more to it than that. Is there something in your past? Some trigger we've not discussed? Or is it something to do with me?" There it was on the table.

To his relief, she looked shocked by the question. "*You*? No, Sir, it definitely isn't you."

"Then something from your past?"

She shook her head slowly. "No, nothing like that. At least, I don't think so. I wasn't quite sure what the issue was myself. I just thought it was my nature to be reserved, but you're right, there's nothing reserved about the scenes we have already done."

"Exactly. Do you have any thoughts on what the issue might be?"

"You know, Sir, it's a funny thing. I think most people go their whole lives without thinking about sex."

He laughed. "I'm fairly certain that's not true. It has been suggested that men think about sex several times an hour."

She smiled and blushed. "That's not what I'm talking about, Sir. What I mean is, most people don't think about the minutiae. The tiny details that make us think and act the way we do during intimate moments, and what makes the experience bad, good or fantastic. I'd be willing to bet that for the vast majority of people, if it works, they don't care why. And, for many, if it doesn't work they don't do what it takes to figure out why. I knew girls in college who had sex regularly, but said they'd never had an orgasm. And they just accepted it, believing that there was something wrong with them."

"Well, as much as teenage boys might hate to admit it, having a strong sex drive doesn't automatically equate to knowing how to please a woman, and porn doesn't help. Ten minutes of just plowing into her doesn't work for most women. So the answer he gets to 'Baby, was it good for you?' is nearly always a lie."

She laughed. "Yeah. I had a clueless boyfriend who said that to me once. I might have been a little too honest for my own good."

Tristan chuckled. "Oh, no. How badly did you destroy his ego?"

"I said, if he had to ask, the answer was probably 'no'." She smiled. "He never asked me out again. But this all just goes to my point. Simply understanding the mechanics of sex is all a guy needs to know to get off. And an awful lot of women sort of stumble onto what makes them feel good. I suspect most people find this whole experience of trying something, talking about it, figuring out what works and what doesn't, and maybe why it works or doesn't, entirely new. Over the last few months I've done way more thinking about this stuff than ever before. Last night, I think I figured out what my issue is."

"And what do you think it is?"

She sat up a little to look him directly in the eyes. "Everything we've done, everything I've done to you and let you do to me has been recreational. I understand that. You made the boundaries very clear and I chose to accept them. I tend to compartmentalize things in my life quite a bit. Things we do here go into my 'fun club stuff' box. What I didn't realize until last night is that I have a boundary regarding sex."

"I understand that. It's why you have it as a soft limit."

"But what I discovered last night is that it isn't exactly a limit. You agree that there is a difference between just having sex—fucking—and making love?"

"Yes, of course."

"Well, in setting emotional boundaries around what I do here, I have discovered a line between those too. It might be okay to just recreationally fuck in the club. But for me, making love isn't recreation. It won't fit in my 'fun club stuff' box. Don't get me wrong, I don't mean one has to be *in love* to make love, but I think there is a deeper connection when making love. It's not just you giving me pleasure or me giving you pleasure. I think it's a moment where we're joined, physically and emotionally, giving and taking from each other. I don't want to share such an intimate event with others, at least not the first time. And I don't want someone to fuck me before they make love to me. Do you understand that, Sir?"

"More than you know, little bird. I also admire how well you understand and respect the emotional boundaries that we put in place. The fact is, the boundaries are there to protect both the Dom and the trainee. But like anything else, after a while it becomes a point of negotiation."

And now was that time. He just needed to put it on the table. "If you are open to it, I'd like to take our relationship to a new level. I want to see you outside of the club. Would you be open to that?" Christ almighty, he had never felt so unsure about a woman before. A little voice from deep within him said, *that's because you've never wanted a woman's heart before and was never willing to offer your own.*

"Are you serious?"

He couldn't read her expression so he simply answered, "Very serious."

To his delight, she gave him a warm, bright smile that completely lit her face. "Yes, Sir. I would love to see you outside of the club."

He hugged her close and was completely aware of the tension draining from his body. "That makes me very happy." Until this conversation, he hadn't realized how unsure about her he'd been. But his little bird was a rule follower. The rules had been laid down at the outset and because they hadn't changed, she'd observed them.

They sat for a while in silence, him simply relishing the feel of her in his arms. He would like to have stayed like this all night, but he knew he couldn't. "It's getting late, Cassandra. Are you staying with Julia again tonight?" Maybe he could buy a few more minutes if she didn't have to drive to Lutz.

"No, Sir. I'm going home. I have things I need to do tomorrow."

"When do you get home from the conference?"

"My flight gets in Saturday evening, a little after eight, Sir."

"I'm going to miss you. I'd tell you to come by the club for just a little while, but I know you'll be exhausted. Besides, we have a date on Sunday to look at beach condos."

She smiled. "I'm looking forward to it. Where shall I meet you?"

"Meet me? That isn't the way a date works. I'll pick you up at your house at ten. We'll go to brunch, then we'll look at condos."

Again, she gave him a brilliant smile. "Okay. Next Sunday at ten."

"Perfect. Now, go change and I'll see you to your car."

He walked her to the women's locker room. Then he waited for her in the reception area until she'd changed into her street clothes. Once they reached her car, he gave her a kiss on the cheek. "Good night, Cassie. I'll see you next Sunday."

"Good night." She tilted her head to one side, looking a little confused. "You called me Cassie. You almost never call me Cassie. In fact, I don't think you ever have."

"Cassie, that's part of the protocol I follow. In the club you call me Master Tristan or Sir. I call you by your given name, *Cassandra*, or by my nickname for you, *little bird*. We aren't in the club now."

"Well then, good night, Tristan."

Chapter 14

By mid-morning on Sunday, Tristan had just about come to terms with the fact that he wasn't going to see Cassie for a full week. Then his cell-phone rang just before noon. He frowned, a little worried. Cassie almost never called him.

"Hi, Cassie."

"Hi...um...Tristan. I...uh...I need some help."

"What's wrong? What's happened?"

"Nothing's wrong. Not really. But this morning I was offered a contract on my house."

"Was it a good offer? You shouldn't take a low-ball contract. You live in a very nice area and $675,000 is an extremely fair price."

"How do you know what I'm asking?"

"Cassie, I'm in real estate. When you told me you were selling your home, I looked it up. I ran the comps and you probably could have started with a higher asking price."

"That's what my agent said, but I really didn't want the hassle of it being on the market for a while. I had no idea I'd get an offer this quickly."

"What was the offer?"

"They offered me a full price, cash contract. Plus another $75,000 if I'm willing to leave most of the furniture."

"*Full price, cash*? Take it. That almost never happens."

"But they have a contingency. They want to settle as soon as possible and move in immediately."

"Well, that adds a wrinkle. Did your agent tell them they're crazy?"

Cassie laughed. "No. Their agent said they were ready to put a contract on another house until they saw mine. They like mine better. The other house isn't furnished but it is empty and they can move in two weeks or less. So I have to either take it, or lose it."

"How do you feel about the furnishings?"

"My grandmother liked nice things so it's all very good quality, but not exactly my taste. I want to keep my bedroom and office furniture which I bought when I remodeled things. I'd also like to keep the furniture from the breakfast area. That was where we always ate or sat and talked. When grandma was in good shape, it seemed like she lived in the kitchen. There is one glass case full of memory-laden things in the living room that was in my parents' home. And there's a painting in the family room that was also from their house. Other than those things I'm fine with leaving the rest."

"Okay, how much do you owe on the house?"

"I don't owe anything. I inherited it from my grandmother and any mortgage was paid off long ago."

"Well, then things are pretty straight-forward. It will take at least a week, maybe a little longer for the title company to do their thing. Since you will only be moving a few rooms, professional movers should be able to pack you up in less than a day and move you in somewhere else the next."

"The somewhere else is the problem."

"So, that's what we need to focus on. Go ahead and take the contract. I know you were going to finish preparing for your conference today, but in light of this, how about we go look at properties. We'll see what's out there."

"But what if I can't find anything?"

"Don't worry. If we can't find a place before you go, or what you want isn't available immediately, we'll work it out. If it's only a matter of a couple of weeks, your furniture can go into storage and you can stay at Island Treasures."

"Okay. I'll sign the paperwork and get things started."

"And I'll pick you up in a little over an hour."

Just as he'd promised, about an hour and ten minutes later he pulled into her driveway. Her home was impressive.

He'd have to see the inside, but based on the neighborhood and the curb appeal, her asking price had been more than fair. He jumped out of his car, went to the door and rang the bell.

Cassie answered it wearing a designer sundress and sandals. "Hi…uh…Tristan. Come in."

He leaned forward and kissed her cheek. "Hi, Cassie. I'd love to."

"I know you had intended to take me to brunch when we did this next week. But the crazy contract has changed all that. I thought it would save time if we just had a bite here before we leave. I made chicken salad."

"You didn't have to do that. We could have picked up something quick. But I have to be honest, I love chicken salad."

She smiled. "So do I." She led him from the entryway, down a hall to a huge, bright kitchen with a dining area larger than most formal dining rooms in suburban homes. A basket of rolls, a plate with grapes and watermelon slices, another plate with lettuce and tomato slices and a bowl of potato chips were already on the table, which was set with china and cloth napkins. He smiled. Her old-fashioned manners were showing.

"Everything's ready." She took a bowl of delicious looking chicken salad and a small dish of mayonnaise from the refrigerator and put them on the table. "I don't have a lot of drink options. Would you like unsweetened iced tea, lemonade or water?"

"Lemonade sounds good."

She poured two glasses of lemonade and brought them to the table. "Please sit down."

"After you." He held her chair for her before taking his own.

"I wasn't sure what you might like on your sandwich, so I thought you might like to make it yourself. Or if you prefer, tell me what you want and I can make it for you."

Although he'd never wanted a sub to serve him outside of the bedroom, this was just too tempting. "I like the works. Lettuce, tomato, a little mayo and a few shakes of pepper."

She made the sandwich and offered him the plate of fruit and the chips before she served herself.

He took one bite of the sandwich and was in heaven. "Cassie, this is the best chicken salad I think I've ever had."

"Thank you. I put in chopped apples and toasted almonds."

"Do you like to cook?"

She smiled. "Yes, but I do much less of it since my grandmother died. In the last year or two there were always caregivers here, so there was someone to eat what I made. With just me, if I cook more than two or three times a week, I wind up with more leftovers than I can eat."

"What's your favorite thing to make?"

She shrugged. "It depends on the mood I'm in. I like Italian food. I love lasagna, but it's too heavy for hot weather. I make good shrimp scampi and veal piccata. But I also just like a nice steak or a burger."

His mouth watered. Those were some of his favorites.

"Do you like to cook?" she asked.

He grinned. "No. I make great reservations though."

She laughed. "Really? You don't cook at all?"

"If it weren't for K-cups, I couldn't even make coffee. I have a full-time housekeeper who cooks Monday through Thursday, if I'm going to be at home. I usually stay at Island Treasures Friday and Saturday nights. There are several really excellent restaurants in the resort."

They continued to make small talk while they ate. Although she was as sweet and polite as ever, Tristan had the sense that Cassie was on edge. Finally, he called her on it. "Cassie, you seem nervous. What's wrong?"

She stood up and started to clear the table. "I'm not nervous."

She reached for the basket of rolls, and he clamped a hand on her wrist. "Cassandra, look at me."

She did, but her brow was furrowed.

"Now is not the right time to begin hiding things from me. What's bothering you?"

"Honestly, it's nothing. It's just...well, I didn't think about what it would be like to be with you outside of the club. I don't know what to do. It's like a first date, only sooo not like a first date because we've...we've...I guess, I just feel awkward."

"Come here," he said as he stood and pulled her against his chest.

She responded by wrapping her arms around him.

"Cassie, are we strangers?"

"No."

"Lovers?"

"No...not really."

"Then we're somewhere between strangers and lovers. You called me today as a friend would, because you needed my help. Is it fair to say we're friends?"

"Yes."

"Perfect. The best relationships start as friends. You said you were very good at compartmentalizing your life. So maybe, for a little while, you can keep Master Tristan and Cassandra who are in a D/s relationship in one box, and Tristan and Cassie the friends who are exploring what kind of relationship they might have in another."

She sighed and he felt her relax. "I think I can do that."

"Good. Let me help you clear the table, then I'd like to see your home before we go."

"Okay."

It only took a couple minutes to put things away. Then she showed him around. It was a typical Florida design, built in a U shape, with a screened lanai and swimming pool in the center of the U. The main living areas were in the front of the house. The master suite was in one wing and three bedrooms with two full bathrooms were in the other wing.

As they were walking back through the house to leave, Tristan said, "Cassie, your home is fantastic and worth every penny of the price."

"Thank you."

"It's huge."

She nodded and gave a little shrug. "It's almost like two houses. The idea was that eventually I would be able to live here, comfortably, even with a family, and help care for my grandmother as she grew older. But that was before she was diagnosed with Alzheimer's." A shadow of sorrow crossed her features. "Still, having so much space made things easier. She deteriorated so quickly, I needed live-in help for a while and the house could certainly accommodate that. Plus, there was plenty of space in the master suite for all of the equipment needed to care for her. But now…"

"Well, I can understand wanting something a bit smaller. I have a list of available properties in my car. Are you ready to go see some?"

"Very ready."

He saw her into his car, then got behind the wheel and headed out.

"You said you were thinking about a beach condo. Do you have anything specific in mind?"

"Not really. I would like to be right on the beach. I like the idea of a condo because I wouldn't have to worry about maintenance, but I would consider a house. I'd really like to have three bedrooms."

He frowned slightly. A beach front property that size would likely cost more than she would make from the sale of her house, meaning she would have to finance some. "Cassie, you said you didn't owe anything on the house, right?"

"That's right. I have realtor fees and such to pay, but with the sale of the furniture too, I should net over $700,000."

Ceci Giltenan

"How much do you make a year as an editor?"

"It depends, but I can typically earn about $60,000 if the work is there."

"So, you can probably qualify for a mortgage of $120,000 to $150,000. I'm not sure we'll be able to find beachfront property for that but we'll try."

"Oh, I don't need a loan. I have other money."

He glanced sideways at her. "What's your price range then?"

"I can afford to buy any home that I would want to live in."

"That's not what I asked."

"Maybe not, but the purpose of the question was to figure out what I can afford. The answer is, I can afford what I want. So if there is a three-bedroom, beachfront property available I'll look at it, regardless of the price."

"Even if it is priced at twelve million."

"Is it likely that something with only three bedrooms on the beach would be twelve million?"

"No."

"Then we don't have to be concerned about that."

He frowned at her.

"Don't worry, Tristan. Like I told you before. I have been thinking of moving for quite a while now, so I've been looking at the listings. I know the general price range for the kind of condo I want and I can afford even the most expensive ones."

She earned $60,000 a year but could afford a condo potentially priced at over a million? *Who is she?* He wanted to ask her, but he refrained. He hated hearing that question every time some acquaintance realized he was wealthy. "Okay, then, beachfront it is."

They spent the next few hours looking at the available properties from Clearwater to St. Pete's Beach. Unfortunately, there weren't many on the market and there were problems

129

with all of them. In some cases, while they were in buildings on the beach, they didn't have views of the Gulf. A few had been poorly maintained and were overpriced. But most were not available for immediate occupancy—requiring a minimum of three months to vacate.

After seeing the last condo on the list, Cassie said, "I guess of all of them, that one is the best. It is on the beach and has a view. The owners can be out in six weeks. I really wanted at least three bedrooms and the kitchen was a lot smaller than I'd have liked. Not to mention the fact that it's still over an hour away from the club."

Tristan nodded. "Honestly, I think you could find something much better with a little more time.

"Maybe I should look at rentals instead. I could rent for a while and watch for something that suits me better to come on the market."

That changed everything. The more time he spent with her, the closer he wanted to keep her and he might have just the thing. "Well, if you are open to a rental, I may have the perfect place for you. There is nothing for sale in any of the buildings I own. However, an elderly couple, the Tillmans, who live in a three bedroom unit, are looking to sub-let their home for a few months. Mr. Tillman's health is failing and Mrs. Tillman wants to move into a senior-living center where they have access to assisted living services. But Mr. Tillman flatly refuses to sell the condo. He's convinced he doesn't need assisted living and will hate it."

"That's a shame. A few of my grandmother's neighbors have moved into those kinds of communities over the years and they've all been very happy with the choice."

"Honestly, I think he would like it too, but he's pretty stubborn. Then about a month ago, Mrs. Tillman hurt herself trying to help him in the shower. After that, she was finally able to talk him into a six month trial during which they won't sell the condo. If he hates it, she's agreed to come back. They are scheduled to move in two weeks and haven't found anyone who wants to sublet the condo from them yet. They can get by without a renter, but it will be easier for them if they have one."

"Wow, I wouldn't have thought finding a renter for beachfront property would be that hard. This is nearly the perfect time of year to find someone who wants a short-term rental."

"*Nearly* being the operative word. Most northerners don't come down until October or November and they like to stay until the end of March or so. They also usually want something furnished. The Tillmans need their furniture for the new place."

"It does sound like it might be just perfect for me then, and it would give me time to find exactly what I want."

From Tristan's point of view it was perfect too. They would have the opportunity to spend a lot of time together outside of the club. And maybe the ideal place she was seeking was in his arms. But even if six months wasn't enough time for that, there was the chance for more. "Or, if they are happy in their new place and you fall in love with their condo, you could just buy it when they are ready to sell. I'd love having you as a neighbor."

"A neighbor? When you said it was one of your buildings, I didn't know you lived there too."

Damn. He hadn't made that clear. Would she back out now? "Is that a problem?"

She appeared to think about it, then smiled. "No. I don't think it's a problem at all."

Relieved, he grinned at her. "Good. I'll give them a call."

Cassie shook her head. "I don't want to inconvenience them. It's probably too late this evening to go see it. Maybe I could make an appointment for tomorrow."

"Nonsense. It's only six. I know them very well and I'm certain it's not too late. Let me phone them. If you like it, you'll have to meet with the building manager to sign the paperwork before you leave for your conference. So, the sooner it's all started the better."

The Tillmans were home and they were thrilled at the opportunity to meet a potential renter.

As Tristan drove into the complex, it was great to see Cassie's eyes widen with real pleasure for the first time that day.

"Wow. This is what I had in mind. It's gorgeous. I love the Spanish style of the buildings. The red tile roofing has wonderful character."

"I've always liked it. When the complex was being designed, we considered an Art Deco theme, but somehow there's a coziness to stucco and red tile that Art Deco lacks."

"You're right. It feels old-fashioned and homey."

He smiled broadly. "That's what we were going for. However, there is more to it than meets the eye. There is a guard at the entrance 24/7, who not only monitors the gate, but also the security videos from the parking garage and other public areas. There is a pool that's heated in the winter, hot-tub, tennis courts, fitness center, private beach access, and reserved parking in the garage."

"Everything I was looking for."

"I thought you'd like it. So, we'll go see the Tillmans' unit. After that, we'll stop by my place for a few minutes and then I'll take you out to dinner."

"I've taken up your whole day, you don't need to take me to dinner."

"Cassandra, do I need to go all Dom on you? I would like to take you out to dinner. It would please me. If for some reason you can't, I understand, but please don't try to second-guess my invitation."

She smiled and blushed. "Thank you, I'd like that. But I thought we were keeping 'Master Tristan and Cassandra who are in a D/s relationship' and 'Tristan and Cassie the friends who are exploring what kind of relationship they might have' in separate boxes?"

"Well, I'll admit you might be better at keeping things in boxes than I am. And when *Tristan* has asked his friend *Cassie* for something perfectly reasonable that she overthinks, I can't promise that *Master Tristan* won't slip out and remind her of that."

She laughed. "Okay. I'll try not to overthink things."

He parked and took her up to the Tillmans' corner unit. Just as he thought she would, Cassie loved it.

"Oh, wow, the view is amazing. The sunset over the white sand is simply breathtaking."

Mrs. Tillman smiled proudly. "It is spectacular and because it's a corner unit with an open floor plan, you can see it from every room except the bathrooms and the utility room."

Mr. Tillman, who was normally reticent warmed up to Cassie immediately. "I love the balcony. It's a little hot on summer afternoons, but the rest of the year it is my favorite place to relax with a martini."

In less that forty-five minutes, they had the details worked out. Cassie had even offered to let them use one of the bedrooms to store any furniture they wouldn't need at the new place—just in case they decided to move back in six months.

On their way up to see his condo he said, "Cassie, you know it wasn't necessary for you to let them use one of the bedrooms for storage. They could have put anything they weren't going to need into a storage unit. You said you wanted three bedrooms."

"I know. But I was going to have to buy furniture for the third bedroom and it's probably better to wait until I have something permanent before I do that. Besides, while I like the idea of having a guest room, I never have guests so it really isn't all that important in the short-term."

"As long as you're sure."

"I'm sure. And look how relieved Mrs. Tillman was. You could tell the idea of putting things in storage worried her."

He caressed Cassie's cheek, leaned in and kissed her.

When he pulled away, she smiled, looking a little bemused. "What was that for?"

He laughed. "Primarily because I've wanted to do it all afternoon. But seeing the side of you that is so kind and thoughtful, and being reminded of how very sweet you are, I couldn't resist another minute."

Chapter 15

When Cassie's real estate agent had called with the offer just after nine that morning, she could barely process it. It was an excellent offer—she knew it was. She didn't want to refuse it, but how could she find somewhere else to live and move in two weeks?

Just last weekend Tristan had offered to help her find a new home and only last night they'd made plans to go house hunting next weekend. She'd never called him to ask for help on anything before...come to think of it, she rarely asked anyone for help. In fairness, she hadn't really had many people to ask. She had become responsible for so much at such a young age, she learned to figure stuff out as it came up. But she had never bought a home before and the offer left her with no time to waste. She figured if Tristan didn't think it was possible for her to find a place to live in two weeks, she'd have to say no to the offer.

So she called him and for the first time in years, Cassie didn't have to solve a massive problem on her own.

He'd arrived at her house an hour later with a list of properties and appointments his assistant had made for them. He had known just what to do and took care of things. All she had to do was let him. So, a day that had started out filled with tension and worry, ended up being fun. Even though none of the available properties had appealed to her, she had the overriding sense that everything would work out.

And it did.

One look at the Tillman's unit and she was beyond thrilled. It was precisely the kind of place that she wanted to live. She was a little surprised but very happy to learn that Tristan's condo was in the same building. Well, referring to it as a "condo" was a bit misleading. The entire top floor of the building was his. But she guessed that was one of the perks of owning the entire complex.

The interior of his home was not at all what she had imagined. She'd expected sleek, modern industrial décor—lots of black, white and steel. On the contrary his home had an overall Caribbean Colonial flavor. It was light and airy. Small touches of dark wood and rattan were contrasted by bright island colors. The master bedroom was spectacular. A four poster, king size bed stood in the middle of the room. The headboard was huge, creating the effect of a wall, and the canopy frame was draped with gauzy mosquito netting. Floor to ceiling windows opened onto a shady balcony with an amazing view of the Gulf of Mexico. Briefly, she had allowed herself to imagine drifting to sleep in his arms in that bed and waking in the morning to the glorious view.

After a quick look around the outside of the complex, he took her to a charming local restaurant for a great dinner. Then he drove her home and kissed her senseless at her door. Just before he left, he said, "Oh, there's something I need to remind you about."

"What is it?" she asked, wracking her kiss-addled brain for something she might have forgotten.

"Even though our relationship is changing, your orgasms still belong to Master Tristan, Cassandra." With that he turned to walk to his car.

"That's not fair! You're rearranging the contents of my boxes, Tristan."

He got in his car and called, "I never promised to play fair. Call Master Tristan if you have an issue with that."

It didn't matter. She had too much to do to worry about sex.

Of course, once he'd placed the idea in her mind, it was all she could think about. She tried to polish her slides for a while. When she couldn't focus on them, she gave up and went to bed, but she couldn't sleep either. Finally, after thirty minutes of staring at the ceiling, she decided to take him at his word. She dialed his number.

He answered the phone with his rich, sexy Dom voice. "Cassandra, do you need something?"

"Yes, Sir. You know I do. But I wouldn't if you hadn't planted the idea."

"Tsk, tsk, Cassandra. Mind your tone of voice. If I hadn't *planted the idea*, what would you be doing now?"

"Finishing my slides for this week."

"And what are you doing instead?"

"Lying in bed, frustrated, unable to sleep, talking to you."

"Which is more fun?"

She chuckled. "Talking to you."

"You see, Cassandra, your Dom knows what's best for you. Now, my little bird, I want three orgasms before you go to sleep and I am going to tell you exactly what to do."

She smiled. They'd never done this before. "Okay."

"Get out of bed and go to your purse."

"My purse? Why?"

"Cassandra, do you remember who you're speaking to?"

"Uh…I forgot for a moment, Sir, I'm sorry." She hopped out of bed. "I'm going to my purse now." Her purse was on her dresser. "Okay, Sir, I have it."

"Now look inside. You will find something about the size of a salt shaker that resembles a pink and white penguin. I slipped it in there earlier."

Sure enough, it was there. "I found it, Sir." At the tip of the small end was a white, silicone cup about as big as the end of her forefinger. "What is it?"

"It's a clit stimulator. Push the button on the front and put your finger over the silicone tip. "

"Yes, Sir." She did and felt a gentle vibration combined with a slight pulsation. "Oh, my."

He chuckled. "The lower button changes the speed and pattern. Now, go back to bed, make yourself comfortable, position the cup over your clit and experiment. Orgasm number one is all up to you. Do what feels good, but let me hear it. Put the phone on speaker."

She could scarcely believe she was doing this. She climbed back in bed, put the phone on speaker and laid it beside her on the pillow. She touched herself with her fingers first. She was dripping wet and her clit was puffed up and ready to play. The fact that he could do that to her simply by telling her she couldn't come was a little mind-boggling.

She turned the penguin on low and positioned the cup over her clit. It hadn't felt like much against her finger, but the vibrations encircling her clit felt amazing. "Mmmm."

"Feel good, little bird?"

"Yes, Sir."

"Try increasing the speed."

She did. The pulsations became a little more pronounced. "Oh…wow, that's…that's good." The feeling wasn't like a regular vibrator. She changed the speed again, and gasped at the new sensation.

"By the sound of things, you upped the intensity."

"Oh, yes, Sir. Oh…it's…oh…" Before she realized what was happening, she came hard, crying out as she did. She pulled the wicked little thing away from her sensitive clit and panted as she drifted back down.

"It sounds like the pink penguin, which cannot fly itself, sent my little bird soaring."

"Yes, Sir. That was…wow."

He chuckled again. "Now that you know how it works and how very effective it is, I want you to do it again. Only this time, I want you to get to the edge and stay there. Do not come and do not ask me for permission. You will come when I am ready for you to come, do you understand?"

"Yes, Sir." She would be the one in control of the toy. She would just have to be careful not to go too far.

"But, Cassandra, do not shy away from the edge. You must be ready to come *when I tell you to.* I'll know if you are playing it safe."

"Yes, Sir." Stay right on the edge? With this pulsating wonder on her clit? That was a much harder thing to do.

"Are you ready?"

"Yes, Sir."

"Turn the penguin off and on again so it is at its lowest speed."

"Yes, Sir."

"Then, let's go. Position it over your clit."

She relaxed into it. She could do this. The lowest speed was amazing, but didn't bring her close enough to make holding back hard.

"Are you at the edge, little bird?"

"Not quite, Sir."

"Then increase the intensity...two clicks."

It was the third speed that put her over the edge the first time. "Yes, Sir." In moments, she was lost. She was on the edge. She'd move the penguin away ever so slightly to keep from coming, but not enough to lose the edge. It was incredible and maddening, all at once. *Just come, Cassie. He's on the other end of the phone. What's he going to do?* The answer to that was *be disappointed* and she didn't want to disappoint him. So, she fought to stay on the edge. She panted and moaned until her moans almost became sobs because she needed to come so badly.

"You are amazing, Cassandra. Come for me, little bird."

She exploded. It felt as if every nerve ending in her body was alive and firing jolts of pleasure.

It took much longer to recover from that orgasm than the first one. His voice was in her ear the entire time, telling her how wonderful and beautiful she was.

When she had regained her senses, he said, "Now, one more."

"Sir, I don't think I can."

"Of course, you can. You'll do what I tell you to do because you are an obedient sub."

"Yes, Sir," she answered, still not sure she had another orgasm in her.

"Spread your legs as wide as you can."

"Yes, Sir."

"Now imagine that I have tied your ankles so that you cannot move your legs."

"Yes, Sir."

"Also imagine that your thighs are tied down, as is your waist. You are unable to move anything below your chest, do you understand?"

"Yes, Sir."

"Good. Now position that rather amazing little toy over your clit and turn it to level three. If you had been naughty and disobeyed me, we might have to set it higher—it has eleven speeds. But you've been a very good girl."

Higher? Dear God, she didn't think she could have stood it. "Yes, Sir."

"Now just hold it there. Don't move your hand, don't move your lower body. Just absorb the vibrations."

At first, it was easy enough to do. But as the sensations built, she wanted to move, she wanted to reach for it. *Just move a little. He won't know and it will feel so good.* But she would know and she wanted to do this for him. She wanted to please her Dom. She let out a ragged groan.

"Hold perfectly still, Cassandra. That's a good girl. You don't need to hold back this time. When the orgasm comes, just let it take you."

The constant, unchanging sensation was almost unbearable simply because one tiny twitch of her hips would send her over the edge, but she didn't allow herself to move. Then it was as if every muscle in her body pulsed at once. She practically screamed. It was uncontrolled, powerful, awesome and unbelievably draining. She was completely spent.

Again, she heard his rich voice, praising her, soothing her as she returned to earth.

"Sir, that was…that was…I don't know how to describe it."

"It was three completely different and yet all-consuming orgasms, courtesy of the Dom who knows you well and sees to your needs."

She chuckled. "That pretty much sums it up, Sir."

"Now, my beautiful little bird, drink some water and get some rest. I trust sleep will no longer elude you."

And he'd been right. She was asleep almost instantly and slept soundly until the phone woke her at eight-thirty.

"Hello?"

"Good morning, Miss Hastings. My name is Caroline Preston and I am Mr. Cabot's assistant. He filled me in on everything that happened yesterday and asked me to help make a few arrangements for you."

"Uh, okay. Thank you."

"First, you will need to meet with Margot Weber, the building manager at Cabot Towers to take care of the sublease agreement. Both she and the Tillmans are free at nine-thirty, can you be there by then?"

"Yes. Thanks for setting that up."

"It's my pleasure. Mr. Cabot said you have to leave town late tomorrow afternoon and won't be back until Saturday. If you would like to give me your real estate agent's contact information, I will coordinate the closing with her for you."

"Okay, that'd be great. I'm going to be at a conference, in and out of sessions. I wasn't sure how I was going to do this."

"I'm happy to help. Do you have a real estate lawyer? If so, I'll need his contact information. Otherwise, Mr. Cabot's attorney will handle it for you."

"I do have an attorney."

"Excellent. Then the last thing to set up is the move. I've made an appointment for you with an extremely reliable mover we've used in the past. He will meet you at your house at four this afternoon to take a look and give you an estimate. The Tillmans have had their move scheduled for several weeks now. Their movers will pack on Thursday, load the truck on Friday and move them into their new home on Saturday. We can schedule it much the same for you. Margot will arrange for a professional cleaning crew to clean the condo after the movers leave on Friday. That way it will be ready for you to move in on Saturday."

"Okay. But we don't know when closing will be yet."

"Don't worry about anything. I will do my best to see that it is scheduled for Friday, but if it has to be earlier in the week, arrangements can be made with the new owners for you to stay in the house past closing."

"Great. Thank you. This is a huge help. I really appreciate it."

"No worries at all."

Cassie gave Caroline the contact information she needed before getting off the phone. Then she took a quick shower, dressed, grabbed a cup of coffee and was heading to Cabot Towers in less than thirty minutes. Margot was an efficient, middle-aged German woman. She had all of the paperwork ready and it took less than an hour to go through it with the Tillmans.

Cassie was home by noon. Thanks to Tristan, everything was done. She didn't have to worry about anything.

She sat down with her computer, a sandwich and a glass of iced tea. By the time the doorbell rang at four, she was finished with her presentations.

The mover was very pleasant and professional. "So, we are essentially packing up everything in the master bedroom, office, kitchen and the breakfast area, bathrooms, closets, utility room, one glass case in the living room and a single piece of art. It shouldn't take more than a few hours. We can take care of it on Thursday afternoon. We'll pack the truck on Friday morning. That won't take long at all. Two hours tops. We could move you in that day, if you want."

"The people who own the condo where I'm moving won't be out until Friday afternoon and the management company will have it cleaned before I move in. So if Saturday is okay with you, it will be fine."

Since the house wasn't going to be completely empty, she could stay here Friday night. She could also probably stay with Julia, but somehow she thought she might want one last night here.

So, with Tristan's help, everything to do with the sale of the house and the move was well in hand. All she had to do was pack for the conference and enjoy the rest of the week in Boston. When she got back, a new chapter of her life would start.

Chapter 16

Jim Donovan sat nursing a beer at the end of the bar in Mike's Place, a pub near the hotel where he always stayed when he had business in downtown Boston. He'd been in town since Tuesday, and even though his entire family lived in the area, he usually stayed in the city, to be close to work, then visited family on the weekend. With so many of them it wasn't always easy to see them all. But it was Friday evening and the Sox were playing the Mets in New York. Seizing the chance to get the whole family together, Jim's dad had invited them all to come to the house for a cookout and to watch the game. Jim had two brothers who worked in the city who'd been supposed to meet him here at six so he could ride out to Medford with them.

His brothers were late as usual. The Dom in him hated that on a normal day, even when they were just a few minutes late. Tonight, they were over thirty minutes late, neither one had called to explain why and the game was scheduled to start in about a half hour. There was no way they could make it home before then. And even though he'd called Dad and told him not to make everyone wait for dinner, his Dad refused.

"We'll wait for you guys, Jimmy. No one's in any rush."

He looked up as someone entered the bar. He'd hoped to see at least one of their mugs coming through the door. When he saw it was a woman, he started to turn his attention to the television screen, but did a double take. It wasn't just any woman. It was Cassandra Hastings, the cute, shy sub from Hidden Gem who Tristan was training.

She clearly hadn't noticed that Jim was there. As she stepped into the bar, she didn't spare a glance to any of the patrons. A smile split her face and she went straight to the bartender.

"Baby, it's been ages," said the bartender, who Jim figured was about his own age.

"Davy! I'm so glad you're here."

"Come on, baby, I'm here every Friday night. You know that."

"Yeah, but it would be my luck, the one Friday I'm in Boston, you'd be on vacation or something."

"Vacation? Me? Never. I love my job too much. Come give me a hug."

The bartender, Davy, stepped from behind the bar and gave her a bear hug, lifting her from the ground. "How the hell are you?"

She laughed. "Great. As long as you haven't broken my ribs."

He grinned and put her down. "So you're doing okay?"

"Yeah, Davy. Things are good. You?"

"Couldn't be better. Sit down. I'll make you the usual."

She laughed. "Really? The usual? Can I never break free from that?"

"Not a chance, baby. At least not the first drink of the night."

"Then work your Hollywood magic. I'm going to run to the ladies' room. Could you also put in an order for a burger and rings? I'll share the rings with you."

"You got it. Hey, do you have to be anywhere tonight?"

"No. Why?"

"Mike will kill me if I don't let him know you're here. The only thing worse would be if I called him and you left before he got here."

"I'd love to see him," she called over her shoulder as she went through the doors that led to the restrooms.

Jim wasn't sure what was going on here. It certainly looked like Cassandra was hooking up and he knew Tristan would be livid. When Tristan was in any relationship, he had one nonnegotiable rule: he didn't share.

The bartender stepped into the kitchen, presumably to put in Cassandra's order. When he came back out, Jim got his attention.

"What can I get you?"

"Another beer, please."

"Sure thing. You want a cold mug?"

"Yeah, that'd be great." Jim nodded toward the end of the bar where Cassandra had been. "She's cute. Is she your girlfriend?"

"Nah," said Davy as he got the frosted mug from a freezer under the bar and started to fill it.

"An ex?"

Davy frowned. "No. She's way too young for me. I've known her since she was a kid."

Well that was good to know. At least she wasn't two-timing Tristan with the bartender. "So she's from the neighborhood?"

"Sort of. Her Uncle Harvey—or I guess he was her great-uncle—lived nearby. He was a regular for years. He was like family, you know? So she is too."

"Her parents were okay with her hanging out at a bar with her uncle?"

Davy frowned, appearing affronted. "There is nothing wrong with a kid being here. Lots of regulars bring their families. It's a neighborhood pub, not a dive."

"Sorry, Davy, I didn't mean any offense. I was just surprised her parents didn't come too."

"Baby's parents and her dad's parents were killed in a car accident when she was just a squirt. Seven, I think. Most of the time she lived with her grandmother, Harvey's widowed sister. Baby visited him a couple times a year at least and when she did, he'd bring her here for dinner most nights." Davy slid the frosty mug of beer across the bar and started making two more drinks.

"She's not your girlfriend and you call her *baby*?"

Davy laughed. "Harv called her 'baby girl', so his friends here called her baby girl too, or eventually just Baby. Harv didn't have any other family and he absolutely adored her. You would have thought his baby girl hung the moon. I'd never seen the man so excited as when she was accepted at Boston College and decided to go there. Baby was finally going to be living in Boston. At the time, I was kind of worried. You know, her being a teenager and all, I figured after she was in college she wouldn't want to hang out with her old uncle much and he'd get his feelings hurt. But she was in here with him at least once a week. A real sweetheart of a kid."

"She sounds like it."

"The worst part was that he had to leave Boston when she was a sophomore."

"Wow, he sounds like he was a fixture here. What could make him do that?"

Davy hesitated.

Jim had been coming here regularly enough to see how they treated frequent customers. Davy was as open and chatty a bartender as Jim had ever met and he didn't consider Jim a stranger but perhaps that question was too personal. "Sorry, I didn't mean to pry."

"No, it's not that. Harvey would tell you himself if he were here. It's just really sad. His sister lived in Florida. He told Baby he needed to move somewhere warm for his health. The truth was his sister had Alzheimer's and it was getting to the point where it wasn't good for her to be alone. They kept it from Baby. He knew she'd want to leave BC and help. Neither Harv nor his sister wanted that. She finished in five years with a Masters degree in English. *With honors*," Davy added, clearly as pleased with her accomplishments as if he were family. "Harv came up to Boston for her graduation and threw a huge party for her here in the bar. Damn, he was proud of her. We all were. Like I said, she's family. Harv had some connections and had gotten her an entry-level position at Harcourt. Unfortunately, that was the last night I saw him."

"What happened?"

"He had a massive heart attack a few days later and died. Baby backed out of the Harcourt job so she could go home to Florida and take care of her grandmother. Since then, every time she comes to Boston for anything, she comes here. Either my dad or I make her a Shirley Temple." He raised one of the drinks he'd made in one hand. "And we make Harv a vodka tonic." He lifted the other glass. "My dad is the 'Mike' in 'Mike's Place'."

Jim was stunned. Cassandra had the reputation of being a sweet sub and he'd heard something about how she'd come to Florida to take care of her grandmother. His heart ached when he learned just how much she'd lost in her young life. "Poor kid."

"Yeah, she's alone in the world now. Her grandmother passed away a year and a half ago or so. Dad and I flew down for the funeral. We tried to talk her in to coming back up here where she has friends."

"She doesn't have friends in Florida?"

"Of course, she has friends. She's a doll. You can't help but like her. It's just that they're all older folks. Neighbors or friends of Harv and her grandmother. But at the time, the loss was too fresh and she wasn't ready yet. She hasn't been in Boston for months. We almost had her convinced last time. Maybe this time she'll change her mind."

Jim hoped not. Tristan would be crushed. For all his talk of keeping things professional, Jim knew his friend was falling hard and fast.

Cassandra walked back into the bar from the restroom.

The bartender picked up the drinks he'd made and took them to her. "Here's your drink, Baby. The food's been ordered and dad's on his way."

"Thanks, Davy." She sat down, took a sip of her Shirley Temple and glanced around the bar for the first time. She saw Jim and, based on her expression, recognized him. She smiled warmly and nodded her head in greeting, but didn't speak. The general rule for club members who meet unexpectedly in public is not to acknowledge each other. It could result in a violation of one or both person's privacy relating to their membership in the club.

He smiled, nodded back and raised his glass to her.

A group of about eight guys entered the bar. They were loud and rowdy, and by the looks of them, were planning to hang out there to watch the game—reminding Jim that his brothers were now forty-five minutes late.

The newcomers all eyed Cassandra as she sat alone at the end of the bar.

One of them said, "I got dibs on the wicked hottie at the end of the bar," before making a beeline to her. "Hey, gorgeous, you are smokin'. How 'bout you join me and my buddies to watch the Sox."

"No, thank you," she said with a polite smile.

"You here with your boyfriend?"

"No. My uncle."

He looked around. "I don't see nobody and you are too pretty to be drinking alone." He put a hand on her shoulder.

"Please don't touch me." It was worded as a polite request, but the command in her voice was unmistakable.

The man ignored her, running his hand down her arm. "Come on, gorgeous. Don't be that way. I'll buy you a drink."

Jim saw red and was off his barstool in an instant. But before he could take a single step, Cassandra had grabbed the man's wrist with one hand, twisted it and with her other hand was bending his little finger back so hard another fraction of an inch would break it.

"I asked politely. Now, when I let go, you are going to go back to your friends and leave me alone. Or I see three men in this bar who are going to beat the ever-loving shit out of you."

Jim's focus had been solely on Cassandra, but at those words, he glanced around. Davy had stopped what he was doing and stood poised to fight. And an older man who, by his resemblance to Davy, could only be his dad, Mike, had just come through the front doors. If he'd been a cartoon, steam would have been issuing from his ears.

"Okay. Let go of me, bitch," said the piece of shit who had hit on her.

That was all it took. Mike was across the room in a heartbeat and had the guy by the shirt dragging him to the door. "That's my baby girl. Get the hell out of my bar, asshole. And you'd better never fucking come back."

One of the guys with the asshole said, "Come on, Mike. We always watch the Sox here. He didn't know she was your daughter. He was just hitting on a pretty girl. He's harmless."

"If my baby was about to break his fingers, he's not harmless and if you hang with garbage like that, I don't want you in my bar either. All of youse, get out."

The other men left, looking more irritated with their asshole friend than Mike.

After shutting the door behind them, Mike turned to Cassandra and opened his arms. "Baby, it's good to see you."

She stepped into his embrace, hugging him tightly.

"That jerk didn't hurt you, did he?"

"No, Mike."

Mike's gaze swept the bar and landed on Jim. "Hey, I've seen you before. You come in every now and then when you're in town. Were you the third man who was, to quote my sweet girl, gonna 'beat the ever-loving shit' out of the asshole?"

"Yes, Sir. The name's Jim Donovan."

Mike let go of Cassandra to shake Jim's hand. "Mike Quinn, I own this place. Your tab's on me tonight."

"Thanks, but it isn't necessary. I have no use for jerks who can't take 'no' for an answer. And in fairness, your *little girl* was holding her own."

Cassandra smiled. "But you were willing to step in. Too many times people sit back and pretend they don't see or it's none of their business. Thank you, Mr. Donovan."

"Don't mention it. And you can call me Jim." Out of habit, he didn't offer her his hand. Generally, a Dom didn't touch a sub who wasn't his, without her Dom's permission.

"Thank you, Jim. I'm Cassie Hastings."

At that moment, the door opened and his brother Kevin stepped in. "Hey, Jim, sorry to keep you waiting, bro. Since we're a little late, Chris didn't look for a place to park. He's waiting out front. We gotta go."

Jim snorted. "A little late? Try an hour late." To Mike and Cassandra he said, "I have a family thing to get to. It was nice meeting you, Cassie. You take care of yourself."

Jim would have liked the chance to speak with her alone, to make absolutely certain she was okay, but it couldn't be helped. And she seemed to be in the care of men who considered her family. He threw a twenty on the bar and left with his brother, wondering exactly how much of Cassie's background Tristan knew.

Chapter 17

The conference had been fantastic. Cassie's presentations were well received and she made quite a few new contacts. She always enjoyed Boston. It was home to her best memories of Uncle Harvey and many of those included Mike's Place. Mike and Davy were the closest thing to family that she had left. They tried to talk her into moving back every time they saw her. Even though she didn't want to trade her tropical paradise for Boston, as time passed she considered the idea more and more seriously, just to be near them. But for the first time since her grandmother had passed away, she wasn't tempted. This time, she'd assured them she was happy and making friends. She loved the community at Hidden Gem and was beginning to feel very close to several of her friends there.

Seeing Jim Donovan in the bar had shocked her. Still, it had been obvious by his accent that he was originally from Boston and she knew he often travelled on business. It had been one of those crazy small world moments. She'd have liked the chance to chat with him privately.

Having to fend off an overzealous loser was never fun to do. But she was pretty proud that she'd been able to. She wasn't helpless and having embraced her submissive side didn't change that. If anything, it empowered her. Submission was a gift and she had the power to say yes or no to anything in her life. Still, the fact that there were friends ready to step in if she needed it had warmed her heart. She would tell Tristan about it. She wanted to be able to thank Master Jim.

She'd had a great visit with Mike and Davy that evening. She told them about the sale of the house and her plan to buy something on the beach. She also mentioned that she had met some new friends and was happier than she had been in ages. Finally being able to quiet some of their concerns for her, lifted her spirits considerably. She hated that they worried.

The conference finished Saturday afternoon and as nice as it had been, she was ready to go home. This would be a busy week. Just as promised, Tristan's assistant, Caroline, had taken care of all of the details. The move would go as initially planned. The settlement was scheduled for Friday morning and the buyers agreed to let her stay in the house until Saturday morning.

When she arrived at the Tampa airport, part of her wanted to see Tristan badly enough that she nearly went to the club. But she was exhausted and he wasn't expecting her, so she went home. They had a date the next day anyway.

Or did they?

When he'd set up the date, it had been to go out for brunch and look at properties. That was before the contract she'd received changed everything and they had gone out last Sunday.

Maybe she should call him to confirm?

But he would be in the club for hours still. Then if he got the message and he hadn't planned on taking her out, it might make him feel bad that he hadn't clarified that. He wouldn't want to call her that late. He might decide to take her out just because of the misunderstanding, even though he hadn't planned to.

She could wait and call tomorrow morning when she knew he'd answer. But if he wasn't planning to take her out, he might sleep in. She wouldn't want to wake him unnecessarily and, again, he might decide to take her out simply because he felt obliged to.

Damn. This is why submission felt so comfortable. She didn't have to overthink things.

Then it occurred to her. That was the answer. *Submit.* She would be ready to go to brunch with him at ten. If he intended to keep the date, he'd be there. If that wasn't his intention, he wouldn't be. She'd know that he was doing exactly what he'd planned and would not have rearranged anything because of what he thought she wanted.

She told herself, either way, she'd be happy. She'd love to go to brunch with him. On the other hand she also had things to do to get ready for her move. But when the doorbell rang shortly before ten she was thrilled.

She opened the door. "Hi."

"Hi, Cassie. You look fantastic."

Because it was a typical hot August day, she wore a retro blue and white cotton summer dress and white sandals. In a further attempt to stay cool, she had captured her hair in a smooth French twist.

He wore light tan trousers and a crisp white linen shirt.

"Thank you. You look pretty good yourself."

"Thank you. However, after not seeing you for a whole week, polite greetings at the front door simply will not do." He pushed her into the house, swung the door shut behind him and kissed her deep and hard.

She slipped her hands around his neck and returned the kiss.

When he finally came up for air, he rested his forehead against hers. "I missed you."

"Mmm. I missed you too. I was tempted to stop by the club last night on my way home from the airport."

"I would have loved seeing you. But I'm glad you didn't. I'm sure you were exhausted and then I would have had to punish you for not taking proper care of yourself."

"Then I'm glad I gave in to my fatigue. I don't like being punished."

"I know. And as much as I love to see that gorgeous ass turn red, it's much more fun when you are enjoying it."

He kissed her again. "Do you remember what we had planned for today?"

"Brunch and house-hunting."

"Yes, well we did the house-hunting last weekend and there is nothing new on the market for you to see. So we'll go to brunch, but we haven't had a chance to play all week and I don't think I can wait until next weekend. How would you like to play a little today?"

"Not in the club?"

"Not in the club. Since this is the first time away from the safety of that environment I promise to keep it low-key."

"I trust you. I'm not worried."

"I'm glad you trust me. Just like everything else in this lifestyle though, it is important to start slow. One's ability to trust is affected by environment. Trusting me in the safe environment of the club will be different than trusting me when we are completely alone. So, today, no bondage—nothing very intense."

She smiled. "I think I'd like that."

"Good. To start with, give me your panties."

"My panties? But we're going out."

"Cassandra, I said, give me your panties. You have earned five spanks for questioning me."

"Yes, Sir." Cassie wasn't sure what he intended, but she'd go with it. She took off her panties and handed them to him.

He put them in his pocket. "Now bend over. Put your hands on the table and count."

He lifted her skirt and gave her one spank. She knew instantly this wasn't really punishment. It felt oh-so-good as soon as the initial sting passed. "One."

He gave her the remaining light, stinging blows that had her ass feeling warm and tingly.

She didn't move after the fifth spank. She waited for his command.

"Very good, little bird. We'll get back to this later. However, there *is* something I'd like you to wear this afternoon, instead of your pretty little panties." He massaged her bottom allowing his fingers to slide into her soaked pussy. He knew exactly what to do to turn her on.

She closed her eyes and gave a low moan. It had been too long.

He slid his fingers backwards, and circled her anus. "You particularly like anal play, don't you, Cassandra?"

"Yes, Sir, I do."

He reached into his pocket with his other hand and held up a butt plug for her to see.

Her eyes went wide. "B-but we're going out. I...I can't..."

"Of course, you can. You don't like to be exposed in public and you won't be. That beautiful dress you are wearing more than adequately covers your delicious ass. No one will see it, or the little accessory wedged into it. The plug isn't even very big. You'll just barely feel it and it will keep your thoughts on the wicked side. Besides, we're going to one of the restaurants at Island Treasures for brunch."

"And that makes it different because...?"

"It's an adults-only resort." He leaned in to whisper in her ear, "I bet you won't be the only one there with your little butt nicely stuffed."

She remembered the first day she'd met Julia. Julia had been wearing a butt plug that day and had said *it keeps me deliciously turned on all day*. A slow smile spread across Cassie's face. She had been introduced to all kinds of wild things in the club, but this was the kinkiest thing she'd ever considered doing outside of that environment and she loved it. "Okay. I'll do it."

"Excellent. Spread your legs a little wider, bend over and hold your skirt out of the way." He pulled a tube of lube from his pocket.

"You certainly came well prepared," she said as she followed his instructions.

"Oh, little bird, you have no idea how much I've been looking forward to this." He put a little lube on his finger and massaged her tight opening before working the lube inside.

She did love the way it felt and gave another little moan of pleasure.

"That sexy little noise you make when you enjoy something turns me rock hard." He added a little more lube, continuing to slide his finger in and out. He kissed the sensitive spot at the base of her spine, sending a delightful shiver through her. Then he removed his finger, replacing it with the small plug.

"Now, stand up and walk a little. Tell me how it feels."

She straightened up, repositioned her skirt and walked down the hall towards the kitchen.

He followed her.

He was right, it was just the perfect size to feel it occasionally and be turned on. "It feels good. Fantastic, in fact."

"Excellent. I'll just wash the lube from my hands and we'll go." He went to the sink.

"Um…Tristan…can I ask you something?"

"Of course."

"Well…I guess I'm not sure…um…what are the rules?"

"The rules?"

"I understand the rules in the club. And you said outside of the club they don't apply. But when I questioned you a minute ago, you called me Cassandra and spanked me."

He dried his hands and turned to her. "Cassie, sweetheart, it wasn't a punishment. Not a real one."

"I know and I liked it. But I don't want to make a *real* mistake. I like to know the rules."

He gathered her in his arms. "I'm sorry, little bird, you're right. I should have made my expectations clearer. Except for showing each other respect, club rules do not apply outside of the club or the bedroom. Period. Nothing you do will result in a punishment."

"You're sure?"

"Absolutely. If something changes, we'll discuss it before it becomes a rule."

"And inside the bedroom, club rules apply?"

"Not always."

"Then how will I know?"

"If we are in private and I address you as Cassandra, that is your sign that we are shifting into a D/s relationship and club rules apply. Will that help you?"

"Yes. I think so."

"Good girl. But, Cassie, you have a voice. You have the words to stop anything you don't like. Always. You know that, right?"

She nodded. "I do. I just wanted to understand everything."

"I know. It's what makes you such a lovely sub." He took a step back. "Now, are you ready to go?"

She wiggled her ass and grinned. "So ready. Thank you."

"You are a very bad girl. Wiggling that sweet ass at me when it'll be at least two hours before I can get my hands on it again."

"Was I meant to be the only one having naughty thoughts?"

"My lovely little bird, when I'm with you, all my thoughts are naughty, no matter what you do. If you fan those flames too much, I'm not sure I'll make it to the restaurant." He put a hand in the small of her back and guided her to the front door.

She picked up her purse and a light sweater from the entryway table. It was a blistering hot day, so restaurants and other public places tended to set their air-conditioning to arctic.

Once they were in the car and on their way, Tristan asked her about the conference.

"It was great. It's the biggest indie conference in the world."

"Indie conference? I thought it was something to do with editing."

"That's part of it, but it's way more. The conference focuses on all aspects of independent publishing. So, indie-authors, small publishing companies, cover artists, editors, aspiring authors and a variety of others attend. There were workshops on everything you could imagine related to creating, publishing and marketing a book."

"What did you speak on?"

"One workshop was on why professional editing is important and the different kinds of editing that a book often needs. And the other workshop was on self-editing techniques."

"Those sound like diametrically opposed topics. If an author needs a professional editor, self-editing seems redundant."

"It isn't really. There are a lot of little steps that an author can take to improve the quality of their writing."

"Are most of the workshops aimed at authors and aspiring authors?"

"Yes, but even many of those are helpful to editors too. It's very interesting to hear a successful author talk about character development, or building suspense or even what makes for a good sex scene." She wiggled in the seat, feeling the plug in her ass and thinking her experience with good sex had expanded exponentially over the last few months. "By learning some of this myself, when I'm working with an author on a content edit, I can provide more concrete guidance about what needs to be fixed."

"I can see how that would be helpful."

"And, of course, for freelance service providers like editors and artists, it's a nice opportunity to network and make new business connections. The evening social events were great for that."

"So you lived and breathed the publishing industry for four days."

"Pretty much. Except on Friday evening when I went to see old friends at their bar. Which reminds me, I ran into Master Jim there."

"You didn't greet him as *Master Jim* did you?"

She glanced sideways at him and huffed. "I may be new to this, but as important as privacy is to me, that is not a rule I'd forget. He was sitting at the bar. I smiled. He nodded. It was a standard greeting for two strangers who accidentally make eye-contact."

Tristan reached over and patted her knee. "Good girl. I shouldn't have doubted that. It's a bit of a knee-jerk reaction with me. As the club owner, one of my primary concerns is confidentiality."

"I do need to thank Master Jim, though."

"Why?"

"A guy hit on me who wasn't taking no for an answer."

Tristan's expression turned furious.

"Don't worry. I handled it. I'm tougher than you think. Then my friend Mike, who owns the bar, kicked the guy and his buddies out. But just before that, Master Jim looked ready to take the loser down."

Tristan still frowned. "What were you doing in a bar alone?"

"I already told you. I was there to see old friends and I wasn't alone. Mike owns the bar. His son Davy was the bartender. I was in good hands."

"Are these friends from your college years?"

Cassie was a little surprised that he'd remembered that detail. They'd only talked about her past during their first meeting. "They were actually my great uncle's friends. Then when Uncle Harvey had to move here to help grandma, Mike kind of filled in for him as a sort of father-figure. Mike and Davy are the closest thing to family I have."

"I see. I'd like to meet them someday."

"If you're ever going to be in Boston, let me know. I think you'd like them."

"I'm sure I would. And we can thank Jim this weekend. He's usually at the club when it's open, unless he's out of town."

"*We* can thank him?"

"Cassie, in our world, a kindness done to you is a kindness done to me as well."

She smiled. She liked the idea of being part of "we".

"So, now you know about my family, as sparse as it is. But I know next to nothing about yours. You mentioned once that your parents were divorced when you were a teenager. Do you have any brothers or sisters?"

He frowned. "It isn't a particularly heartwarming story. My father was seventeen years older than my mother. He inherited a modest amount from his grandfather, forty thousand, just as he was graduating from high school. Most of his friends were drafted and went to Korea, but he had polio as a kid and his left hand was paralyzed, so he wasn't drafted and went to college instead. He studied economics and began investing his inheritance in the stock market almost immediately. He had an uncanny skill for making sound investments and was a millionaire by the time he was thirty-five. It was the sixties and he became the consummate playboy." His tone of voice held a note of disapproval.

She glanced sideways at him, but refrained from making a comment.

He chuckled. "I know, I own an adults-only resort and a sex club. What I just said might sound a little judgmental. But my father looked at women as conquests. He subscribed to the 'do anything, say anything, pay anything to get the piece of ass you want' school of thought. Once he did, he moved on.

Cassie was a little confused. "But I thought casual sex was kind of an accepted thing in the lifestyle."

"It is. But it is all built on honesty and trust. Both parties know the rules going in. If it's casual sex, it's casual sex. There is no lying or manipulation to get one party to do something he or she isn't ready to do. I think that is one of the aspects of the lifestyle that first attracted me. I like sex and I like being in control. I expect I'm like my father in that. I also like pushing limits and exploring different paths to pleasure for both parties." He paused for a moment, frowning. "But my father's only goal was his own pleasure and he relished the conquest, no matter what it took or who it hurt. That's what I find reprehensible. I hate manipulative behavior. Actually, that is the main reason I started the club."

She smiled, remembering Julia's punishment on Cassie's first evening at the club. "I know you don't like scheming subs."

"But I like devious Doms even less."

"Devious Doms?" she asked playfully.

His expression turned deadly serious. "Cassie, you have only experienced the lifestyle in my club. There are other clubs and communities all over the world as well as individuals who practice BDSM outside of any organization. And even though mutual consent should be the foundation of the lifestyle, occasionally it isn't. It is all too easy for a Dom to pressure a sub into doing things she doesn't want to. I wanted to create a space where that was less likely to happen. That's why there are no truly private areas. It's one way of protecting submissives from charming bastards like my father. Not that he was into the kink. I think it was just about his needs and the thrill of the conquest. But the fact is, he left a trail of embittered women behind."

Cassie found this nothing short of amazing. "Wow. I'm impressed. Most of the guys I've known in the past were exact replicas of their dads, good or bad. I knew one guy in college who seemed to think making lots of babies with lots of women was his duty in life. Apparently his father had kids with five different women."

"Well, thankfully, my dad didn't do that. He was either careful, or lucky, or both."

"How did he meet your mom?"

"It's almost stereotypical. They met in 1973. She was a pretty, twenty-one year old flight attendant for BOAC."

"BOAC?"

"British Overseas Airway Corporation, the predecessor of British Airways."

"So she was British?"

"Still is. She was the first woman—maybe the only one—he ever met who didn't fall into his bed easily. But with his eyes on winning the prize, as they always were, he did what it took to get her. Only what it took was a wedding."

"Good for her for standing on her principles."

He shook his head and frowned. "Don't be too impressed. She makes no bones about the fact that she wasn't in love with a man who was nearly twice her age. Just like all the other women in his life, my mother was attracted by his net worth. But unlike the others, she wanted the life he could give her over the long term and not just for a few weeks or months. She was just the first one to figure out how to get him to marry her."

"She made him fall in love with her?"

He gave a mirthless laugh. "I don't think it was love. Not really. He was certainly in *lust* with her. But he was also in his forties and it was time to find himself a trophy wife. She was beautiful, poised, and she had a very cultured sounding British accent. She fit the bill perfectly, so marriage was the price he was willing to pay. They were married a year after they met. It was six years before my mother became pregnant with me and I think the marriage was already on the rocks by then. I don't ever remember them being happy and I'm certain neither of them were faithful. They were finally divorced when I was thirteen and weeks later, in Vegas, my mom married a longtime business associate of my father's."

"So, you don't have any siblings?"

"Actually, I do. I have a nineteen-year-old half-brother, Nick. My mother had him when I was fifteen. She divorced his dad a few years later and moved to London where she still lives. Nick is at University there. Then when Dad was in his late sixties he married another woman—half his age—and they had a little girl." Tristan frowned, looking uncomfortable.

"You don't have to tell me more. I'm sorry if I'm getting too personal."

"No, it's fine. Talking about my half-sister just always reminds me that my dad was an ass right up to the end. Her name is Madison, she's fourteen and a nice kid. My father divorced her mother when Madison was barely two. He was a total piece of shit about the whole thing. He had a pre-nup in place and he wasn't budging, even though a child was involved. Don't get me wrong, they weren't destitute by any stretch of the imagination, but Madison is as much his child as I am. When he died a few years later, I tried to make amends. I put half of the estate in a large trust fund for her."

"That was a very decent thing to do."

He shrugged. "It was fair."

"Yes but I haven't run into many people in my life whose first instinct is to be fair with money."

"By the time my father died, I was worth more than he was anyway. And that was probably because of the advantages I had growing up as his son. If he had things his way, she wasn't going to benefit from that. Maybe it's just easier to be fair when others need it more than you do."

Cassie shook her head. "No. I go back to my first statement, it was a very decent thing to do. In my experience, money doesn't improve people's judgment, it clouds it. The more they have the cloudier it gets."

"In your experience? You've had similar trouble?"

"Not exactly."

The fact was, she had experienced both sides before. She was orphaned and left nearly destitute when her parents and grandparents were killed in an accident. The new car her father was driving careened out of control and crashed. Witnesses reported that it accelerated suddenly to a dangerous speed and her father appeared to be desperately trying to stop it. Even the police suspected a mechanical malfunction. But the car was so badly demolished, there was little evidence to go on and nothing conclusive was found. In later years she saw photos of the crash and those images still haunt her. If it hadn't been for her other grandmother and Uncle Harvey, Cassie would have ended up in the care of social services.

Oddly, it was also because of Uncle Harvey that she'd experienced the opposite. He was wealthy. She hadn't realized just how wealthy until after he died. But clearly other people knew. In college, particularly, there were more than a few people who, finding out who her uncle was, pretended to be a friend because of what she might be able to do for them. Even though she should have known better, Cassie had always managed to let herself get hurt by these people. It was one reason she preferred to keep her life as simple as possible. She was less of a target if no one knew. She had already revealed much more to Tristan than she ever would have to most people, because he had his own wealth and he didn't consider her a potential benefactor.

But all of this was in the past where it belonged. She didn't like to talk about it. Just remembering it made her uncomfortable. She fidgeted in the seat, and becoming suddenly aware of the plug in her ass again, gave a little groan.

He chuckled. "Is that delightful toy having the desired effect?"

"You could say that."

"Knowing it's there is having nearly the same effect on me. I assure you, we won't linger long over brunch."

"Good, because I fear no matter how fine the meal is, food is not what will satisfy me."

In spite of that bold statement, brunch was fantastic and she enjoyed every morsel. But when they stood to leave, and she felt the little toy, she was reminded once again that the afternoon held even more promise.

They left the restaurant and he led her back to his car.

"Where are we going?" She knew he had a suite here and had assumed they'd be spending the afternoon there.

He put his arms around her and kissed her. "Cassie, even though this is a five-star, world-class resort, and I have a permanent residence here, it is still, technically, a hotel. I don't want to make love to you for the first time in a hotel. I want you in my home, in my bed."

She smiled, pleased by his thoughtfulness.

It was only a ten minute drive to Cabot Towers. In a week, this would be her home and the thought thrilled her. She had already decided exactly where her furniture was going to go and how her office would be arranged. The idea of glancing up from the computer every now and then and seeing the beautiful Gulf beach out the window quieted any concerns about possibly missing her old home.

The condo being so much closer to Hidden Gem was definitely an advantage, but it also meant she would be closer to Julia and her other friends from the club. She finally had friends to do things with, but living so far away had been inconvenient, to say the least. She spent a lot more time driving than she ever had in the past. Julia and Cyndi always managed to find cool festivals and things to go to near the beaches. Denny, who lived in St. Petersburg, shared her love for movies.

In his sweet, thoughtful way, he always picked a theater somewhere between the two of them. But that still meant they both had at least a thirty minute drive.

Living so close to Tristan would seem to be a perk too, even though not knowing exactly where their relationship was going concerned her a little. But that was the beauty of subletting from the Tillmans. Within six months, she would surely have a better handle on everything. Even if the Tillmans decided to sell, she didn't have to buy it. If it wasn't working, she could move elsewhere.

"You seem pensive all of a sudden," said Tristan as he parked the car. "Is everything okay?"

She smiled. "Absolutely. I was just thinking about how nice it's going to be to live here. I was imagining what it will be like to have such a wonderful view from my office."

"I think you are going to love it." He got out of the car and came around to open the passenger door for her. "Are you ready to play?"

She wiggled her hips. "Very ready."

Once they were in the elevator, he said, "I know how you like rules, so I want to be very clear about what I expect this afternoon."

Just hearing him say that helped her relax. "Okay."

"Club rules are in effect starting now."

"Yes, Sir."

"As soon as we step into my apartment, you will take your hair down, remove all of your clothes and kneel by the door until you are given other instructions. You will remain completely naked for the rest of the afternoon."

She frowned, her thoughts going immediately to the number of windows in his condo.

"Cassandra?"

"Yes, Sir. I just…well your condo has lots of windows."

They reached the top floor. He guided her off the elevator, which opened just outside the door to his condo.

"It should go without saying that I am fully aware of your limits. But even if public nudity wasn't a soft limit, I would never choose to parade you in front of my neighbors. All the windows in the building are tinted to block the sun. It keeps the units cooler and makes it nearly impossible to see in from outside. Furthermore, this building is two stories taller than all the other buildings in the complex, and since the entire top floor is mine, no one has a direct line of site into my condo anyway.

"I'm sorry, Sir. It was a gut reaction. I see what you mean now about trust being affected by environment."

"So, you will spend the rest of the afternoon naked. Is that understood?"

"Yes, Sir."

"I intend to make love to you this afternoon. Because that is a hard limit at the club, I need to know I have your consent."

She smiled. "Yes, Sir. You have my full and eager consent."

"Excellent. I like the sound of *full and eager*." He opened the door to the condo and stepped back, allowing her to enter first.

She stepped inside and just as he'd asked, removed her dress and bra, folding them neatly and placing them on the table by the front door. She slipped the sandals off her feet as she pulled the comb out of her hair, putting them with her dress.

She started to kneel beside the table and he tapped her shoulder, stopping her.

"Kneel there." He pointed to the other side of the door where a small pillow lay. "The tile is cold and hard."

She smiled. "Yes, Sir."

"What has caused that happy smile to light your face?"

"I always smile when I am reminded how wonderful you are."

He chuckled. "And what reminded you of that?"

"I don't recall seeing a random pillow on the floor by the door the last time I was here, Sir. I believe you put it there for me before you left this morning. Thank you, Sir."

"You're very confident about that."

"Evidently as confident as you were that I'd want to do this, Sir."

"Not confident, my beautiful little bird. Hopeful."

"I guess that makes two of us then, Sir. I was hoping you'd ask."

Chapter 18

Tristan couldn't take his eyes off Cassie. She was the picture of perfect submission, kneeling naked by his door. Eager. Hopeful.

Normally, before he played with Cassie in the club, he put great thought and care into planning the scene. His goal being to push Cassie's boundaries little by little while they both had a good time. He'd had a scene planned for today as well. Looking at her now, he threw his plan out the window. He wanted to simply enjoy her. To see her come, over and over again. To see her lips or hands wrapped around his cock. To bury himself in her and come with her.

He hadn't brought many women to his home in the past. He didn't have a separate "playroom" as some Doms did. However, like the alcoves at Hidden Gem, his bedroom furniture and décor had been designed with some modifications to allow for kinky play if he chose to engage in it there. But simply seeing her naked in his entryway made him want to do more than take her straight up to the bedroom. She wasn't just another sub. Nor was she a casual girlfriend. He loved her. And suddenly his plan for the day became clear. This was his chance to make certain she knew that.

"Cassandra, this afternoon we are going on a quest. A treasure hunt. I'm certain there are priceless treasures to be found here if we just look."

"What sort of treasure are we looking for, Sir?"

"Ah, my beautiful little bird, today we are in pursuit of orgasms."

A smile flirted at her lips. "Whatever you wish, Sir."

"We will search this condo from top to bottom and see how many we can find."

"Yes, Sir."

"I think we should start in the living room. Stand up and come with me."

She rose gracefully and followed him.

"Cassandra, I want you to sit on the sofa, spread your legs and put your feet on the edge of the coffee table."

She did as he asked, sitting up somewhat stiffly.

"Lean back, little bird. Make yourself comfortable."

"Yes, Sir." She looked a bit confused. He suppressed a smile.

"Spread your legs a little wider." He nudged her heels farther apart. "That's right. That is simply beautiful, little bird. Now, you need to find that first orgasm for me."

"Excuse me, Sir?"

"You heard me correctly. That delightful butt plug has had you turned on for hours now. Use those very talented hands and make yourself come while I watch. You needn't wait for permission, come whenever you're ready."

She blushed, just as he expected she would, but immediately began to touch herself. Soon she was writhing and making the sexiest little noises, her hands moving ever faster. When he was certain she was just about to come, he pulled out the butt plug, causing her to crash over the edge in a shuddering climax.

"Good girl. You found a lovely little orgasm. Once you've caught your breath, let's see if we can find another."

He took her hand and led her to the kitchen.

"The kitchen, Sir? I'm not sure about this."

"You doubt me? Tsk, tsk. You have just earned yourself a punishment. Bend over, hands on the counter, feet apart."

"Yes, Sir."

He opened one of the drawers and pulled out a silicone spatula. "This should do nicely." He spanked her lightly, turning her backside pink.

She moaned and arched her back to meet the blows, clearly enjoying the sensation.

He caressed her dripping pussy with his left hand as he increased the intensity just enough to have her flinching a little with each blow. Still, she had started panting as if staving off orgasm.

He grinned. "Will you ever doubt me again?"

"Oh…no…no…Sir. Never."

"Good girl." He dropped the spatula and plunged two fingers into her. "Come for me, little bird."

She tightened her grip on the counter, cried out and came with force, slumping forward onto the cool granite when her orgasm passed.

"That's two, my beautiful girl." He grabbed a bottle of water from the fridge before scooping her into his arms and carrying her to his study. He sank into a cane plantation chair, cuddling her against his chest. "Have some water before we continue our quest."

She took the bottle he offered and drank half of it. "Thank you, Sir."

"Have you revived enough to continue our mission?"

"Ah, Sir, about that. Am I the only one allowed to find the orgasms on this expedition?"

He chuckled. "That was my plan, but I suppose I could help too. What do you have in mind?"

She sat up and caressed his hard length through his trousers. "Well, I think there might be one here somewhere."

"Then I give you permission to do whatever is necessary to find it."

She smiled, coyly. "Yes, Sir."

She climbed off his lap and fetched a throw pillow from another chair. "May I use this, Sir?"

"Whatever you wish."

She dropped the pillow on the floor in front of his chair, and knelt on it between his knees. She unbuckled his belt and unzipped his fly. She tugged a little at his trousers to gain better access, then released his dick from its fabric prison.

He shifted his hips lower in the chair and relaxed as she gave him an expert blow job, his balls cupped in one of her small hands. Simply seeing her on her knees with his cock disappearing in and out of her mouth was nearly enough to bring him off. When he couldn't stand it any longer, he came.

She swallowed every drop, then sank back onto her heels with a very pleased expression on her face. "I believe that was number three, Sir."

"Indeed it was, my little bird."

"Now, where shall we look, Sir?"

"Let's see. We've found one in the living room, the kitchen and right here in my office. I think it might be worth searching the dining room."

Her eyebrows shot up. "The dining room, sir?"

"Yes." He stood up, adjusted his clothes and took her hand. "Do you doubt me?"

"Oh, no, Sir."

"Then come along." He grabbed a throw from the back of a chair before leading her to the dining room. "Yes, there is definitely one here somewhere. Besides, I'm up for a little snack." He went to the head of the table and spread the throw out in front of him. "Come here and sit on the table."

She did as he asked.

"Now, lay back. You can put your feet on the arms of my chair."

"Am I meant to be your *little snack*, Sir?"

"Mmm, yes." He lowered his head to her pussy and tickled her clit with his tongue. "Delicious."

Before long he had her crying out in yet another orgasm.

He pulled her onto his lap again and wrapped the throw around her as she recovered.

"How are you feeling, little bird?"

"Amazing…incredible…and a little tired."

He laughed. "Ah, yes, maybe a little break in our quest is in order?"

"That would be good, Sir."

"Then come with me." He took her hand and walked with her to his bedroom.

She glanced around. "This is such a beautiful room."

"I'm glad you like it. Shall we curl up for a Sunday afternoon nap?"

"Mmmm. Yes, Sir. I'd like that."

"Well, get in bed then." He removed his clothes and joined her, pulling her into the curve of his body.

She sighed and not surprisingly was asleep almost instantly.

He rarely took a nap during the day but he was more than happy to simply hold her and watch her sleep. Still, surprisingly, he did fall asleep. When he woke, dusk was falling and she was no longer in his arms. Had she left? "Cassie?" There was an unmistakable note of panic in his voice.

"I'm here. The sunset is breathtaking."

He looked up, relieved to see her standing in all of her naked glory looking out the window. "Come here, little bird."

"Yes, Sir."

She joined him on the bed.

"Are you rested now, my beautiful girl?"

She smiled. "Yes, thank you, Sir. It's funny, I never take a nap."

He chuckled. "Neither do I. I suppose a quest such as ours is not undertaken without expending a bit of energy."

He pulled her down on the bed and planted a tender kiss on her lips, then along her jawline to her ear.

"Speaking of which," he continued, "I think we are up to four but I'm certain there are a couple more orgasms hiding in this very room."

She giggled. It was a sound he loved.

"I'm game if you are, Sir."

"Oh, I am. I'll be right back." He climbed off the bed. He had promised not to use any bondage today, and he wouldn't. But he didn't want her thinking about anything except what he was doing to her. He returned to the bed with wrist cuffs and rope.

"Do you remember our first scene?"

She blushed. "I'll never forget it."

"Do you remember that I didn't want you to think that night? I just wanted you to feel?"

"Yes, Sir."

"Well, I want the same thing now. I'm going to put these cuffs on your wrists and bind them to the head of the bed. But they are just there to remind you not to move your hands. They'll be on loosely enough that you could easily pull out of them."

She smiled and offered him her wrists.

God, she was wonderful. This was the woman he wanted in his arms, his bed, his life, forever.

When her hands were bound over her head, he kissed her fingertips, palms, wrists, slowly moving down her arms. He kissed her eyelids, her lips, her earlobes, her throat. He worshipped her entire body with his mouth and his hands.

Soon, he was rewarded with the throaty sounds of pleasure that he so loved to hear.

When he reached her pussy, he spread her labia and blew gently on her swollen clit.

She let out a ragged breath, raising her pelvis towards him.

"Don't move, little bird. You will be punished if you do. Lie very still and take everything I give you. I will tell you when you can come."

A little frustrated groan escaped her lips.

"What was that?" His voice had the steely edge to it that she always responded to.

"Yes, Sir. I'm sorry, Sir. I'll be still."

"Good girl."

With tongue and fingers he brought her to the precipice. He watched with joy as she panted, struggling to remain still and not to come, simply because he'd asked her to. This was the moment for which he'd waited for months. He sheathed himself in a condom, knelt between her legs and gradually entered her. His first thrusts were almost painfully slow. He wanted to keep her back from the edge for just a little bit longer. But he wanted it too badly himself. He picked up the pace and when Cassie shook with the effort it took not to come, he said, "Let me feel you come, little bird."

She arched against him, crying out with the force of her climax. Her internal muscles gripped his cock, contracting around it as he thrust into her and found his own release. It was the heaven he'd imagined it would be.

When the final convulsive shudders of orgasm had passed, he withdrew from her and released her wrists from the cuffs. Then he pulled her close, enfolding her in his arms.

She began to tremble and he felt a drop of moisture hit his arm where her head rested.

"Cassie, are you okay?"

She nodded. "Yes. I just…" her voice broke on a sob.

"Oh God, Cassie, did I hurt you?"

"No…no…of course not. That was just…that was…I've never felt anything like that before. I…well…I'm sorry. I'm being silly. I'm so sorry."

"No, Cassie, you're not. It was the same for me. It's never been like that for me before either."

"That was…that was…look what you've done to me. I can't even find a word for it."

"Transcendent?"

She swiped at the tears on her cheeks and chuckled. "Yeah, that one will do."

Chapter 19

It had been the most incredible day of Cassie's life. And that was considering that the previous six months had been pretty remarkable on their own.

After they had both recovered from making love, they went back to the kitchen, naked. She rummaged through the fridge and found the ingredients to make a rather delicious pasta primavera.

There was something altogether wonderful about making and eating dinner together in the nude.

"I guess I should go home before it gets too late," she said as she finished putting the dishes away.

"Would you like to stay here tonight?"

She turned to look him in the eye. She wanted nothing more. But she knew it would be a serious inconvenience. "Thank you. I'd love to, but I probably shouldn't. I have so much to do this week. I should try to get an early start. And I'm sure you're busy. It will take two hours out of your morning to drive me home and come back."

"Cassandra, when are you going to stop overthinking everything? If you need to get an early start we will. I have a meeting with some investors in Tampa at ten tomorrow morning. Taking you home first isn't a problem. If we leave here by eight, I'll have you home by nine and have more than enough time to make my meeting. Now, I'm going to ask again. Would you like to stay the night?"

She blushed. "I'd like that a lot."

He smiled. "So would I."

Sleeping with him throughout the night and waking up next to him in the morning was wonderful.

A round of shower sex raised the orgasm count to eight. She could get used to this.

He had her back home by nine as promised, and before leaving had kissed her into a stupor.

"Cassie, I would love to see you again tonight. However, I know you have an insanely busy week ahead so I won't ask. But call if you need anything. If I don't talk to you before then, I'll meet you at the bar in the club on Friday."

"Okay. I'll see you then."

From the moment Tristan pulled out of the driveway, it seemed everything went downhill for Cassie.

The phone rang almost instantly. The caller ID said *Margot Weber.*

"Hi, Margot."

"Hello, Cassie. I'm so sorry to call you this early."

"No worries, I've been up for hours." She smiled and stretched, feeling the pleasant soreness of well used muscles.

"Yes, well, Mrs. Tillman called a few minutes ago, wondering if it would be possible to postpone your move for a month or even six weeks."

"I don't think so, Margot. The closing for my house is set for Friday afternoon. The new owners want to take possession immediately."

"I understand but you see, Mr. Tillman was taken to the hospital last night. It is his heart. He will be having bypass surgery this morning."

"Oh, I'm so sorry. Mrs. Tillman must be terribly upset. Is she okay? Does she need anything?"

"She's worried, as you might imagine. But, given all that is happening, you can see that the Tillmans can't move out of their unit this week. She's certain that a month will be enough time to sort everything out. But it would be nice to be able to give them up to six weeks, just to be sure. Could you perhaps talk with your buyers and explain what has happened? Maybe they will be willing to reschedule."

Cassie seriously doubted it. "I can try."

"Thank you, Cassie. Mrs. Tillman said if it isn't possible for you to wait, they will release you from your sublease agreement."

"I appreciate that you called me right away, Margot. I'll let you know what I can arrange."

Cassie dialed her real estate agent immediately and explained the situation.

"Cassie, I will call and ask, but I'm not hopeful. The other property that they were interested in is still on the market. If it were only a week or so at the most, it would be in their best interest to give you the extension. But in a month's time they could close on the other property, move in and be settling into their new home. If you can't close for a month, the sale will fall through and you will be responsible for covering a number of their expenses related to the contract on this house."

"I don't mind covering any expenses."

"You are not likely to get another offer this good."

"I know that. Look, just ask them. Tell them about Mr. Tillman's heart attack. If they won't budge, I'll see if I can find someplace else to live in the short-term."

It came as no surprise when her realtor called an hour later with the news. "If you can't settle on Friday, and be out of the house by noon on Saturday, they are pulling out of the deal."

"Okay. Thanks for asking. Leave everything as it is for the moment. I'll see if I can find something temporary." Her calm politeness belied the sheer panic that was setting in. She only had a few days to find some place to live.

She spent the rest of the day on the phone and internet. She found a couple of furnished "winter rentals" available to lease for no less than four months. That wasn't really a problem. She didn't mind paying for a full four months, even if she wouldn't be staying the whole time. She'd have to put her stuff in storage but she'd be able to do without most of it for a month or so. Still, she worried. What if that wasn't long enough? What if the Tillmans still weren't ready to move then? And once tourist season had fully started, what if she couldn't find anything else?

As much as she wanted to help the Tillmans, she didn't want to risk not having a place to live. She decided it would be better to find an available, empty rental, with a longer lease and continue to look for the home she wanted to buy. So she called Margot to let her know the lease would have to be canceled. Then she shifted into apartment hunting mode, spending most of Tuesday evening and Wednesday driving to look at them. None that were immediately available were great. But she found one that the owners had moved out of, and were going to have to abandon their lease.

The rental agent explained. "If you assume their lease before the end of the month, they'll only lose their security deposit and last month's rent, instead of owing us for the full eight months. If you like the apartment and want to stay, you will have to sign the regular two-year lease at least a month before your current lease expires."

"And I can move in immediately?" She sounded desperate to her own ears.

"Sometime next week probably—after the paperwork is processed."

Oh, dear God, could this be more frustrating? "How long will that take? I really need to move in this weekend?"

"I'm not sure about that. If everything's in order we might have it all done by Monday."

"Monday? Why so long?"

"The thing that usually holds everything up is the credit check."

"I can promise you, my credit is fine. But if it will make things easier, I could just pay the entire eight months in advance."

"Well if you can do that, plus the security deposit, you can definitely move in on Friday, if it's what you want."

It wasn't what she wanted. She didn't want to be moving into this crappy apartment near Long Bayou in the first place. But at this point, there weren't a lot of options and the location was only about twenty minutes away from the club and ten minutes from Tristan's place on Redington Beach. "Fine. Let's go sign the paperwork."

With the paperwork signed, she went home and began to pack.

The professional packers came on Thursday morning. Then the movers came to load the truck first thing Friday morning. Although she had intended to stay in the house until Saturday morning, because the Tillmans' condo wasn't going to be ready for her to move into until then, she realized she might not have to do that now. She wanted to go to the club tonight but after the week she'd had she was tired. She didn't want to drive all the back to Lutz if she didn't have to.

She asked the guy who seemed to be in charge of the movers, "Would it be possible to move my stuff into the new place this afternoon?"

"Sure. The guys will like it better. It means they won't have to work tomorrow."

The truck was packed by eleven so the new owners could do a walkthrough, the closing started at noon and by one-thirty her furniture and boxes were being unloaded at the new apartment. By six the moving van was driving away.

She unpacked linens and made her bed. She was certain she'd be too tired to make it when she got back that night. Then she made a peanut butter sandwich for supper, showered and got ready to go to the club. She put on a matching dark pink bra and thong and pulled a sundress on over them. She'd change into her lace tunic dress once she got to the club. Tonight, of all nights, she needed to turn her head off, put the disappointing week behind her and relax.

Chapter 20

Friday was finally here and Tristan was looking forward to seeing Cassie again. Not calling her all week so that she could focus on the move had been torture. He lost himself in a daydream about what it was going to be like having her so close. He looked up, startled, when someone knocked on the door. "Come in."

Sean Casey opened the door. "Do you have a minute?"

"For you, I have two. What's up?"

Sean came in and shut the door.

Tristan frowned. "This looks serious."

"It is. I need to tell you something. I wish I didn't have to, but I think it's important."

"What's happened?"

"Nothing. At least, I don't think so, not yet."

"Damn it, Sean, get to the point."

"It's about Cassandra Hastings. Did you know she edits romance novels?"

"She edits all kinds of novels, but, yes, I knew that."

"So you know she's editing a series of books about a BDSM club?"

No. Tristan frowned. "Who told you that?"

"No one told me, exactly. I overheard it. Cyndi and my fiancé are friends. She came over to the house yesterday evening to hang out with Amanda because I had to work late. When I got home, after an exhausting day, my ears were assaulted by Cyndi's never-ending stream of chatter from the kitchen. Honestly, it's enough to make anyone nuts. I went to the kitchen fully prepared to suggest Cyndi might enjoy wearing a ball-gag all night tonight. But Amanda was telling her about a stand-up comedian we saw a few weeks ago who did a pretty funny bit on what it would be like to have sex with a romance novel author. Then Cyndi said, 'Master Tristan could tell us what it's like'."

"Cassie's an editor, not an author."

"I know, and Amanda made that point too. But then Cyndi said, the writer only comes up with a good plot, the editor is the one who fills it in and makes it a bestseller."

"What gave her that idea?"

"She probably heard it from Julia."

"How would Julia know?"

"She works as a virtual personal assistant and apparently some of her clients are authors. One is pretty famous, Mona Moore. She writes shifter and sci-fi romances. It's all pretty hot."

Tristan frowned. "How would you know?"

"I'm not gonna lie, Amanda got me hooked on sci-fi BDSM romance. Mona Moore's stuff is off the hook."

"But according to Julia, she doesn't really write it herself?"

"She writes it, but apparently complains her books are almost unrecognizable when she gets them back from an editor."

Tristan frowned. He knew next to nothing about the publishing industry but he'd heard that editors with big publishing firms hold a lot of power. "Is this Mona Moore the one writing the BDSM series?"

"No, the author is Scarlett Turner, a friend of Mona Moore's. She isn't one of Julia's clients. She's one of the authors who Cassie edits for. What worried me was that Cyndi went on to say the first book isn't due out until the spring, but she can't wait to read it and see who she *recognizes*."

"*Who she recognizes*?"

"Yeah. She seems to think Cassie only came to this club to get authentic material."

Sweet, shy, Cassie? The girl who found the calm center of her world in submission? The girl he was beginning to love?

Hell, not *beginning to love*, he'd already lost his heart to her. There was no way Cassie had joined the club simply to get information. "She signed a confidentiality agreement, just like everyone else."

"I get that, Tristan, but think about it. If she did put memorable scenes that she saw here into a book, it would be disastrous. Sure, she would change names and stuff, but if one of our members reads it and recognized it as having taken place here, it will destroy Hidden Gem. And no one would even have to file a suit for that to happen. In fact, it isn't likely that anyone would go public with their accusations. They'd probably just quit. But you know how fast things spread in the BDSM community. Before long no one would want to be a member of the club, or play here, if it meant they might risk winding up as a character in a book."

"I'm sorry, Sean. I don't believe she'd do that. This is Cassie we're talking about. Shy, reserved Cassie is definitely not the type to kiss and tell."

"Maybe that was the first clue. I don't think I've ever met a sub who didn't have a little bit of an exhibitionist in them. Maybe she's been on a mission from day one to get as much as she can while giving as little as possible."

Tristan frowned, shaking his head vehemently. "No! Her discomfort with nudity is not a sign that she *gives as little as possible*. She is the most genuine and giving sub I've ever encountered. I'm telling you, she isn't a security risk."

"Are you willing to bet your club on it? For that matter, the taint of indiscretion might have a negative effect on the entire resort."

Tristan frowned. Sean was right about that. The resort was a romantic retreat for adults. The beach was clothing optional. There were clothing optional pools and hot tubs. There was a spa that offered a variety of sensual services for adults. There were two nightclubs open to guests, one of which regularly had sexy theme nights. The resort was known to be open and accepting of all lifestyles. Very often members of BDSM clubs from other places in the country would arrange group vacations to Island Treasures. There was even a designated event space set up as a BDSM club, specifically for their use, separate from Hidden Gem. Discretion was one of the pillars on which the entire operation was grounded. If people began to question that, the entire resort could fail.

"Listen, Tristan, I know you don't want to even consider the possibility that she came here with another purpose. You like her and she seems nice, but you can't ignore this. You have to find out. At least ask her about it. If there's been a mistake and she's not editing that series, we can put the rumors to bed."

Tristan gave a heavy sigh. He didn't believe she'd do this—at least he didn't want to believe it—but Sean was right. The best course was to get the facts and quash the rumors. He'd do it as soon as she arrived tonight. "Fine."

"Wasn't it Julia who introduced her?" asked Sean.

"Yes. Mutual friends introduced them."

"Mutual friends? Authors?"

"I believe so. Someone Cassie works for who knew someone Julia works for."

"Don't you think that is a little too much of a coincidence?"

Was it? Could he have misjudged Cassie so? Had she and her author friend manipulated Julia and the entire situation, simply to ensure that Cassie had access to a private club? Had everything been a performance? No. This past Sunday was evidence that he and Cassie had a deeper connection.

"Surely you haven't forgotten the last time. Don't fall for it again," Sean warned.

The last time. He couldn't possibly forget that. It was one of the reasons he had founded Hidden Gem and set such strict entry criteria and confidentiality rules, not to mention iron-clad non-disclosure agreements. Over ten years ago, before he opened the club, when he was much younger, he had fallen for a girl he'd met at charity function, Tara Ash. After a couple of dates, he'd introduced her to a little kink and she seemed to love it. Eventually, he took her to a club both he and Sean played at regularly. Only visitors weren't vetted as rigorously there. They only needed a medical certificate, the funds to buy a one month pass and to sign a basic non-disclosure agreement that had no teeth in it.

Unfortunately, a month was long enough for her to find what she sought. Tara identified three members who were particularly ripe targets for blackmail and went after them. One of three was Adam, who'd been a friend of Tristan's since prep school. He was a member of a prominent southern political family and in medical school at the time. The other two were subs, a young gay man who hadn't come out of the closet publicly, and a middle-aged woman who was a professor at a local university.

Adam went straight to Tristan. He didn't want to be fucked around by the girl, but his family could be seriously damaged if stories about their "deviant" son were made public. Tristan stepped in with enough money to keep her happy and a strong enough legal team to keep her quiet.

At the time, the guilt he felt was crushing. He had been the one who'd brought her to the club in the first place. He'd fallen for her almost instantly.

Just like I did for Cassie.

The pieces were falling into place and he didn't like the picture. *Damn it all. How could I have been so trusting? Did I fall for the sweet, innocent act again?*

"Sean, I certainly haven't forgotten the last time. I really think there must have been some misunderstanding. Julia's working tonight, so she should be here early. Send her up as soon as she arrives." If Sean's allegations were true and Julia knew about this…there would be consequences for her as well.

"I'll take care of it."

"And if I'm not downstairs when Cassie arrives, call me."

"You got it."

After Sean left, Tristan tried to put his anger aside and get some work done until he had more information. Focusing on the problem, worrying about it, would do no good. But the possibility that Cassie betrayed him in this way ate at him as nothing ever had.

Finally, fifteen minutes before eight, a tentative knock drew his attention. Julia stood in the open door. "Master Sean said you wished to see me, Master Tristan?"

"Yes." His tone was short and clipped. "You introduced Cassandra Hastings to me. How well do you know her?"

"I know her pretty well. She's one of my best friends."

"So, the two of you have been friends a long time?"

"No, Sir. I wouldn't say that exactly."

"What does that mean?"

"It means we are good friends but I haven't known her long. We became close really fast."

"How long had you known her before bringing her here?"

"A few weeks I guess. Yeah, we started the paperwork for Hidden Gem about a month after we first met. It was an author friend of mine who introduced us. A friend of hers knew Cassie and they knew we both lived in the same area. Cassie didn't know many people. Cassie's such a lovely person, we became instant friends."

Tristan could scarcely believe what he was hearing. "You brought her here after only knowing her a few weeks?"

"Yes, Sir. But it was a perfect fit. You know what she's like. She was born to be a sub. She's made so many friends and learned so much about the lifestyle."

Of course, she did. That had probably been her goal from the start...*just like Tara.* "What else do you know about her?"

"I know she spent several years caring for her grandmother. That's one reason she didn't have many friends down here, according to Scarlett."

"Scarlett?"

"Yeah, Scarlett Turner is an amazing author. I don't know her personally. She's a really close friend to one of my clients, Mona Moore. I think they went to college together. Apparently, Scarlett ended up marrying one of Mona's old boyfriends."

"Is your friend, Mona, in the lifestyle?"

"Sort of. I think she likes the kink in the bedroom. I'm not sure it goes beyond that."

"She doesn't play in clubs?"

"No, I don't think so."

"But her friend Scarlett lives the lifestyle?"

Julia shook her head. "Apparently not. Once I found out that Mona knew Scarlett, I said something in a message about Scarlett's books being almost as hot as Mona's are. Mona answered with an LOL. She said something about Scarlett having a great imagination for someone who is so vanilla."

"So she writes erotic novels that involve BDSM but she isn't in the lifestyle? She doesn't play in clubs?"

"No, Sir. Based on what Mona has said, I wouldn't think so."

"But they both know you play in a club?"

"Well, Mona does. She asks me about it from time to time. I think she'd like to try a club sometime."

Tristan's anger was rising rapidly. He could feel a muscle in his jaw ticking. "Julia, did you know what Cassandra did for a living before bringing her here?"

"I knew she was a friend of Scarlett's and that she works from home. I thought it was something with computers, but I found out a few weeks ago that she's Scarlett's editor. How cool is that?"

"Did you know Scarlett Turner and Cassandra are working on a series of novels set in a BDSM club?"

"Scarlett announced the series in a newsletter recently. I didn't realize Cassie was editing them. I can't wait to read them. But now that you mention it, with Cassie working on the project, I bet they'll be very realistic. Especially since Scarlett isn't into the lifestyle."

Tristan had had enough. Julia wasn't the brightest woman he knew, but that meant she'd been careless, not malicious. She hadn't intentionally let in someone who could destroy them.

"You can go, Julia."

"Yes, Sir. I'll see you later."

This was bad. Tristan hadn't been willing to believe Cassie, the sweetest sub he had ever encountered and the only one for whom he'd ever developed such strong feelings, could actually do something so low. But he feared history was repeating itself. It was possible that just as Tara Ash had been, the apparently wide-eyed, innocent Cassandra Hastings, was actually a master manipulator. She was an editor for Scarlett Turner, an author who wrote erotic BDSM novels, but didn't live the lifestyle herself. She had a series of novels planned set in a BDSM club, but had never been to one. So she and her author friend used Julia to get her editor in.

He thought back to his first meeting with Cassie. She'd talked about how readers want the fairytale and she wanted to know how much reality varied from fiction. So she'd asked an author of BDSM romance—the one who had introduced her to Julia—about it. Cassie had said, "I think she must be in a particularly wonderful relationship. She would have me believe her life perfectly imitates art." But according to Julia's friend, Scarlett Turned didn't live in a D/s relationship, and neither author played in clubs.

He scowled. If the author wasn't in the lifestyle, life couldn't very well imitate art. It had all been lies. How could he have misjudged Cassie so?

His phone rang.

"Cabot here."

"It's Sean. She's here."

"Thanks. I'll be right down."

Tristan dreaded this. He'd prefer to just revoke her membership and send her away, but it wasn't that simple. He had to ensure the confidentiality of his members and the integrity of his club was maintained. He hardened his resolve and went downstairs.

His eyes immediately found her. They always did. Her ability to make ordinary clothes extraordinarily sexy never failed.

Cassie was chatting with Tina. She and Cassie had bonded immediately from Cassie's first days in the club. "Good evening, Cassandra, Tina."

Tina lowered her gaze. "Good evening, Master Tristan."

Cassie too was the image of a polite sub. "Good evening, Sir."

"Tina, excuse us, please."

"Yes, Master Tristan. Have a good evening."

Cassie remained standing with her head bowed and hands folded.

"You have put me in a very bad position, Cassandra."

"I'm sorry, Sir. What have I done? Does this have something to do with the condo?"

"No Cassandra. You lied to me about your interest in this club and have breached confidentiality."

She looked up. "Excuse me, Sir?" Her voice was incredulous. "I have never uttered a word to anyone about this club."

"You are the editor of a series of novels set in a BDSM club, correct?"

"No. I mean, not yet. I've been contracted to edit them."

"Cassandra, how could you do this? How could you betray everyone here like that?"

She looked baffled. "I don't understand why you are so angry or why any of this is relevant. I signed a confidentiality agreement with the club. I have not broken that agreement."

"For the moment, perhaps, but that is only a technicality. You weren't honest. Trust is the single most important aspect of a D/s relationship, but you hid something from me. And in doing so, you misled everyone here."

She tried to convince him that she'd done nothing wrong. She insisted she hadn't come to the club to develop material for a book, and she couldn't understand why her profession was a problem.

But he knew the truth. The *shy* girl who didn't like to be on display, who preferred not to have an audience, hadn't told him the complete truth about her interest in the club and was prepared to expose everyone here. She actually believed she could explain, but there was no justification for this. The damage was done and he had to do what he could to repair it. If she truly had no ulterior motive and wanted to regain the members' trust, she would acknowledge her error in not disclosing her professional interest in the club and accept the consequences. If she didn't, if she had been lying the entire time, she would leave…and his heart would break.

He stared at her for several long moments. "So, this is what you will do. You will submit to a *public* punishment of my choosing, willingly, here and now. Or, you will leave and never return. If you choose to accept the punishment and reconfirm that you will never disclose anything that occurs within these walls, your slate is wiped clean. If you choose to leave, you will never be welcome back here. Additionally, should there ever be any question that you violated your confidentiality agreement, I will pursue legal actions against you."

Hurt flashed across her beautiful features for a moment. Then she straightened her back and nodded. "Yes, Master Tristan."

He laid out her punishment in detail. "Very well. If you consent, you will go to that spanking bench," he motioned to one in a highly visible area of the main room, often used for demonstrations, "and remove all of your clothes. I will secure you to the bench and place a vibrator against your clit. I will administer ten strokes with a cane. I will touch you with my hands in any way I see fit during the punishment. You will count the strokes and when we are done, you will come. Do you understand?"

"Yes, Sir."

"Do you consent to this punishment? Even though it includes several things on your list of soft limits?"

"Yes Sir, I consent."

"As always, you can use your safewords at any time. The punishment will stop and you can leave."

"I understand, Sir."

"Then, go to the bench, remove your clothing and kneel beside it until I am ready."

"Yes, Sir."

He watched her walk, back straight, through the gathering crowd to prepare for her punishment.

"Have you gone soft, Tristan?" asked Luke, a younger Dom. "You believed she was going to throw confidentiality out the window and you're only going to give her ten strokes of the cane?"

"That's not the punishment," said Maurice, a Dom in his sixties.

"Then what is?" asked Luke.

"He's doing to her what she was prepared to do to us. Exposing her, allowing her to keep nothing private. But, Tristan, son, if you mean to do this, spare nothing. It will be a hard, but valuable, lesson for her to learn."

Tristan nodded, not taking his eyes off of her. "My thoughts exactly. She needs to experience what it feels like to have things you don't want to share made public." He hoped that the experience, more than any signed agreement, would make her think and remember that.

He let her kneel naked and wait for him longer than he normally would have. When he finally walked over to her, he said nothing. He took time to adjust the bench while she continued to kneel silently. When he could practically feel her tension, he stepped in front of her.

"Except for counting, you will not speak until your punishment is over. Stand up."

She rose gracefully to her feet. She did everything with poise. Simply walking through a room, she had the elegance of a dancer.

"Position yourself on the bench."

She did and he restrained her before adjusting the bench to position her ass high in the air and spread her legs wide enough for easy access. Last, he positioned the vibrator against her clit and turned it on low. He caressed her body lightly, feeling her relax and respond to his touch.

Ah, little bird, I'm sorry, but you will not enjoy this long.

He massaged her beautiful backside before doing something he knew she would hate. He spread the cheeks of her ass to display each intimate nook. "Every inch of you is beautiful, even if you are shy about sharing it."

As the crowd responded, he felt her stiffen. She closed her eyes.

He gave her backside a little swat. *Spare nothing.* "No, you don't. You will not hide anything from us. Not even your lovely eyes."

Everything he did, every word he said, was intended to make her feel good and then become aware that all eyes were on her. It was the exact opposite of how he had handled her up until this moment. Even as close to her limits as he was pushing her, he felt her arousal. He brought her to the edge of orgasm before delivering the first blows.

Somewhat to his surprise, she didn't cry out.

He knew the cane hurt—each stroke left an angry red stripe—but other than counting, she made no sounds.

After the fourth stroke, he stopped and rubbed her ass to ease the sting a little, before increasing the vibration speed and bringing her to the edge of orgasm again.

Then he repeated the process. Four blows followed by sexual stimulation intense enough to bring her to the precipice. Still, she remained silent. It was not what he'd expected and it was breathtaking to watch. He couldn't help but praise her.

"Good girl. You are amazing."

Tears ran down her cheeks, but other than that, she was in absolute control.

The last two blows would be the worst. He would deliver them to the most sensitive spot, just below the curve of the buttocks.

"Nine."

"Ten."

He felt her relax slightly, but he knew the next part would likely be the very hardest for her.

Once again he brought her to the brink of orgasm. She hovered there, almost as if she was fighting desperately not to come. *Oh, no, baby, this is the most important part.* He knew how to make her topple over the edge. He said the words. "Come for me now, little bird."

Her body trembled in a violent orgasm during which she didn't utter a single sound.

Tristan immediately moved the vibrator away from her sensitive clit. "That was beautiful, little bird. I'm proud of you."

Sounds of approval came from all around.

Tristan removed the straps holding her to the bench, and helped her stand, before putting his arms around her. She still trembled and his only goal became giving her the comfort and care she needed.

"That was absolutely magnificent," he whispered. "When I said don't speak, I didn't expect you to be completely silent." He kissed the top of her head.

She nodded but then rather than sinking into his embrace, she stepped backwards, away from him and started to clean the spanking bench.

Tristan touched her arm. "You don't need to do that, Cassandra. One of the subs on duty will. Come with me and we'll talk."

She pulled away from him. "I do need to do it, Sir."

What was happening here? She was always content to cuddle in his arms after a scene and this had been more intense than anything they'd ever done. He tried again. "It's done now, little bird. Come with me."

She shook her head and before he processed what she was doing, she'd put on her thong and bra.

He picked up the lace covering. "I didn't tell you to dress, Cassie."

"No, you didn't, Sir. But it has been a long day and a very long week. I need to go home and get some rest." Her tone was even and unemotional—almost nonchalant.

He put his hand around her waist, pulling her towards one of the more private areas provided for aftercare. "Not before we talk."

She pulled away again and in the same, soft, calm tone said, "Perhaps we do need to talk, but not now. Not in here. May I please have my dress, *Sir*?"

"No. Cassandra, this isn't the way it works as long as you are wearing that collar. Come with me now."

Chapter 21

Cassie was determined not to draw any more attention to them tonight. She went with him until they were away from public view. Then she stopped, unfastened the collar and handed it to him, her heart lurching. "I don't wish to embarrass you or make a scene. I have told you that I need to go home and rest now. Because I respect the rules and boundaries of the club, I do not wish to discuss anything else here, even if we are in a less open area. Good night, Tristan." Tristan. Not Master Tristan. That was over.

She made to leave and he put a hand on her shoulder to stop her. "No, Cassandra, you will not walk out."

She turned, looked him squarely in the eyes and said one word. "Red."

He looked as if she'd slapped him, but it had worked. He dropped his hand. She calmly walked away, wearing nothing but her bra and thong. As a good sub should, she didn't make eye contact with anyone as she strode steadily towards the doors to the locker room.

She had almost made her escape when Tina stopped her. "Cass, sweetie, are you okay?"

"I'm fine."

"That was intense. But you were so great. Everyone was very impressed, and it's all over now."

Cassie forced a semblance of a smile and nodded.

Tina frowned. "Are you sure you're okay."

"I'm certain. Thank you for the concern, but really, I'm fine. I'm just tired, so I'm heading home. Good night, Tina."

"Good night, hon." The woman frowned, looking less than convinced.

And Cassie was through the doors. Thankfully she met no one in the locker room. She pulled on her sundress, slid her feet into her sandals and grabbed her purse. Tristan still had her lace tunic but she could live without it. It took her less than thirty seconds and to her great relief, when she stepped into the reception area, Denny, who was working the desk, was distracted, signing in several members.

"Goodnight, Denny," she called and was through the door, out into the warm night air before he could answer.

She looked up as she headed to the parking lot and her step waivered for a moment. Tristan stood leaning against her car.

Well, at least they were outside the club.

She continued walking towards him, stopping in front of him, just beyond his reach. "Goodnight, Tristan."

"Cassie, I'm not letting you leave until we talk and you said you couldn't talk in the club. So, we can talk here, or go to my suite or somewhere else if you wish. You're upset and I'm your Dom. You can't just walk away like this."

She had hoped to allow her own anger to cool before they did this, but so be it. "Fine. You want to talk here? We'll talk here. But you *aren't* my Dom anymore, and you've already had your say, so it's my turn now. You said the single most important aspect of a D/s relationship was trust. I have trusted you with everything. This whole world is new to me and not a little scary. I have given you absolute control, trusting that you would not harm me. But tonight you have."

"You consented to the punishment."

"That isn't what I'm talking about. *You* didn't trust *me* and you suggested to the members of the club present that I had betrayed all of you."

"You hid your professional interest in the activities occurring in this club."

"And *that* is where you're wrong. My first day here you asked my profession and I told you I was a freelance book editor. You asked what kind of books I edited. I told you, romance including erotic romance with BDSM elements."

"You didn't tell me you were editing a series of books *set in a BDSM club.*"

"No, I didn't, because the author was only just beginning to write them. The first one still isn't finished so I haven't started editing them. I have no idea what they contain—I haven't read a single word. So while it is true those books are in my queue, even if I were actively editing them, the fact that I have played here at this club, with you, has nothing to do with what's in them. *The author writes the content.*"

"But you have ultimate control."

She practically snorted. "What gave you that idea? I make suggestions regarding pacing, I find plot holes, I fix errors, but the content is the author's alone."

She looked away, still trying to gain some control. "Tristan, I came here because I was curious and yes, I became curious because of my work. I think it's fairly clear that I was beginning to like what I found. My only professional interest in this club was to be able to identify inaccuracies and inconsistencies. Even that was absolutely secondary to my desire to learn about the lifestyle. Personally, I would think you'd want that. I've seen review after review of erotic romances stating that the author misrepresented elements of the BDSM lifestyle. It's like I said, I don't have that much pull with an author. But if I thought something was really egregious, and they refused to fix it, I would separate myself from the project."

"You still should have told me."

"Well, you've made that pretty damn clear and you can cloak yourself in righteousness if you wish, but I did nothing wrong. I didn't lie to you and I didn't betray you or anyone else."

He ran his hands through his hair. "Then why did you submit to that punishment?"

"Because you made it a public issue before you spoke to me about it. You decided that simply being contracted to edit that series had violated your trust and that of everyone in the club. You gave me no opportunity to explain anything."

"You could have just left."

"I could have. Unfortunately, I was beginning to think of many of the people inside as friends," her voice broke and she looked away for a moment. If she were being truly honest, she was certain he had destroyed any chance she had at friendship with them now. She took a deep breath and met his gaze. "If I had left with them believing what you led them to believe, I could never have looked any of them in the eye again. You destroyed my credibility with everyone and the fact is, a public punishment doesn't fix that. The idea of a clean slate is ridiculous. They'll always think, 'oh, we need to be careful around Cassie, she might put us in a book,' even though I don't write the goddamn books. So, submitting to the punishment didn't give me a *clean slate*, it simply allowed me to walk away with my head up."

"Cassie…"

"*No!* Now, we're done. Excuse me, I'm going home." She stepped around him, opened the car door and climbed in.

He held the door when she tried to close it. "Cassandra, I can't let you go like this. Please, you're upset. At least let me drive you home."

"No. Good night, Tristan."

"Cassandra…"

"I said *no*. Does *red* work better for you?" she practically shouted.

He shook his head in frustration. "Fine. Drive carefully and we'll talk tomorrow."

She didn't disabuse him of that notion. If she had her way, she would never see or speak to him again. When he stepped away from the car she shut the door, started the engine and drove away.

As Cassie drove out of the Island Treasures resort she was instantly thankful she'd moved into her new place earlier today. The hour drive north to her grandmother's old house, after everything that had happened, would have been more than she could take. She was also glad she wasn't moving into the condo with the breathtaking view in Tristan's building. Who knew the snafu that had turned her life upside down and sent her scrambling to find a place to live this past week, would end up being a blessing.

In her rush, she hadn't given anyone her new address yet. No one had her cell phone number. The phone she had always used, the number she gave to friends, was her grandmother's old land-line. She could transfer the number to her new apartment, but why bother now? She needed a fresh start. So, since they had no way to contact her, she should be able to leave her ruined reputation, Hidden Gem and everyone in it behind. *That* was a clean slate.

A lump rose in her throat when she thought of the friends she had made, the sense of belonging that she was beginning to feel. But in that community, trust was everything, and after what had happened tonight…well, she would simply have to start again.

She hadn't loved the apartment near Long Bayou, but it was all she could get on short notice. It was closer to the Gulf and would give her time to find the perfect condo on the beach or even to think about whether she wanted to stay in Florida at all. She had nothing to bind her here anymore. She could go to Boston. Hell, she didn't even have to stay in the United States if she didn't want to. She could do her work from anywhere in the world as long as she had access to the internet. Maybe she'd move to Australia. The possibilities were limitless.

But for now, she and her broken heart would go to her crappy new apartment, have a good cry and try to put this all behind her. She'd figure out the rest later.

~ * ~

The next day Tristan tried calling Cassie. She would have had time to calm down and perhaps she would listen to him. He wanted her to come to Hidden Gem tonight. She needed to see that she was wrong. Everyone who had witnessed her punishment the previous evening had admired how well she had accepted it. She had publicly and profoundly reaffirmed her commitment to the privacy of club members and that was all anyone needed to let the matter drop. But he had gone even further than that by returning to the club after she left and admitting his error.

Her phone had been disconnected.

It didn't matter. She was supposed to be moving in today. He'd keep an eye out for the movers, then go downstairs and talk to her in person. That was better anyway.

But by early afternoon, when the moving van still hadn't shown up, he called Margot Weber.

"Hi, Mr. Cabot, how are you?"

"I'm well, thanks, Margot. I'm just wondering, I thought Miss Hastings was moving in today, but I haven't seen any movers."

"Uh…no, sir. That fell through."

"What do you mean it *fell through*? The Tillmans were supposed to move out yesterday. The sublease agreement with Miss Hastings was signed."

"But, sir, Mr. Tillman was put in the hospital last Sunday morning with heart problems. Mrs. Tillman called first thing on Monday, absolutely distraught, needing to postpone the move."

"For how long?"

"She asked for another month but said if Miss Hastings couldn't wait they would release her from the agreement."

"Cassandra *can't* wait a month. She was supposed to settle on the sale of her grandmother's house yesterday. The new owners had agreed to let her stay there last night because the condo wasn't going to be available until this morning. She had to be out today. She'd have no place to go."

"Miss Hastings told me that, but when I explained the Tillmans' position she completely understood. She couldn't have been nicer. She said she would ask if the new owners would let her rent a little longer. If they wouldn't, she'd try to find a temporary place."

Fuck. The night before, Cassie had told him it had *been a long day and a very long week.* And he hadn't asked what she'd meant by that. "Was she able to stay in the house?" But he knew the answer to that. Her phone wouldn't have been disconnected otherwise.

"No, sir. She called Wednesday to say the terms of the closing hadn't changed, but she was able to find an apartment."

"Where?" he demanded.

Until that moment, Margot had seemed blissfully unaware of his increasing irritation. "Uh—I don't—what I mean is—she didn't say."

He could not suppress the angry Dom rising within him. "Why didn't you call me when this happened? I could have perhaps helped Mrs. Tillman, or at least found Miss Hastings something temporary in another of my buildings or even at the resort."

"I-I-I'm sorry, sir. I didn't think you would want to be bothered. I didn't know you had any interest in this."

Tristan tried to rein in his temper. Margot was an employee, not a sub. "Margot, I realize the sublease agreement was between the Tillmans and Miss Hastings, but I own these buildings and the complex management is my responsibility. I don't like asking people to simply back out of a contract that will more than inconvenience them, without looking for other possible solutions first. You should have called me for that reason. Moreover, Miss Hastings is a friend of mine. I was the one who sent her to you. I assumed you knew that."

"No, sir, I didn't. I'm terribly sorry, Mr. Cabot. Miss Hastings seemed willing to work things out with the Tillmans."

"I'm sure she was. That's the kind of person she is." Sweet Cassie always sought to please people. It's what made her a good submissive, but it also made her willing to bend over backwards for anyone, while giving very little thought to herself. That wasn't always a problem: the world needed kind, considerate people, but it certainly could make it easy for people to take advantage of her.

"Just because someone is willing to seek a solution to a problem, doesn't mean they should have to. We could have tried first."

"I understand that now and I'm sorry, sir. Is there anything I can do?"

"No. There's nothing to be done now. But if she calls, get a cell phone number from her then transfer the call directly to me."

"Yes, sir."

Damn it. Now his only hope of seeing her today was if she came back to Hidden Gem tonight.

But she didn't.

And she didn't come back the following weekend or the one after that.

He tried several real estate sources to which he had access, to see if she had leased something somewhere in the area. But there was no record of any such transaction. Which meant she was probably subleasing from someone else.

He felt sure Julia would know how to reach her, but she didn't.

"I only had the one number for her, Master Tristan."

"What about email?"

"When we first met it was because Mona Moore sent me her phone number. I don't have her email."

"Could you call Mona Moore, or perhaps allow me to?"

"I don't actually have her phone number. I don't need it. Everything is done electronically. But I have emailed her already. She said she'd check with Scarlett. I got a message back earlier today that Scarlett said Cassie was upset and preferred to be alone for a while."

He checked with Tina, Cyndi, Denny and several other people at the club who seemed close to her, but, like Julia, none of them knew anything and they were all upset and worried by Cassie's sudden disappearance.

He scoured social media searching for her profile finding nothing. That wasn't surprising. After all, she didn't even use a cell phone. Either she wasn't on social media or she had strict privacy settings in place.

He tried reaching out directly to the author, Scarlett Turner, via social media contacts, but she didn't respond.

He simply couldn't find Cassie, and she never came back to the club.

He had to face facts. She was gone. He had lost her and it was his own fault. He had opened himself as he never had before and allowed her in. Love was something he wasn't sure really existed so he never expected to feel it so profoundly. Nor could he have imagined the bitterness of its loss.

I should never have given in to it.

Never have given his love to Cassie or felt hers in return? No. As soon as that thought crossed his mind, he rejected it. Tennyson might have been right when he said, "'Tis better to have loved and lost than never to have loved at all." But, damn, it hurt like hell.

Chapter 22

Six months later.

Cassie was elbow deep in the manuscript she was editing—a young adult romance chocked full of hormones and angst—when the phone rang shortly after noon.

"Hello?"

"Cass, it's me, Dani, and I have a huge favor to ask."

Dani, Danielle Ashford, lived in the apartment across the hall. Her husband had left her and their three-year-old daughter, Emily, a month after Cassie had moved in. Not surprisingly, he had yet to pay a dime of the court-ordered child support. Dani, who initially had worked only part-time, had taken a full-time position as an administrative assistant for a company in St. Petersburg three months ago. Her *huge favors* nearly always involved her little girl. Typically, it was because Dani had to be at work early or stay late and needed someone to take Emily to, or pick her up from, daycare.

Cassie didn't mind doing this. Emily was adorable, the daycare center was literally right around the corner and usually it didn't take much more than thirty minutes of Cassie's time. The center opened at seven and closed at six. In most cases, Dani just needed a few extra minutes. She'd never called so early in the afternoon before.

"What's up, Dani?"

"I don't know what to do. The daycare just called and Emily is sick, she's running a fever. I have to pick her up, but my boss is on a telephone conference and I don't know how long it will last. I can't just leave."

"I can get her for you. When do you think you'll be home?"

"That's just it. I don't know. I don't want you to have to watch her for hours. I thought maybe you could bring her here."

"You can't take care of a sick kid at work."

"I know I can't, but by the time you get here, my boss might be off the conference and I can tell him I have to leave.

"But what if he is on it for hours? Are you sure you don't want me just to bring her here until you get home? I really don't mind."

"Cass, that is so nice of you, but I can't ask you to do that. Plus, I think she needs to see the doctor, her pediatrician's office is closer to here than home."

"But, Dani, I don't have a child seat." Cassie usually just walked to pick her up or drop her off.

"The center keeps a few on hand to loan out when stuff like this comes up."

Cassie sighed. "Okay, I'll bring her to you. What's the address?"

"I'll text it to you. And I'll call to let them know you're coming."

Cassie was dressed for work, which for her was sometimes pajamas. Today, she wore sweatpants and a T-shirt. She considered changing—or at least putting on a bra—but she didn't want to take the time and she was glad she didn't. When she arrived at the daycare center and saw Emily, she called Dani back. "Sweetie, her temp is 101.5 and she looks miserable. Are you sure you don't want me to just take her home and take care of her until you can get here?"

"Oh, poor baby. No. I can't just leave and I was able to get a doctor's appointment in an hour. The doctor's office is only ten minutes away from here. That gives me fifty minutes for my boss to get off the phone before I have to leave. I'm sure he'll be done before then and it won't be a problem."

Cassie had her doubts. Dani's boss didn't seem to care that, allowing for driving time, she had a ten-hour window when she could work. Happily letting her leave early seemed unlikely. "Okay, if you're positive this is best."

The daycare center staff made sure the child seat was installed in Cassie's car correctly and thirty minutes later Cassie pulled into the enclosed garage. Dani had said she'd meet Cassie there, if she was able to. But if not, Cassie was to bring Emily up to the CEI office.

Dani wasn't in the garage.

"I want my mommy."

"I know, princess, we're going to go find her right now." Cassie held Emily as they rode up the elevator.

"I want my mommy," the little girl whimpered again.

"We're almost there, sweetie."

"My tummy hurts."

Cassie rubbed her back gently. "I'm sorry it hurts, Emily. Mommy's going to take you to the doctor and I'm sure you'll feel better soon."

Emily put her chin on Cassie's shoulder and continued to whimper. They got off the elevator on the top floor. "Mommy said the office was just beyond the elevator lobby," murmured Cassie, more to herself than to the little girl. Sure enough, she saw double glass doors and Dani was at the desk just inside.

Unfortunately, they were barely through the door when, without warning, Emily vomited down Cassie's back.

Stunned, Cassie just stood there, holding her.

Dani cried, "Oh, no, Emily," and rushed from behind her desk with a trashcan. "Cass, I'm so sorry."

Cassie went down on one knee, shifting Emily off her shoulder to a sitting position on her other knee. With one arm around her waist, she held Emily's head with her other hand while the child finished emptying her stomach into the trashcan. With that accomplished, Emily began to cry.

"Oh, honey, let mommy get some water to clean you up."

Dani grabbed napkins from her desk drawer, wet them from the water cooler and began wiping the mess from her daughter's face, all the while Emily continued to wail.

"What's going on here?" said an all-too-familiar voice from behind Cassie. *Tristan? Tristan was Dani's demanding boss?* Her mind was instantly filled with images and sensations from their time together and the pain was almost unbearable. Facing him now was the absolute last thing Cassie wanted to do. Maybe, if she played it right, she would be able to just slip out, unrecognized and unnoticed.

Dani lifted Emily from Cassie's knee, trying to console her while also explaining the situation. "I'm sorry, Mr. Cabot. This is my daughter. The daycare center called to say she was sick, but I didn't want to leave without telling you and you were in a conference. I asked my friend—she helps me sometimes if I have to come in early or stay late—anyway, I need to take Emily to the doctor so I asked my friend to bring her here to me. She…uh…threw up. Emily that is—not my friend."

"I can see that."

"I'm really sorry, sir. I'll clean up the mess."

"Ms. Ashford, your child is ill and needs to see a doctor. Please go now and take care of that."

It was his Dom voice and it made Cassie's stomach flutter. She stood up, keeping her back to him.

"I'm really sorry, sir." Dani sounded as if she were about to cry.

Cassie's protective nature rose to the surface but before she threw caution to the wind and turned to tell Tristan he was being an ass, he said, "These things happen."

His voice lost its sharp edge. "I wasn't aware that you had a child, but I certainly would have understood your having to leave suddenly to care for her. In the future, if your little girl needs you, just leave a note."

"I'm not fired?"

"Of course not, Ms. Ashford. See to the child. I expect you'll need to stay home with her tomorrow. If she's still ill on Monday, let me know."

Good. He was being reasonable.

"Yes, sir. I'll just get my purse and we'll go."

Perfect. Dani was too flustered to introduce her and Tristan had given no indication that he recognized her. It was probably rude to continue standing with her back to him, but it was the only way to escape this situation.

"Do you need your friend's help?" he asked Dani.

"No, sir."

"Then I'll show her to my washroom where she can clean up. I hope Emily feels better soon."

No! She still didn't turn around. "Thank you but—uh—I'll go with Dani. I'll shower when I get home."

Dani shook her head. "Cass, don't be silly. You've got puke in your hair. It'll make your car stink. Thank you so much for bringing her here. I'll see you later." With that, Dani was out the door.

Cassie started to follow Dani anyway.

"Cassandra, stop." It was his Dom voice again.

She sighed and turned to face him.

He shook his head slightly. "Did you honestly think I wouldn't recognize you?"

"Hope springs eternal."

"You *hoped* I wouldn't recognize you? That may be worse."

"Would you prefer I lied?" The bitter tone of her own voice surprised her.

"We're not going to have this discussion here, Cassandra. Come to my office."

He reached for her elbow and she took a step back. "I'm not your sub, Tristan."

His eyes narrowed. "Are you *anyone's* sub?"

Surprised by the question, Cassie shook her head. "No."

"Then you are standing in my lobby, covered in vomit. I have a fully equipped shower suite in my office. And Ms. Ashford was right, your car will smell like vomit forever if you drive home in it like that."

"Speaking of *Ms. Ashford*, I thought your assistant's name was Caroline."

"Caroline resigned in September. Her husband took a job in San Diego. But that has nothing to do with your current circumstances. Come get cleaned up."

She was a disgusting mess. *And you're a grownup. Act like one.* "I…you're right. Thank you. A shower would be good."

He raised an eyebrow, but motioned down a small hallway.

As she walked past, he took her elbow and guided her into his office. "The bathroom is through that door. You'll find everything you need. We'll talk when you're through."

She just nodded and went into the bathroom. She was surprised by how unsettled she felt in his presence. She thought she had long since exorcized her feelings for him. She'd closed the door on that part of her life and had promised herself never to open it again. She stared at her reflection in the mirror.

It wasn't that she regretted it. Not any of it. She wasn't sorry she had gone to Hidden Gem or experienced the lifestyle. She certainly didn't regret submitting to him. There was a peace in that, a freedom that she had never dreamed possible and that she'd never felt since. No, she was glad that she'd experienced these things. However, she also believed she'd made the right choice that night.

He had said it. Trust was the most important element of the D/s relationship. It is the ultimate source of the freedom and peace a submissive feels. Cassie didn't give her trust to people easily, but she'd given it to him and he broke that trust. What's more, not only had she given him her trust and willing submission, somewhere along the way, she had given him her heart. He had broken that too.

The pain she felt afterwards had been a terrible price to pay. So, while she didn't regret anything, neither would she ever do it again.

With that resolved, she undressed. She thought it best to wash out her clothes so they could be drying while she showered. She was glad now that she hadn't bothered to change into nicer clothes to pick Emily up. Her T-shirt had received the worst of it. She washed it as best she could with the hand soap, blotting it dry with a towel before hanging it on a towel rack. Thankfully, only a little of the sour mess had splattered on her sweats. She spot washed those and also hung them to dry, before climbing into the shower.

Cassie hadn't realized how tense she was until the hot water hit her body and she felt herself relax. She just stood there for a moment, letting the warmth work its magic. She used his shampoo and body wash. Surrounded by the scents she associated with him, she let herself feel, for just a moment, the comfort and calm she had once felt in his presence. But the pleasure she gained was short-lived. In giving into it, she also felt the hurt that inevitably came with those memories.

She sighed, turned the water off and stepped out of the shower.

"Cassie?" He called through the door.

"I'm almost done."

"I assumed you were. I keep a change of clothes here. I have a clean shirt for you."

"It's okay. I washed mine."

"Then yours is wet and it's a chilly day. Take this dry one."

She smiled at his Dom voice. It wasn't a request. It was an order. She didn't have to follow it, but getting out of this mess would be much easier if she did.

She wrapped herself in a towel and opened the door. "Thank you."

He handed it to her. "My pleasure."

"I'll be out in a minute." She closed the door. The shirt he had given her was a crisp white dress shirt. Not the best thing to be wearing with no bra, but in truth, even though her T-shirt was dark blue, as wet as it was, it wouldn't have been much better. She had a small brush in her purse that she ran through her heavy, wet mass of hair. The white shirt would be soaked as soon as she put it on if she left her hair down. Another quick search of her purse turned up a butterfly clip. She gathered her hair on her head and clipped it in a messy bun.

That was all the damage control she could do. She dressed, rolled the sleeves up on the shirt that was way too large for her, steeled herself and left the bathroom.

He looked up from where he sat behind his desk. "Better?"

"Yes, thank you. And thank you for the shirt. I'll launder it and send it back with Dani."

"Keep it. It looks better on you."

She wouldn't keep it, but she wouldn't argue. "Well, I'll leave you to your work and get back to my own."

"No, Cassandra, you won't. You'll sit down with me and talk about what should have been discussed that night."

"Tristan, that part of my life is over. Clean slate, remember?"

"Oh, little bird, the slate is far from clean. Part of me wants to blister your ass."

Cassie's irritation rose. "I did not intentionally mislead you. I hadn't then, nor have I since, breached confidentiality."

In fact, because of how badly it had hurt, she didn't want anything in her life that would remind her of her time at Hidden Gem, so she found another editor to handle the series. To further close away that part of her life, after she had finished what was already in her queue, she no longer accepted manuscripts containing BDSM themes. But she wouldn't waste her breath telling him this. Clean slate.

Tristan's jaw clenched. "And that statement illustrates why we need to talk. You disappeared before anything could be resolved. The only reason I let you leave that night, as upset as you were, was because I believed I'd see you the next day so we could discuss everything. You drove away allowing me to believe that, all the while knowing you never intended to see me again."

"Look, that was months ago and I've moved on. You don't need to concern yourself with me any longer." She walked toward his office door. "I'll give the shirt to Dani."

She reached for the handle, but he was across the room in a few strides. He placed his palm on the door to prevent her opening it. "God damn it, Cassie. Don't walk away again. I know I hurt you, but I can't fix anything if you don't give me the chance."

"I told you, I'm fine. I don't need to be fixed."

"I don't believe that you're *fine* and I know I'm not."

No, he didn't look fine. He looked as torn apart as she felt. He was in pain and she couldn't bear seeing it. She looked away from him, still holding on to the door handle, trembling. She most certainly was not fine either. She believed, if she didn't leave right then, she would shatter and she didn't want to do that here.

He caressed her cheek, gently turning her face towards him. "My beautiful little bird, please don't fly away again."

It was all too much. Surrounded by his scent and overwhelmed by his nearness, she burst into tears.

Chapter 23

When the child's wail had rent the otherwise calm professional atmosphere of his workplace, he'd ended his call and left his office to see what was going on. He froze when he saw a woman, on the floor on one knee, with a little girl screaming on her lap and his assistant hovering over them, trying to clean vomit off the distraught little one.

He'd had no idea his new assistant had a daughter but that wasn't what had taken him aback. Kneeling in his lobby was the woman he adored, who had left him six months ago, seemingly without a backwards glance. At that moment he hadn't known if he'd wanted to scoop her into his arms or turn her over his knee.

When she'd pulled away from him, saying, "I'm not your sub, Tristan," his heart nearly stopped. Did she belong to someone else? He didn't think he could have handled that.

Now she stood in front of him, sobbing.

He wrapped his arms around her. "Shh, little bird. Please don't cry."

"I-I-I can't—I can't do this."

"Come sit with me and let's talk."

His office was large, with a sitting area to one side of his desk. He urged her towards the couch there, sitting beside her with his arms around her until she'd stopped crying.

He wiped the tears from her cheeks and wanted to kiss her so badly it hurt. But he wouldn't. Not yet. Not until they had sorted this out.

"I was worried about you. You disappeared. No one knew where you were or how to contact you."

"Tristan, I told you everything that needed to be said that night."

The bitterness in her voice pierced his heart. "You believed that I had broken your trust. And you were right. I should have spoken with you alone first. I'm sorry. I was upset. I was worried about the integrity of my club and the privacy of my friends."

"How could you think I'd break confidentiality?"

Looking at her now, reading the hurt in her expression, how could he have thought that? He hadn't wanted to believe it, but if there was any chance the accusations were true, he couldn't ignore it either. "Because there were already whispers about what your involvement with that series might mean and I had faced something like this before. I couldn't ignore it, even though I didn't want to believe it. I knew the only way to quash the rumors was to address them publicly. I let those concerns rule my actions. Still, I should have spoken to you first."

She shook her head, clearly angry. "You knew me. I had revealed more of myself to you, given more of myself to you than I have ever given anyone. But that is a mistake I will not make again."

No! He could not lose her again. "Cassie, please don't say that. Over the past few years, I have played with many submissives and even entered into exclusive relationships with some of them. Never have I encountered anyone like you. I know you gave yourself fully to me and I royally fucked it up that night. I thought I was doing the right thing. But, I am human. I do make mistakes."

"But your mistake destroyed me and my reputation."

"No, Cassie. That is where you are absolutely wrong."

"I'm not wrong," she practically shouted. "I understand human nature."

"Perhaps. And as far as the wider population goes, you are probably right. But that is not true within our community." This was the crux of the issue. "You don't understand it as well as you think. Everyone in that club knew how incredibly difficult that punishment was for you. They knew it took you to the very edge of your limits. They also knew that if you had joined the club solely to gather material for books, you had that already. You could have walked away. There was no need for you accept the punishment unless you wanted to remain in the community. Even though you hadn't told me specifically about the BDSM club series on which you would be working, after you did, no one believed you would reveal private details from the club. It was over. You were forgiven."

Cassie shook her head, an expression of utter disbelief on her face. "You can't unring a bell. *You can't.* The accusation was there and it will always be there. The slate will *never* be clean."

He wanted to touch her so badly. To pull her onto his lap, comfort her and never let her go. But he couldn't. Not yet. "You're wrong. On top of everything else, when you left that night, I went back in. I told everyone in the club the full details of your role as editor. Many people believed, as I had, that an editor had much more control over a book's content. I confessed the error I had made by not clarifying all of that first. Cassie, at that moment you became an awe-worthy hero. Even though you were in the right, you had chosen to accept the punishment in order to maintain your honor and the respect of the club members. And you did both. If you had come back Saturday night, you would have learned that."

She shook her head. "I won't ever go back."

That statement chilled him to his core. He couldn't lose her again. "Why? You blossomed there. Your submission not only gave me joy but it brought you peace."

She calmly met his gaze. "Yes it did. Tristan, I liked how connected I felt to you and I will own that I enjoy the kink. I like the intense sensations. I like role-playing and the sensual punishments that are a part of that. But real punishment is something else. The whole concept of ever *needing* to be punished is absurd. The fact that I had to submit to the punishment you dictated, but once you were aware the fault was yours, not mine, you were able to stand in front of your peers and apologize makes my point."

"Cassie, reward and punishment is a fundamental of the lifestyle. It is part of the roles we adopt in the club. I thought you understood that. It's why, even though you don't believe me, the slate is clean."

"I did understand it and when we were playing that was fine. But that punishment was not part of a scene." She looked away. "I had given too much of myself to you. It was probably a colossal newbie mistake, but with my trust, I had given you my heart. I figured you didn't love me, but I loved you. And in that moment, when you wouldn't believe me or listen to me...you broke my heart."

She figured he didn't love her? "*Jesus Christ.* I fucked this up, Cassie. I know that, but how on earth could you believe I didn't love you?"

She looked confused. "You never said it."

"Since when do words mean more than actions? From the moment you walked through the doors of my club, I never played with another sub. I never touched another woman. It's why I never allowed you to play with anyone else as part of your training. I couldn't bear to watch it. You became my sole focus. Everyone knew I loved you."

"I don't understand. I thought you played only with me because I wore your training collar."

"God, no, Cassie. That only meant that you were under my protection and anyone wishing to play with you had to negotiate with me. I didn't *allow* anyone else to play with you—and believe me, there were plenty who wanted to. Other than those in committed relationships, do you know a single Dominant or submissive who only plays with one person?"

Her brow furrowed. "I guess I hadn't noticed."

"Cassie, I'm sorry. I let you down. Not just by not believing you. I forgot how green you were. You were such a perfect sub for me. You delighted me with everything you did.

It was as if you had years of experience. I knew you didn't, but your flawlessness made me forget that."

"But if you loved me and I was so perfect for you, why didn't you collar me?"

"Because I was afraid of overwhelming you, of pushing too hard. You had your whole life put in neat boxes. I was in the BDSM club box but I wanted more from you. To me you weren't simply a sub I enjoyed playing with. You were a woman I wanted to build a deeper relationship with. I'm afraid a collar is not enough for you. Again, it belongs in one box. You proved that by simply taking the training collar off and handing it to me. No, my beautiful little bird, I wanted much more from you. I wanted to be a part of every aspect of your life. Ultimately, I wanted vows and a lifelong commitment. I intended to give you a ring before I gave you a collar. Tell me I haven't truly lost you." He didn't try to hide the desperation in his voice.

She met his gaze again. "Tristan, I can't go back to the club. I was destroyed. I know you see it differently but I can't face them. I don't want to. Not yet."

At least she wasn't pushing him away. "Fine. No club. Leave the box where Master Tristan and Cassandra were in a D/s relationship shut for the moment. But Tristan and Cassie were just beginning to explore a different relationship. We'll start over there, in a more traditional way."

"You mean…like…dating?"

"Yes. Just the two of us—alone. Tristan and Cassie. Without any protocol or a club full of people. Allow me to win your trust again."

~ * ~

Cassie wanted to. She wanted to so badly. Simply being with him for this brief time reawakened the great many good memories as well as the bad. She wanted to love him and be loved in return. "I don't think I could stand to ever be hurt like that again."

"Cassie, I would like to swear that I will never hurt or disappoint you again. But that is foolish. We are both human. Like all people who love each other, we are destined to make mistakes occasionally. What I will swear to you is that I will do my best not to, and I will try to learn from my mistakes when I do. Please, give us another chance."

Until that moment, Cassie had been prepared to leave. As much as she wanted what they could have together, she feared the horrible pain of loss that she had already experienced. It was better to build walls and never let anyone in, than to risk that devastation again. If he had promised her eternal, undying love without heartache, she would have run.

He didn't do that. Although he promised to try not to, he acknowledged that he might hurt and disappoint her from time to time—as all people who love each other sometimes do. He was totally honest...and said he loved her. She looked into his eyes. They were full of hope...and fear...and love.

She nodded. "Okay. I will."

He gathered her in his arms and kissed her. Oh, how she had missed this.

When he broke the kiss, he caressed her cheek, saying, "There is one more thing, little bird. When problems arise, the only way to fix them is to address them head-on. If you hadn't disappeared that night, all of this would have been resolved then. I thought I was giving you a little space, and you ran away. Cassie, it is a colossal mistake to allow a problem to go undiscussed and thus unresolved for long. When it comes to talking about an issue, I will never again respect a safeword. I know it might be really hard sometimes, but failing to deal with a problem is in no one's best interests. Do you accept this?"

He was probably right. A tremendous amount of heartache could possibly have been avoided had they talked sooner. Still, remembering how angry she was that night, a discussion might not have gone well. "I accept that dealing directly with a problem is best, but I also think sometimes it's a good idea to take a little time to cool off before discussing hard topics."

"I don't disagree. That's why I let you go that night. I was under the impression that I would see you the next day. You let me believe that, knowing differently. You essentially lied to me."

She frowned. "I was upset."

"I know. And in the future, I'll understand if you need a little time and space to get your head together. Just ask for it. But don't use a safeword. I won't honor it. I don't ever want you to run away like that again."

She paused to consider this. It was reasonable. "Okay. I won't use a safeword to avoid a discussion. I promise."

"One last thing. After this discussion, do you believe you did the right thing that night? Intentionally leaving me with the mistaken impression that we would have a chance to discuss things the next day? Disappearing without a word? Leaving me and other friends worried about what happened to you?"

A lead weight settled in her stomach. Her goal had been to escape a heartbreaking situation. She hadn't thought beyond that. "No."

"Is it a pleasant feeling?"

"Of course it isn't. Maybe deep down I thought you deserved it but I didn't think about anyone else at the time. I feel awful now."

"You need to apologize to several other people. I would have you do that at the club in person, but I know you aren't ready to return to Hidden Gem yet. So, if you don't have them, I will give you telephone numbers and as soon as possible, you should call Tina, Denny, Julia, and Cyndi. They were particularly worried. I suggest meeting them somewhere so you can speak in person, but even if it's over the phone, you will apologize to them. Mistress Diana and Master Jim were extremely concerned as well. If you are willing, I will make arrangements to meet them with you so that you can make amends to them too. Do you agree?"

"Yes, of course. I really am sorry about causing stress to so many people."

"And in the future, when you think about everything that has happened, what do you think you'll feel?"

"The same thing. Guilt. Remorse that I caused you and others to worry."

"Even if I tell you—if everyone tells you—we understand what led up to it and forgive you?"

She mulled that over before answering. "Yes, I expect so."

"Then I'd like you to consider something. In the lifestyle, that kind of behavior would have earned you a punishment."

Her eyes went wide. *A punishment?*

Tristan continued, "But once the punishment was completed, it would be over. You would have paid the price for your behavior. Most subs find letting go of guilt in this manner is freeing. So, I forgive you, either way, but you might be better able to forgive yourself if you accept a punishment."

She frowned. "I'd never thought of it that way."

"I know."

"I don't like punishment."

"I know that too. The choice is yours. Which do you prefer?"

~ * ~

This was perhaps the hardest thing that Tristan had ever done. As, Cassie's frown deepened his resolve wavered. There was something so young and vulnerable about her in that moment, he nearly jumped in to take punishment off the table. He truly didn't want to discipline her, not now. Not when he'd just found her. But this wasn't about what would make him feel better. Carrying baggage into a new relationship wasn't healthy either. He really believed she needed to make this choice and if she chose punishment, the relief it would bring her would be worth it.

Finally, she said, "I'm still not sure I fully believe the concept of a clean slate, but I do feel awful about the stress I caused you."

"So, you'll accept a punishment?"

"Yes…Sir."

"Okay. Cassandra, you are being punished because you effectively lied to me when you left the club that night. You were angry and upset and as your Dom that night, I needed to know that you were okay. You refused to discuss the incident then, and allowed me to believe we would have the opportunity to talk the next day. But, instead, you disappeared, leaving everything unresolved. By doing that, you caused not only me, but other people who care about you, no small amount of stress and worry. Do you agree?"

"Yes, Sir."

"So, your punishment will be a spanking on your bare backside, over my lap, right now. I will give you twenty spanks with my hand. You will count each one. When we are done, you will apologize and I will accept the apology and forgive you. Do you understand and agree to this punishment?"

"Yes, Sir." She looked miserable.

"Very well. Pull down your pants to below your knees and bend over my lap."

"Yes, Sir." She did as she was told, blushing profusely as she pulled down her sweats and panties, then hesitating only slightly before laying across his lap.

"Remember you have safewords. Use them if you need to."

"Yes, Sir."

He started easy, distributing the first ten spanks across the fleshy part of her ass and the top of her thighs, rubbing the reddened skin after each blow. He knew they stung by the way she flinched, but her voice remained controlled, so they didn't hurt too badly. He increased the intensity steadily over the last ten.

She was trembling and tears stood in her eyes by fifteen. She let go of a ragged sob after twenty, but it was over.

He pulled up her pants, then cuddled her on his lap as she cried. He stroked her gently but didn't try to stop her tears. This was the release she needed.

"I'm s-s-sorry," she sobbed.

"I know, little bird, and I forgive you. I'm sorry too. It's behind us now." He kissed the top of her head.

When she regained control, she continued to rest her head against his chest, accepting his comfort.

"How do you feel now?" he asked.

"Um…better. I hate to admit it, but I feel a lot better."

"Good. I thought you might."

"But…"

"But what?"

"If accepting a punishment relieves a sub's guilt, how does a Dom accomplish the same thing?"

"We don't."

"What do you mean?"

"We can apologize and seek forgiveness when we foul up. That is what I did. But I will always carry some guilt for having let you down."

"But I forgive you."

He kissed her. "Thank you. And that means the world to me. Still, this is part of the power exchange in a D/s relationship. I give you a means to let go of guilt because I care about you and want you to feel that freedom. I do it knowing that the same outlet isn't open to me. It's the nature of the roles we accept."

"I'd never thought of it like that."

"It's not always easy to understand."

"I still don't like punishment."

"Good. That's the way it should be."

"But I finally understand something I didn't before. When Tyler punishes Greg, Greg always says 'Thank you, Master, for your loving correction.' I just thought that was part of their protocol—part of the punishment even. But there always seemed to be a note of sincerity and genuine relief each time I've heard him say it that I couldn't quite comprehend. He really means it, doesn't he?"

"Yes, he does."

"I really do feel much better." She paused briefly. "But I can't quite say, 'Thank you for your loving correction.'"

He chuckled and held her close. "It's okay, Cassie. It's enough to know you feel better."

She snuggled against him for a few more minutes before saying, "I should go. I've interrupted your afternoon and I'm sure you have things to do."

"Yes, I have some very important business to take care of. I have the woman I adore in my arms for the first time in six months and I need to make absolutely certain she feels well and truly loved for the rest of the day."

She smiled. "What do you have in mind?"

"A date. Dinner and a maybe something fun afterward."

"Okay. But it's hours until dinner time and I'm not dressed for dinner at a drive-thru, much less a place where someone might actually see me."

"Fair enough. We'll do something fun before dinner too. I know just the thing and you don't need to wear anything special for it. But we can go to your house and pick up a change of clothes."

"You're seriously blowing off the rest of the work day?"

"I'm the boss. I'm allowed."

"I live across the hall from Dani. If you go with me to my apartment, I can't guarantee that you won't run into her."

"Do you wish to keep this relationship a secret from her?"

"No. I just thought you might."

"Cassie, I love you. I have already told you I wanted to marry you. I still do. I don't care who knows about us."

Tears welled in her eyes. "I...I don't know what to say."

"You've already said it. You're giving me a second chance. That's all I need to hear for now. The rest will fall into place."

Chapter 24

Cassie left the office with him. He would follow her in his car to her apartment so she could change clothes. Then they'd go together to do whatever fun thing he had in mind. She had the twenty-minute drive to her apartment to process everything that had happened in the last ninety minutes.

Cassie had been shocked by exactly how the spanking had affected her. She had been so caught up in her own anger, embarrassment and loss that night at the club that she hadn't considered how her sudden disappearance might impact others. In the months since then, she had thought about contacting Julia, at least, but she couldn't quite bring herself to do it. She wanted to leave the past in the past and she didn't really believe anyone cared all that much.

When he told her how worried they'd all been, she felt horrible. She would have contacted her friends to apologize even without him telling her to do so. But when he'd suggested the punishment she almost dug in her heels. She didn't believe receiving a punishment resulted in a clean slate. She had agreed to it that night purely to maintain her honor. She had done nothing wrong before then.

She accepted the spanking in his office this afternoon to prove her point, to make him understand that he was wrong. But she failed. She did feel better. She still had amends to make, but she felt free of everything that had been between them.

When they reached her apartment and he got out of his car, he frowned. "This is…well, it certainly isn't where I'd expected you'd be living."

"When the Tillmans' condo fell through, I had to take what was available at the moment. This was the best I could get. I assumed eight months of an abandoned lease."

"That's another thing I must apologize for. I wasn't aware that anything had happened until Saturday. I wish you had called me."

"I guess I assumed you knew."

"No. I didn't know until you didn't move in on Saturday. I would have helped both you and the Tillmans in whatever way necessary. I chewed Margot out for simply dumping the problem in your lap. She never should have done that."

His demeanor was stern and his tone of voice was all Dom.

"Poor Margot."

He chuckled. "You are too soft-hearted for your own good sometimes. As it happens, the Tillmans did move into the senior living community a month later. Mr. Tillman loved it and put the condo on the market immediately."

"I know. I saw. It sold right away."

"Yes it did. I had hoped you would see the listing and buy it. It is exactly what you wanted."

She shrugged and shook her head. "I thought about it, but it belonged in a box that was closed and put away."

"So you are still looking?"

"Only half-heartedly. I've considered leaving Florida."

The look of horror on his face caused her to smile. "Don't worry. I'm not going anywhere. But I do need to find someplace else to live before this lease is up. I don't want to renew it."

"I'll begin making some inquiries again."

When they reached her apartment, Tristan was no more impressed with the inside of it than he'd been with the outside.

Cassie left him in the living room while she changed into a cute, blue tweed, sheath dress with a matching jacket and slipped on a pair of pumps. She brushed out her hair that had begun to dry and twisted it into a neater bun, put on a little blush, mascara and lip gloss and was back in the living room in less than five minutes.

"Wow. That was fast and you look gorgeous. You really do know how to dress for any occasion."

Cassie smiled. "Thanks. I was aiming at dinner. Of course, I might be way overdressed for whatever else you have in mind."

He gave her a salacious grin. "Oh, you are. But we'll have no trouble fixing that."

She laughed. "Then I'm ready if you are."

"After you." He followed her into the hall and once there, took her keys, locked the door and handed them back to her.

Once they reached the car she asked. "How exactly are you planning for us to spend the time before dinner?"

"I thought I'd take you to one of the restaurants at Island Treasures for dinner. And it occurred to me that in addition to the fine dining establishments there, we have a world-class spa. It has been a stressful day on many levels. I thought you might enjoy a massage."

"Are you serious? It's impossible to get a massage anywhere during high season on such short notice."

He raised one eyebrow. "I have a little pull."

She chuckled. "That's right. How could I have forgotten? Frankly, I'd love a massage."

He gave her an enigmatic smile. "Excellent."

They arrived at the resort in less than twenty minutes.

When they walked into the spa, the receptionist greeted them. "Good afternoon, Mr. Cabot."

"Good afternoon, Felicia. This is my very good friend, Cassandra Hastings."

"Good afternoon, Miss Hastings."

"Were you able to schedule everything?" Tristan asked.

"Yes, sir. It's all ready for you. Please follow me."

She showed them to an elevator and took them to the fourth floor, which surprised Cassie a little. "So, only the spa reception area is on the ground floor?"

Tristan shook his head. "No. The spa takes up well over half of this building. The fitness center, including an indoor pool, takes up most of the rest of the space."

"Wow, you must have a huge spa staff."

"We do offer a wide array of spa services, we provide them in unique environments. You'll see what I mean in a minute."

They got off the elevator into what appeared to be a hotel hallway. Felicia led them to one door, unlocked it, opened the door and handed Tristan the key.

"This is your suite for the afternoon. You can have it for as long as you wish. No one is booked in it for the rest of the day."

"Thank you, Felicia."

Cassie tried not to frown or look disappointed. Somehow, she hadn't expected Island Treasures to rent rooms by the hour under the guise of being a spa.

Tristan put his hand in the small of her back and guided her into the room, closing the door behind them.

Once inside, she realized it was not what she had thought. The dimly lit room looked like a relaxation room in a spa. There were several comfortable chairs and a double chaise lounge. Soft, relaxing music played and water trickled down a wall fountain, adding to the peaceful sounds.

Set into one wall was a counter on which stood a carafe of fruit infused water, an urn of hot water, a variety of teas, rock sugar, honey, a small tray of fruit and raw vegetables, and a dish of trail mix.

"Wow. Is this a private waiting area?"

Tristan chuckled. "It's a private everything. Let me show you." He opened the door to the left. "This is the wet room."

It was completely tiled, like a bathroom, and the floor was slightly sloped towards the center of the room to a floor drain. Surprisingly, it contained two whirlpools, each large enough to accommodate four people. "If these are private rooms, why are there two spas?"

"One is cold and one is warm. Going back and forth between the two is very invigorating." He motioned toward two glass doors to the left. "There is a sauna and a steam room too. The cold pool works the same way when using them.

There were two tables, like those used to give massages, at the other end of the room. "So, that is where they give massages?" asked Cassie, pointing to the tables.

"No. That is for body treatments requiring water."

He led her to the right, towards the tables and through a door on their right. This room turned out to be a large, well-appointed bathroom and changing area. There were two other doors. He motioned to one. "That goes back into the relaxation area. And that one," he motioned to the other, "goes to the treatment area. That's where they give massages, facials and so forth."

"This is incredible. But it must cost a fortune."

"It is more expensive to have services provided in these suites but it isn't outrageous. The main floor, where we came in, is a classic spa set-up. There are separate bathrooms, locker rooms, whirlpools and saunas for men and women. Then there is a common relaxation room and a series of treatment rooms. The second floor is set up exactly the same way, only it is gender neutral. Both men and women can use the facilities there as long as nudity doesn't bother them. Booking any treatment gives the patron access to either of those spa facilities."

"I see. So these rooms are more for couples."

He smiled. "Usually. Occasionally three or four people, book these private areas. The rooms can be rented by the hour with or without spa services added. If a treatment is booked, the spa personnel just come up here at the appointment time to provide it. These rooms are cleaned and restocked after each booking."

"I imagine they're popular."

"They are. We have two floors of them. You don't have to be a guest at the resort to book services in the spa, although we always try to keep some appointments open and available for guests."

"So, we are having a couples massage?"

"I have a few things booked. Have you ever had a body scrub at a Korean spa?"

"No. But I've had salt or sugar body scrubs."

"We do offer those as well, but Korean spas don't use salt or sugar. You soak in hot water for a while to soften dead skin, then they scrub you with exfoliating gloves."

Cassie cringed. "Ouch."

He laughed. "Actually, it isn't uncomfortable at all."

"Not even on a freshly spanked ass?"

His brow drew together. "I didn't think the spanking was that hard? Does it still hurt?" His voice was laced with concern and he reached his hand out to caress her backside through her clothes.

She blushed. "No."

He gave it a light swat. "Then it should fine. Frankly, in my opinion, this kind of body scrub is significantly better than a salt or sugar scrub. Are you game?"

She wasn't sure what she was getting into, but she said, "Sure."

That turned out to be the *best decision ever*. It was the most amazing spa experience she had ever had. Ninety minutes later, every inch and crevice of her body had been scrubbed, she'd had a fresh cucumber facial, a soothing shampoo and now she relaxed on the table, her body coated with a rejuvenating green tea mask.

Tristan lay, similarly adorned on the table next to her.

"Tristan, that was amazing. Beyond amazing. If there's a single dead skin cell on my body, I can't imagine where it would be."

He chuckled. She loved that sound.

"Right?"

"What do we do now? Will the ladies be coming back to wash this off?"

"No. When we are ready, we'll shower it off. Then comes the massage."

The shower stall in the bathroom, like everything else, was over the top. It was large enough to hold four people comfortably but that was the least remarkable part of it. Nearly the entire ceiling was a showerhead, from which water flowed like steady, gentle rain. Then there were multiple showerheads set into the walls. One could simply stand in middle and water sprayed from all directions.

Tristan began to gently wipe away the bits of mask that were not immediately loosened by the shower. His hands slid over her breasts, teasing the nipples. Having his hands on her again after so long, felt very good.

She too began exploring his body as she cleaned away the mask. He was so beautiful. His muscles, gleaming with water, were solid under her touch. She slid her hands down his back to his buttocks, cupping each firm cheek in a hand.

"Ah, my beautiful little bird. How I've missed your touch."

She planted kisses down his chest, stopping to swirl her tongue around each small, taut, nipple. He didn't stop her, so she kept going. She kissed her way to his navel, exploring it with her tongue.

He lightly caressed her shoulders but still didn't make a move to stop her, so she kissed her way down his happy trail to the base of his cock.

He groaned with pleasure and that was the only permission she needed. She lowered herself to her knees and took nearly the full length of him in her mouth. She massaged the base of his cock with one hand while cupping and massaging his balls with the other.

She moved her head back and forth on him, taking him deeper with each thrust. She resisted the urge to gag as the head of his cock hit the back of her throat and went deeper. She loved doing this for him. She loved the primal sounds of pleasure that escaped his lips as she sucked him off. She felt him tense, and knowing he was ready to come, she took him as deep as she could. His warm cum hit the back of her throat and she swallowed rapidly to take it all.

He removed his softening cock from her mouth. Then putting his hands under her arms, he lifted her gently from her knees. Covering her lips with his, he kissed her deeply.

"Little bird, that was amazing. Thank you."

"You're welcome."

"Now, we need to get out of the shower and dry off. I have another special treat for you."

After they had toweled each other off and kissed a little more, he led her into what he had called the "treatment area".

In the middle of that room was a massage table that was both longer and wider than typical.

"Have you ever heard of a sensual massage?"

"Is that a euphemism for a massage that is really just sex? Like a happy-ending massage?"

"I suppose it could be, but in most states it's illegal for a massage therapist to have sexual contact with a patron. However, that's not what I'm talking about. We offer a special kind of couples massage here that we call a sensual massage. A couple is joined by a massage therapist who gives one member of the couple a classic, therapeutic massage. At the same time, the person's partner provides a more intimate massage— orgasm, or multiple orgasms being the goal."

Cassie's jaw dropped. "That sounds…that sounds…incredible. Is it legal?"

"Yes, it is. The massage therapist never touches either person in a sexual way. All intimate contact is between the couple. If they wish to be alone at any point, the therapist quietly leaves the room."

"Um…so…that's what you have planned?"

"That is what I'd like for you. But if you aren't comfortable with it, you can have an ordinary, therapeutic massage."

What he had described was a little shocking. Maybe if she'd never had an orgasm where others could see and hear her she wouldn't be quite as open to it. But she had and she wanted to try this. "I think it sounds…mind-blowing."

He grinned. "Well then, let's get on with it."

He removed her towel and helped her onto the table before covering her with a sheet. He kept the towel around his own waist and opened the door to the relaxation room. "We're ready."

In walked a middle-aged woman dressed in white scrubs. She shook Tristan's hand. "Good afternoon, Mr. Cabot."

"Good afternoon, Heather."

"This must be Miss Hastings. I'm Heather, your massage therapist."

"It's nice to meet you, Heather. You can call me Cassie."

"It's nice to meet you too, Cassie. I trust you've enjoyed your other treatments so far?"

Cassie smiled what she feared looked like a goofy, half-drunk grin. "Very much. Thank you."

"Mr. Cabot has explained the concept of a sensual massage to you?"

"Yes."

"So you know, I will be giving you a classic massage. All sexual contact will be from your partner."

"Yes."

"And you consent to allowing your partner to touch you in very intimate ways, while I am performing your massage."

"Yes, I do."

Heather smiled broadly. "Well, then, close your eyes, relax and let's get started."

She folded the sheet down, exposing everything from the waist up. At first the massage started exactly as one normally would. Heather began massaging Cassie's scalp, then moved to her neck, shoulders and arms. Cassie became deeply relaxed.

As Heather moved to her back, Cassie felt Tristan's hands very lightly massaging her scalp, then stroking her arms. When Heather reached the base of Cassie's spine, she stopped momentarily in order to move the sheet again. This time it covered Cassie's back and shoulders, leaving everything below the waist bare. Tristan's hands replaced Heather's at Cassie's lower back and Heather moved to her feet.

Tristan massaged Cassie's ass, his thumbs slipping ever closer to the cleft between her cheeks. She began to writhe under his touch, wanting more, but he gave her a light swat. He leaned close to her ear and said. "Be still. This is on my terms."

She sighed and relaxed into his touch. She was aware of Heather's firm massage on her feet, calves and lower thighs, but Tristan's hands were what held her attention. Finally, one long finger pushed between her legs. It circled her clit once before stroking her from her clit to her anus, leaving her nearly breathless.

Tristan leaned down to her ear again. "It's time to turn over, my love."

She did. The sheet covering her fell to the floor but she didn't care.

Heather continued to massage her feet and legs while Tristan shifted his attention to Cassie's breasts. When Heather moved back to Cassie's head, massaging her neck arms and shoulders, Tristan moved one hand to Cassie's pussy. It had been so long, he had her on the edge in moments.

But he didn't hold her there long. He whispered, "Come for me, little bird."

Cassie's orgasm ripped through her.

Tristan didn't let her come down. Heather's hands continued to gently massage her neck and shoulders, while Tristan stroked Cassie's pussy. He brought her to orgasm again with his hands.

As Cassie was drifting down from the second climax, she was vaguely aware that Heather had left the room. Tristan pulled Cassie to the end of the table, put her knees over his shoulders, and began licking and sucking her clit. She felt so relaxed, so incredibly good, it was as if she were floating. He slid first one finger into her, then two. Part of her wanted to arch into him, to demand more, to push herself closer to the edge.

But the other part wanted to be led, to take what he would give, to simply absorb all of the sensations and trust him to eventually take her where she wanted to be. This part won. She lay absolutely still as he devoured her, his fingers stroking the sweet spot inside her. If she moved a fraction of an inch she would come and she didn't want to. Not yet. Not until she heard the words.

Her breathing became rapid, shallow panting. She would not ask him for release. She didn't have to. He would give it to her when the time was right.

She clung to the edge, savoring this place of pure sensation, outside of time and space until he said the words.

"Come for me, little bird."

It felt as if she exploded into a billion shards of light. She bucked against him, her internal muscles clenching and unclenching around his fingers.

As the spasms of her orgasm subsided, he withdrew his fingers and slid her farther back onto the table. He was gone from her for an instant, but before she could sort out where he'd gone, he was back. He climbed onto the table beside her, pulled her back against his chest, and covered them both with a light blanket.

She felt warm and protected in his embrace as she slowly floated back to earth. She may have dozed momentarily. She wasn't sure. He made no demands of her, seemingly content to just have her in his arms.

"That was...that was..." She realized there were no words.

"Hands down, the most beautiful thing I've ever seen," he said.

She smiled, groggily. "Thank you."

"You're welcome." He kissed her head.

"How many times have you done this?"

"Done what, little bird?"

"A sensual massage like this."

"Never."

"It's new?"

"No. But you are the only person I've ever wanted to do it with."

She turned her head to look at him. "Really?"

"Really. Do you remember telling me that for you 'making love isn't recreation'? That it wouldn't fit into your 'fun club stuff box'?"

"Yes."

"You said you felt a deeper connection when making love that was more than giving and taking pleasure."

"Yes."

"Well, I suspected that this might evoke the same kind of emotional connections and it did. I've made you come numerous times before. But with the exception of one extraordinary day, most of those times were 'fun club stuff'. A series of calculated moves on my part intended to get a certain result. Don't get me wrong, I love doing that. But this was different. Under the effects of the massage you gave yourself over to me perhaps more completely than you ever have. I wasn't thinking about the next move or what response I wanted to get from you. I was experiencing you and you were intoxicating."

"*I was intoxicating*? Christ, I'm not sure I can stand up."

He nuzzled her neck until she giggled. "You can. You're hungry."

She frowned. "You're right. I am. How did you know?"

"Lucky guess. It's almost six-thirty and I'm starving. Let me take you to dinner."

"Well, as much as I'd like to simply curl up and sleep for a while, I am hungry and that's an offer I can't refuse."

Chapter 25

Dinner at Topaz, one of the restaurants in the Island Treasures resort, was spectacular as always. But it could have been a cardboard burger and fries and Tristan wouldn't have cared. His world was complete once more. When he'd realized he'd lost her six months ago, he couldn't come to grips with it. His heart ached. Unable to find her, it felt as if he'd lost her to death. And yet, he knew she was out there. He hadn't been able to let go of the hope of finding her one day.

He hadn't played with anyone in the club since then. He knew he had to get over her first, but he just couldn't let go. His friends were worried about him. Jim had even offered to put him in contact with the bar in Boston that Cassie's friend owned. But to do so would break Cassie and Jim's confidentiality with strangers. The exact thing that he had accused Cassie of. He couldn't do it.

As it turned out, she lived less than ten minutes away and was his new assistant's neighbor.

With Cassie back in his life, he couldn't get his fill of her. He didn't want her out of his sight. The spa at Island Treasures had been a stroke of genius. He was able to spend hours with her in a relaxed and comfortable environment.

Now he was driving her home and he still wasn't ready to let her go. When they reached her apartment, he walked her to her door. He wanted to stay with her, sleep next to her, wake with her in his arms. He did not, however, want to overwhelm her. So, he prepared to kiss her goodnight at her door and leave.

She opened the door, then turned to him and said, "Tristan, would you like to come in?"

"Cassie, I would love to come in. But if I do, I don't think I'll be able to leave."

"I don't want you to leave. I want you to sleep with me."

That was the only encouragement he needed. As soon as she had locked the door behind them, he lifted her into his arms and carried her to the bedroom. He made love to her until she screamed his name as she climaxed. She slept in his arms. Then he made love to her again just before dawn.

Unfortunately when the sun was finally up, he had to leave. "Cassie, I've missed you so very much, and I'm not ready to go back to business as usual. If it were any other day, I'd ask my assistant to rearrange my schedule and handle all my calls, but unfortunately her little girl is sick."

Cassie smiled. "Yeah, I heard something about her puking all over some woman in your lobby."

He chuckled. "I feel terrible saying I'm thankful it happened, but if Emily hadn't gotten sick, I wouldn't have found you. When she's better, I'm sending them on a Disney Cruise."

"Dani would love that. Her deadbeat husband doesn't pay child support and she can barely make ends meet."

He'd see what he could do about that as well. He had lawyers on staff who could help her.

"I have to go to the club tonight. But maybe I can take you to dinner before that."

"How about if I make dinner for you here instead?"

"That sounds great."

"Then if you want to come here at the end of the night...well, I'd like that."

"There isn't a chance in hell I'd turn that down. If you give me a key, I won't have to wake you."

She smiled. "Okay. There's one other thing. I was going to call Julia, Denny, Tina and Cyndi and ask them to meet me for dinner tomorrow evening. I was thinking the easiest thing would be to have them meet me at one of the restaurants at Island Treasures. That way they can have a drink if they want to then go straight to the club when we're done."

"That sounds good. I'll reserve a table for five at either Topaz or Pearl for you."

"They may not all be available."

"That's okay. It's easier to remove people from a reservation than add them. After your dinner, if you want to, you can spend the evening in my suite. I'll join you there when the club closes."

She smiled broadly. "I'd like that."

"Excellent. Then I'll make reservations for us to have dinner on Sunday with Master Jim and Mistress Diana."

"I've been thinking about that. Maybe, instead of eating in a restaurant I can cook for them, if that's okay with you."

That idea pleased him. It was much more personal. "I think that would be very nice. Would you like to use my place?"

She nodded. "I'd love to. You have a great kitchen."

"Perfect. Then, I'll arrange it."

Cassie did meet with the other subs the next evening. He had waited for her in his suite before going to the club and he was glad he had. As soon as she stepped through the door, she fell into his arms and sobbed.

"Tristan, I'm so sorry I ran away like that. They had become such good friends. How could I have done that? They were so wonderful tonight."

"Sweetheart, you were hurt. You've been hurt before and closing off that pain was a coping mechanism. You are only just learning to lean on others once in a while. You've apologized and have been forgiven."

"I was so stupid. And I have to go through this again tomorrow night."

"But then it will be all over."

And it was.

Things went beautifully for the next month. They grew closer and closer. So close that she agreed she would move in with him when her lease was up.

He was planning to ask her to marry him soon. The only fly in the ointment was her reluctance to go back to the club. If she never did, he'd accept that, but she had enjoyed her time there and he knew she would again if she gave it a chance.

Then Wednesday afternoon, while he was in the office, he took a call from Sean Casey. "Hey, Sean, regretting your March Madness picks?"

"No, Tristan, it's something else."

"It sounds serious."

"God, I hate to be the one to do this, but you need to read something. You know the BDSM club books by Scarlett Turner that Cassie edited? The first one was released yesterday and Amanda started reading it."

"Damn it, Sean. That's over. I told you—I told everyone—she doesn't have that kind of control over the content of a book."

"I know you said that. And I believed you. But you need to see it."

"This is ridiculous."

"Tristan, just go on Amazon and buy the book."

"Fine." He pulled out his cell phone and opened the Kindle app. "What's it called?"

"*Newbie: A Club Lace and Leather Novel.*"

Tristan searched for the title, bought it and downloaded it. "Okay. I have it."

"Now go to chapter two and start reading. Basically, Carly, a girl who is new to the lifestyle, is doing her first scene in the club with club owner, Trent."

Tristan started reading. It didn't take long to realize he was reading a description of his first scene with Cassie, almost down to the clothes she was wearing. But Cassie wasn't responsible for this. He knew she wasn't. There was simply no way she would put herself on the pages of a book like this.

"Sean, she didn't do this."

"God, I know you don't want to believe it, but have you ever seen a scene like that in your life? Even first timers usually have some small amount of bondage involved. And this is just the first one. There are others that are a little more generic, but the chemistry between you two is there. Anyone who knows you both will see it."

"Sean, I agree. This is clearly the scene Cassie and I did, but I would stake my life on the fact that she had nothing to do with it being in this book."

"How could it be anyone else?"

"I don't know. But I'm going to find out. Look, if it's possible, keep a lid on this for now. I'll get to the bottom of it."

"Sure, buddy. I'll do what I can."

As soon as Tristan was off the phone he called the corporate lawyer who handled all things relating to the club and resort. Tristan told her what had happened. "All I know is that Scarlett Turner is a friend of the author Mona Moore. Cassie is an editor for Scarlett and Julia Barnes is Mona Moore's virtual assistant. Use whatever means necessary to find out who might be feeding Ms. Turner the information."

"Mr. Cabot, I don't mean to question your judgment, but your girlfriend edited the series. If she didn't influence the content, how could she just let this pass unnoticed?"

"She didn't edit it. That is the only explanation."

"But she admitted to you that she was slated to be the editor."

"That was months ago. The work hadn't started yet. As upset as she was then, I'll bet she turned it down. She tried to put everything related to the club behind her."

"You don't know that for sure."

"I haven't asked her, but I know she didn't do this. You find out who did. Use private detectives or whatever it takes."

Trusting Tristan

"Yes, sir. And what about Julia Barnes herself?"

"I don't think she's behind this, but you can confirm that."

When Tristan ended the call he left the office for the day. Cassie was working at her house. He went straight there.

He knocked first, then let himself in with his key. "Cassie?" he called as he opened the door.

She stepped out of the kitchen. "Tristan, what are you doing here so early? You sent your assistant to the Caribbean, so you're playing hooky?"

"I wish. Cassie, I have to show you something. Come sit with me on the couch."

She frowned, but joined him.

"The first book in Scarlett Turner's BDSM club series was released yesterday and you need to see something."

She shook her head. "Tristan, I didn't edit that book. After what happened, I had it reassigned to another editor as soon as I left the club. I didn't ever want there to be any doubt."

He kissed her. "Without knowing any of that, I knew you didn't have anything to do with this. I am dead certain you have never seen a word of it. It is simply impossible. Please, read it."

She took his phone from him and began to read. Her frown deepened instantly. "Oh, my God. No. This is us." She looked up at him panic stricken. "This was our first scene. Tristan, I would never, ever, share this. It was too special, too intimate. I didn't do this."

"Cassandra, you need to listen to me. I have already told you I firmly believe that you were not involved."

"But anyone who sees this will believe I was," she wailed. "It's like I told you, there is no such thing as a clean slate." The pain and bitterness in her voice caused his heart to ache. "Are there other scenes from the club?"

"Apparently, yes. But according to Sean they are mostly more generic scenes that you and I did but that anyone could have. I have one of my lawyers on it. Clearly this author has other contacts in the club." He frowned. "Julia might know."

"I doubt it. She doesn't know Scarlett. Besides I can't believe Julia would condone this."

"I wouldn't think so. We'll find out. Don't worry. And for now, don't read more of the book. It will only upset you. Let's get to the bottom of things first."

"Don't read it? I have to read it. I have to know what else is in there."

"Why?"

"Be-because. I...I..."

"You don't have to read it. Not right away and not alone. If you trust me on this and give me a few days to sort things out, we can read it together."

"Tristan..."

"I've asked you to trust me. Will you? Will you agree not to read the book yet?"

"I can't believe I'm saying this, but, yes, I won't read the book right away.

~ * ~

Even though she hadn't read the book, Cassie was sick over what had happened and couldn't stop worrying about it.

By the time Tristan arrived at her apartment that evening, she was absolutely beside herself. "Do you know any more about who gave Scarlett the information for the book?"

"My people are still working on it."

"Working on it?" She was so distressed she practically shouted. "This is a disaster, Tristan. What are we going to do?"

"Whoa, Cassie. Yes, I have very skilled people working the problem. We'll know who is behind the leak soon enough, and it will be handled. You have got to stop worrying about it."

"I can't. People who know us will know the couple in that book is meant to be you and me. They'll know someone with access to Hidden Gem broke confidentiality. What's going to happen to the club when that happens?"

Tristan shifted immediately into Dom mode. "Cassandra, stop this instant. You promised to trust me. Do you?"

"I do trust you. It's just—"

"Stop there. You trust me and I said I would handle it."

"I know you did." She wrung her hands.

"But you can't stop worrying anyway." Tristan took her in his arms.

She snuggled into him. "I'm sorry."

"It's okay. Old patterns are hard to break sometimes. But trust is the foundation of any good relationship and outside of the club environment you have relied solely on yourself for so many years, I'm not sure you know how to let go and trust."

She thought about that and frowned. She trusted people. She had financial advisors, and people who managed her uncle's estate for her. She didn't question them. A little voice within her argued. *That's just money and even if all it disappeared, you know you can take care of yourself. You could make enough to live on. You don't trust anyone with anything really important…your feelings…your heart.*

The little voice was right. "I…I…have to protect myself."

"Not anymore."

Chapter 26

Tristan usually worked from his office at Island Treasures on Fridays. He could work as late as he needed to and still be at the club when it opened. It was just after six on Friday evening and the last forty-eight hours had been among the most frustrating in Tristan's life. He had assured Cassie that he would handle the problem, but answers were not coming fast enough for him. He wanted nothing more than to simply go to her apartment and leave the whole mess behind him.

However, that was not an option.

The club would open tonight as always and there was no telling how many people had read the book. The issue would have to be addressed openly and dealt with immediately. So he didn't have the luxury of waiting until he had all the details.

He had called a handful of the most senior Dom/mes of Hidden Gem—Diana, Jim, Adam, Elaine, and Maurice—to ensure they would be there before opening. He did not discuss the specifics, only telling them that a breach in confidentiality had occurred that needed to be addressed. He asked them to make sure no scenes were started until after he'd arrived and had a chance to speak to the members. If what he had planned was to be as effective as possible, everyone had to hear it at the same time.

Now he had one other thing to do and he knew it wouldn't be easy. He had to make certain Cassie would be there too. It was vital that she be there to witness the resolution.

He left the office and drove the twenty minutes to her apartment. He had deliberated for hours about how to do this. He'd come to a hard conclusion. There was only one course of action that would ensure success.

He entered the apartment and called, "Hi, it's me."

"I'm in my office," she answered.

He joined her there, giving her a kiss. "How was your day? Did you get a lot done?"

"Yeah, I did. I'm ready for a break but I wasn't expecting you to come here before the club."

"I know you weren't. Cassandra, I need to ask something of you."

"Cassandra?"

"Yes, I am speaking to you as your Dom."

"Okay."

She had to be in her submissive role for this to work. He adopted the steely, hard-edged tone that he reserved for scenes. "Excuse me?"

She frowned. "I mean, yes, Sir."

"Better."

"Cassandra, do you trust me?"

"Yes, Sir, of course, I do."

"You are confident that I always have your best interests at heart?"

"Yes, Sir."

"Good. Then you will come to the club with me tonight."

She looked stunned. "No, Sir. I'm sorry, Sir, but that's a hard limit."

"I understand and accept that playing at the club is still a hard limit. I don't intend to play. But I need for you to be there."

"Why?"

"Cassandra, you know better than to ask me why. I will not punish you for that lapse because we are treading close to a hard limit. But the answer is the same as always, because it is what I want."

Tears welled in her eyes. "This has something to do with the book, doesn't it? I don't want to do this, Sir."

"I know you don't. But you will because you trust that I know what I'm doing and it will please me for you to obey."

"Will you punish me if I refuse?"

"Yes. And ultimately you will go anyway. Don't put us both through that tonight. Now, go get ready."

Tears slid down her cheeks. "Yes, Sir. What should I wear?"

"Anything that makes you feel strong and confident."

"Yes, Sir. Excuse me." She sounded miserable and it broke his heart. But by her questions, he knew that if he had given her a choice, she would have refused. It truly was for her that he was doing this.

He went to the kitchen. He was certain she hadn't eaten dinner yet and as upset as she was, she would not be comfortable eating out. Not to mention the fact that they really didn't have time. But under her guidance over the last month, he had acquired a few basic kitchen skills. He looked in her refrigerator and found sliced turkey, bacon and everything else necessary for club sandwiches. *I can manage that.*

He microwaved the bacon, toasted the bread and washed and cut the tomato and lettuce. By the time she emerged from the bedroom, he had the double-decker sandwiches on the table with chips and iced tea.

He looked up at her. She had showered and her damp hair was twisted into a smooth bun. She wore a navy blue pencil skirt, a red cotton twinset, navy blue pumps and a navy blue and gold "statement" necklace. He held back a smile. For her, the outfit was as good as armor—she would feel strong and confident in it. If they had been planning to play tonight, he'd have taken her to the "office" alcove and made her his naughty secretary.

He took her hands in his, kissed her and said, "You look gorgeous, Cassie."

"Thank you." She frowned. "Did you make dinner?"

He grinned. "Yes, I did."

Cassie looked genuinely pleased. "Wow! I love club sandwiches. They look great."

"I'm glad you think so. It is the absolute pinnacle of my culinary achievement. Unfortunately, we don't have a lot of time to linger over them. We need to be at Hidden Gem shortly after it opens."

She nodded, still looking none too happy about that. "Then we should start eating."

He held a chair for her before taking his own seat. He was tempted to make small talk but that would not make her any more comfortable. If anything she'd find it annoying. He'd leave the ball in her court.

They ate silently for a while before she asked, "Tristan, please tell me why I must go with you tonight."

He finished chewing what was in his mouth and swallowed. "I've already told you why. I want you there."

"But why?"

"Because I do, Cassie. You need to hear some things that will be said."

"You can tell me what was said afterwards. I really don't want to go."

"I understand that. It's why I didn't give you an option. You said you trusted me and I promise you, this is for the best. Do you understand?"

"Yes. I don't like it. But I understand it's what you want and you think it's best."

"And you trust me?"

"Yes, I trust you."

When they finished dinner, he took the dishes to the kitchen and put them in the dishwasher before she could stop him. He closed the door to the dishwasher and turned to face her as he dried his hands on a towel. "Are you ready to go?"

"Yes, but can I drive my own car?"

"I would rather you ride with me."

"I want to be able to leave as soon as you allow it."

He sighed. "When you are ready to leave, I will drive you home."

"You never leave the club when it's open."

"I will tonight."

"I won't run away again, Tristan."

"I know that. But I also know tonight is not going to be easy. I don't want you to drive yourself home."

"Are you telling me I don't have an option, Master Tristan?"

"No, Cassandra. This is your choice. But it will please me and cause me less worry later if you agree to ride with me."

She crossed her arms and looked away as if considering everything.

He was tempted to call her on her attitude. But he was requiring a lot from her this evening. He knew he needed to give her a little room.

Finally, she said, "I'll ride with you."

"Thank you, Cassandra. I appreciate that."

The ride to the club was silent, but that was as he expected. He knew she was fighting an array of internal battles.

When he had parked the car, he took her hand in his. "Thank you for trusting me and choosing to submit to me, Cassandra. You are an amazingly strong woman and I love you with everything in me."

She sighed and gripped his hand tighter. "I love you too. With everything in me."

He raised her hand to his lips and kissed the back before getting out of the car. He went around, opened the door and helped her out. He held her hand as they walked to the club.

Karla, a sub who had joined after Cassie left, was working at the desk. "Good evening, Master Tristan. Is this a guest of yours? I don't know how to sign a guest in."

"Karla, this is my girlfriend, Cassandra Hastings. She is a member of Hidden Gem."

"I'm sorry. I guess I've never seen you here before."

"I haven't been here in a while," said Cassie in an even, pleasant tone, as she signed in on the electric signature pad.

"Well, enjoy your evening."

"Thank you," said Tristan, taking Cassie's arm and guiding her to the elevator lobby.

"Are we going to your office first?" asked Cassie quietly.

"Not exactly. We are going to my private entrance. I didn't want you to have to walk through the women's locker room alone. If you wish, you can leave your purse in my office."

"Thank you, Sir."

They went up the elevator and down the hall to his office where she put her purse, then on to the back stairwell that led down to the club. When they reached the bottom of the stairs, he turned to Cassie. "Wait here for just a moment."

She nodded. "Yes, Sir."

He punched the access code into the number lock and entered the club, not allowing the door to close as he glanced around. By the time he saw Jim Donovan, the man was already striding towards him. Tristan stepped back into the stairwell, holding the door for him.

When Jim saw Cassie, he beamed. "Cassandra, it's good to see you here."

"Thank you, Master Jim."

Her tone was even and unemotional, but Jim was an astute Dom. He took one look at her and said, "Ah, you don't want to be here."

"No, Sir."

"You clearly have a reason, Tristan?"

"Yes, I do. As I said to you on the phone, Jim, there has been a breach of confidentiality. It must be addressed tonight and I believe it is in Cassandra's best interest to be here when it is. However, I don't want her beside me on the stage. I think that will be much too uncomfortable for her. But I also do not want her left alone. I don't want her to have to field questions from anyone if she doesn't want to. I'm asking you to take responsibility for her when I can't be by her side."

"Certainly."

"You have my permission to touch her in any way necessary to keep her secure."

"Understood."

"Cassandra, I do not want you more than an arm's length from me or Master Jim tonight. Do you understand?"

She frowned. "Yes, Sir."

"Is something wrong, Cassandra?" Tristan asked.

"I...I..." her chin quivered and she seemed to blink back tears. It nearly killed him. He couldn't do it. He'd take her back up to his office and leave her there until this was over.

"Girl, your master asked you a question," Jim snapped. "Did he train you no better than this?"

That somehow shook her from the fear that gripped her. "No, Sir, Master Jim."

"Then answer the question."

She straightened her back and looked directly at Tristan. "Nothing's wrong, Sir."

"Good girl," said Jim. But simple words of praise wouldn't work for Tristan tonight. He took her in his arms, kissed her and whispered, "I love you, little bird."

"I love you too, Tristan," she whispered back.

"Right. Now that we've established that, I believe we have some business in the club," said Jim. He entered the code and opened the door.

Tristan held Cassie's hand as the three of them walked across the room to the main demonstration stage, the same one where he had punished Cassie on the last night she was here. When they reached the stage, he kissed her cheek and whispered, "Remember, stay with Master Jim," before letting go of her hand.

He stepped up onto the stage. He had called earlier and asked the sound engineer to preset the stage with a microphone and to kill the music when Tristan took the stage.

As he had instructed, even though it was twenty past eight, no scenes had started.

"Good evening. I apologize for putting a crimp into the evening, but there is something that needs to be discussed. If everyone will please gather around and give me your attention."

As the members did, many of them noticed Cassie. They smiled, waved and called greetings to her.

She smiled and nodded, acknowledging their greetings, but took a step backwards, closer to Jim. She was clearly not comfortable and Tristan feared it would get worse before it got better.

"Some of you have noticed that Cassandra Hastings is with us tonight."

Murmurs of greeting came from every corner. Just as Tristan expected, the members who knew her seemed pleased to see her there.

"Cassandra left us about seven months ago after I questioned her loyalty and commitment to the confidentiality of our members. I had learned that she was scheduled to edit a series of erotic romance novels by Scarlett Turner, which were to be set in a BDSM club. Although I knew she was an editor and sometimes worked on projects that contained BDSM elements, I did not know about that specific project. It had been suggested that she might have only joined Hidden Gem to gather material for use in these books."

There were a few concerned murmurs from the crowd, but only from new members.

"I was under the mistaken impression that an editor had more control over content than she does. I take the privacy of our club members very seriously and I was worried that because Cassandra hadn't told me about the project, she intended to use things that she'd seen or heard here in the books. At the time, Cassandra assured me that she had no intention of making anything that had happened in the club public. She accepted a punishment for not having told me about the project, even though, as it turned out, she hadn't started working on it yet. For those of you who didn't witness it, she was secured to a spanking bench, caned and was then made to come, publicly."

"And she did it without uttering a sound," said Maurice. "It was spectacular."

"Excuse me, Master Tristan. May I ask you a question?" Tina asked, looking as if she were exceedingly angry.

"Yes, Tina, you may."

"Why are you bringing this up now? She accepted your punishment and it's over."

Tristan nodded. "That's a fair question Tina. You are absolutely correct. She accepted her punishment and it is behind us. However, before I tell you what has happened, I wanted everyone in the room to understand the details of that incident."

He glanced at Cassie and swallowed hard. Her face was beet red and she stared intently at the floor. She didn't see the looks of approval on most of the faces around her, and that wouldn't do.

"Cassandra, don't hide from us. Look around the room." The command in his tone was clear.

If anything her blush grew deeper, but she did as he'd commanded and looked up, glancing around. She was clearly surprised and not a little confused by the warm expressions she saw.

"Now we need to address what has just happened," Tristan continued. "The first book in the series that I just mentioned was released this week. The title is, *Newbie: A Lace and Leather Club Novel*. The title is pretty self-explanatory. It is about a woman, Carly, who is new to the lifestyle and joins a BDSM club. The club owner takes her under his wing. I would like to read you the author's account of the first scene Carly does with the club owner. Because of the ban on digital devices within the club, I have printed this scene out." Tristan pulled the papers from the breast pocket of his suit and began to read.

He was barely into the scene when Maurice called. "Stop reading that now. We've got the gist. That is an uncannily accurate description of your first scene with Cassandra. But I'll be damned if I believe she had anything to do with it."

Adam was shaking his head in disgust. "Maurice is right. You can't possibly believe she wrote that."

Jim looked ready to tear Tristan limb from limb. "Son of a bitch. Tristan, you don't deserve this girl if you think she's responsible."

There were others murmuring similar sentiments.

Tristan looked directly at Cassie. She appeared confused, bewildered. "Cassandra, do you believe in a clean slate now?"

"I...I...but..."

"What is this about, Tristan?" asked Mistress Elaine.

"The night Cassandra accepted that punishment, she did so to maintain her honor. But she hadn't been a part of this community long enough to fully understand what it meant. She didn't believe that she was truly forgiven. She believed at the first suggestion that someone breached confidentiality all fingers would point to her."

"That's not how we roll, girl," said Master Jim.

"I realized, after this breach occurred," Tristan indicated the papers in his hand, "that it might be what it would take for Cassandra to realize that, Jim." He addressed the crowd. "Clearly, those of you who were here the night Cassandra and I did this scene, know that whoever wrote this had have been here too. It was memorable and not remotely like most scenes in a BDSM club—even for a beginner. But like me, those of you who had come to know Cassandra and then witnessed her punishment, knew instantly she wasn't the leak. She gave the project to another editor and never saw the book until I showed it to her this week."

"I had no doubt," said Maurice.

Almost everyone in the room nodded in agreement.

"I agree it couldn't have been Cassandra, but who's behind it then?" asked Diana.

"That's a good question. My legal team has been looking into the author's real identity and if there are other club members who might have some relationship to her. So far, our private investigators have learned some interesting details. For example, Scarlett Turner lives right here in Florida and that isn't her only pseudonym. She also writes under the name Mona Moore."

Many eyes turned toward Julia.

Julia looked shocked. "You're kidding, Sir. I didn't know that, and I'm Mona's virtual assistant. Of course, I've never actually met most of my clients in person. But you'd think she'd have mentioned that, especially when Scarlett wanted me to meet Cassie."

Tristan wasn't surprised that Julia took his statement more as an interesting piece of trivia than an arrow of suspicion pointing directly at her.

Sean shook his head. "Think about that for a minute, Julia."

Julia frowned. "What I meant was…she could have just said she was Scarlett too, Sir."

"Of course, she could have, unless she wanted to keep that a secret from you so you would be less careful about what you said to her," said Sean, clearly frustrated.

"It wasn't Julia, Sir," said Cassandra. "I'm certain it wasn't her."

Julia frowned. "Wait. Master Sean, do you think I told Mona or Scarlett or whatever her name is about Cassie and Master Tristan? I wouldn't do that."

"Mona Moore writes pretty hot stuff herself," said Sean. "Maybe you just told her about the really unusual scene you saw."

Julia looked indignant. "No, Sir. I did not. I would never do that to Cassie. She means too much to me. You all mean too much to me."

"That's enough," said Tristan. "I don't believe Julia is responsible either. But even if all of you aren't convinced, I have one very good reason. We all agree that whoever is responsible for either writing it, or describing it to the author, saw that scene in person."

The crowd murmured their assent.

Julia smiled at Tristan appreciatively.

Tristan smiled back. "Master Adam, care to tell us why it couldn't have been Julia?"

Adam chuckled. "She wasn't there. She was doing a scene with me in the alcoves. I guess I'm off the hook too."

"So do you know who leaked the story to the author?" asked Diana.

"No one leaked the story, although I suspect the author intended for Cassandra or Julia to take the fall. But as it happens, the author was here and witnessed that scene. It was easier to determine the person's identity than I thought." Tristan glanced around the room looking for a tell, and his gaze fell on Cyndi.

She was among the few people who had been quietly watching everything that happened, showing no particular interest. But at that moment, she became highly affronted. "You think I'm Scarlett Turner, Sir?"

He shrugged. "The private investigator said the author was a teacher."

"I'm not the only teacher who is a member of this club, Sir. Tina's a teacher. Amanda's a teacher. Mistress Elaine is a teacher. There are lots of us."

"You're right. And many of the club members who are teachers were there that night. But I decided to go straight to the publisher to find out who Scarlett really is."

Cyndi became livid. "She was under contract never to reveal my identity. I teach elementary school and I'm a good teacher. What I do on my own time is my business. I thought you of all people would respect that, *Sir*."

"You mean like you did? You made Cassie and I the main characters in one of your books."

"I changed your names."

"Right, to Carly and Trent. And you further violated the confidentiality agreement you signed by putting in that scene."

"Oh, come on, it was just a kissing scene. Big deal. There was nothing particularly special about any of the others. They were garden-variety BDSM scenes."

"You are missing the point. That 'kissing scene' was intensely intimate. The fact that you think otherwise is immaterial because, intimate or not, it happened within these walls and thus was private. You had no right to put it in your book and have breached your contract with us by doing so. Like I said, my legal team contacted your publisher this afternoon. She has decided it is in her best interest to remove the book from publication and cancel the rest of the series."

"Well, then I'll sue her for revealing my identity."

Tristan smiled slowly. "Oh, she didn't do that. You did."

"What do you mean? You said you went to the publisher to find out who I was?"

"Yes, I did. But unlike you, she understands the concept of confidentiality. She didn't actually tell me who you were."

"Then how did you know?"

261

"I told you my private investigators found out that Scarlett and Mona were the same person and that she lived in Florida. They also found out that both Scarlett and Mona have posted on social media about being teachers. After that I made a few guesses. First, because of the exquisite detail of the scene, I decided that most likely, it was the author herself who actually saw it. Based on our records, I know who was in the club that night. I simply had to go through the data and try to remember who watched the scene. Once I had a short list, knowing that the author was a teacher narrowed the field. Finally, you were the only one who appeared nervous when I said I knew who the author was. But I didn't know for certain it was you until you became irate about your publisher."

"You tricked me."

"I told you the truth. I contacted the publisher to find out who Scarlett Turner really was. You assumed she had given me the answer."

"This is bullshit. You are making a big deal over nothing."

"Now, you see, that attitude concerns me. After everything that has happened, you don't recognize that what you did was wrong."

"Fine. It was wrong. I'm sorry. Sue me."

"That's not the way we right wrongs in this community. If you are truly sorry, you will acknowledge what you've done, submit to a punishment here and now, and renew your commitment to maintaining the confidentiality of this community going forward."

"Let you cane me? No damn way."

"Well, then your membership is revoked. You are no longer welcome here."

"Fine. I'll leave."

"Before you do, I have a couple of other things to tell you, Cyndi. Your publisher is under contract not to release the true identity of Scarlett Turner or Mona Moore. I am not."

"Are you threatening me?"

"Absolutely. If I ever discover that you have revealed anything else that happened in this club, I will make certain your identity is the lead story on the six o'clock news. *Local second grade teacher from St. Honoria's is a popular erotic romance author.* And once I've done that, I will sue you for violating your confidentiality agreement."

The color drained from her face.

"You wouldn't."

"Has a Dom ever threatened you with a punishment and failed to follow through?"

"Fine. I believe you. But you don't have to worry about it. I won't write anything else about this place."

"Good. Which brings me to my final action. Since you don't seem to recognize the error in what you've done, I intend to contact the owner of every BDSM club that I know of and inform them about what you did here. It's unlikely they'll welcome you with open arms."

"That's breaking *my* confidentiality."

"You already did that by putting that scene in your book. All I have to do is show them the scene and acknowledge that it happened here."

"You're ruining my life." Tears stood in her eyes.

"No, I'm ensuring that you don't ruin someone else's life. If you are ever ready to face the consequences of what you've done, you may be able to gain entry to a private club again. If the lifestyle is important to you, you will. But until that time, no one will risk the confidentiality of their members."

She turned and practically stomped toward the locker room door.

"Diana, would you escort her out please?" Tristan asked.

"Certainly." Diana followed Cyndi to the locker room.

Tristan addressed the crowd again. "Friends, I am very sorry this happened. We try our best to thoroughly screen our members and hold them to the highest privacy standards. Something like this has never happened before. All I can do now is make every effort to resolve it. I believe Cassandra and I were the only identifiable characters from the club in Cyndi's book. So I think the damage is very limited. Also, as I mentioned, the book, which had only been released electronically so far, has already been removed from the market. Of course, there are people who had already purchased it, and nothing can be done about that."

"The good news is, you would have to be a member here and to have seen or heard about that scene and be able to identify you and Cassandra," said Mistress Elaine.

"I think so," said Tristan. "All things considered, I believe we've done everything we can to contain this as much as possible. And for what it's worth, I also believe that Cyndi will honor her promise to reveal nothing else. It's clear she does not want her real identity known."

"It would serve her right if that were the lead story on tomorrow's evening news," said Sean.

Tristan shook his head. "It might. But contrary to what I suggested, we all learned her identity within the walls of this club and are bound by the nondisclosure agreements we signed. Yes, she had broken faith with us, but the only real recourse I have is to file a lawsuit."

Jim chuckled. "So you did, in fact, threaten her with a punishment you have no intention of following through with?"

"Desperate times call for desperate measures. My goal is not revenge for what Cyndi did, it was to prevent it from happening again. Recovering damages in a lawsuit will never be better than not suffering the damage in the first place."

"You're right," agreed Sean.

"So, considering everything, I think the situation is resolved. However, if any of you have lingering concerns, please let me know. And if you are concerned about your privacy here and wish to withdraw your membership, I understand. For now, I hope you can set this unpleasantness aside and enjoy your evening."

Chapter 27

The events of the last twenty minutes had left Cassie stunned. When Tristan began recounting what had happened over seven months ago, she felt the pain and embarrassment of that night all too keenly. She heard Tina ask something, but Cassie was so mortified, she couldn't focus. Why was he making her relive this? She didn't think she could stand it. She wanted to run, but before she had taken one step towards the door, Master Jim put a hand on her shoulder, preventing her.

"See this through, girl," he said softly.

There was nothing to do. She wouldn't make a scene. She could only avoid eye contact and bear the shame until she was able to leave.

Then Tristan told her to look up. She didn't want to. She didn't want to see the same hurt and disappointment in her friends' faces that she'd seen that night. But she'd agreed to trust him, to submit to him tonight, and he'd given her a command.

When she raised her head, she was not remotely prepared for what greeted her. She didn't see a hint of disapproval anywhere. Every gaze she met was filled with warmth and affection…even pride.

Before she could sort out what was happening, Tristan began reading that scene. Had he just built her up to tear her down? She fought desperately not to cry.

Tristan had only read a few paragraphs when the comments started. But the club members didn't disparage Cassie. They defended her, apparently confident that she hadn't been the one who had leaked the content. Master Maurice and Master Adam jumped to her aid immediately. Master Jim looked ready to kill Tristan and said Tristan didn't deserve her.

In the midst of all this, Tristan captured her gaze and said, "Cassandra, do you believe in a clean slate now?"

That's what this had been about. She'd been so certain everyone would think the worst, but the exact opposite had happened. He had known it would, as surely as he knew she wouldn't have believed it without seeing it. He'd asked her to trust him and had only put her through this so she could see for herself.

The fact that it was Cyndi who had betrayed them caused her heart to ache. Seeing her leave, disgraced, brought back painful memories. She knew what it felt like. *No, Cassie, you don't. You weren't disgraced. That was all in your head. Cyndi was given the same opportunity for making amends and she chose not to.* It was a completely different situation. Still, she knew Cyndi was hurting and she hated that.

Tristan finished his speech and stepped down from the demonstration platform. First, he shook Master Jim's hand. "Thanks, Jim. I'm sorry I couldn't tell you more about what was coming. But you understand now why Cassandra needed to experience it as she did?"

"Yes. Until I realized what was happening, I was ready to beat the living shit out of you, but you know your little bird well."

He held his arms out to Cassie and she stepped into his embrace, resting her cheek against his chest. "I think I do. Cassie, you understand now too?"

"Yes, Sir. I know I didn't make things easy tonight. I'm sorry."

"You did rather drag your heels the whole way—for someone who professed to trust me."

"I did trust you...I do trust you...it's just...I...I..."

"I know, little bird. You have relied on yourself for so long, sometimes giving over that last little piece of control is a challenge. You hold firmly to your own beliefs because they've been all you've had to hold on to. Your ability to trust in anything else waivers."

She nodded, continuing to accept the comfort of his embrace.

"Tristan, may I say something to Cassandra?" asked Master Jim.

"Yes."

Tristan loosened his grip on her and she turned to face Master Jim.

"You are one of the sweetest little subs I've ever encountered and I know what you've been through in your life. But even so, if you were mine, I'd blister your ass tonight. You have been told about the dynamics of this community over and over again, by more than just Tristan. You say you love and trust him. And yet, earlier, I nearly witnessed one of the hardest Doms I know cave in to your tears, all because you *didn't* trust him. And if he had done that, you would still not believe that this community supports you and you probably never would."

Cassie swallowed hard. "You're right, Sir. I'm sorry."

"I'll be honest with you. For a minute there, I didn't know where he was going with it all. But I'm not his sub. I'm not the one who professes to love and trust him."

God, he was right. "I don't know what to say, Sir."

"The time for talking is done. Put yourself in his hands, offer him your submission and do a scene with him."

Tristan shook his head. "No Jim. Playing in the club is a hard limit for Cassandra."

Jim arched a brow at her. "Only you can change that, girl. But it's good to see you here again." He kissed her cheek. "She's all yours, Tristan. Don't ever give me a reason to kick your ass."

Tristan chuckled. "I wouldn't dream of it."

Jim grinned. "Now, I think I'll go find Julia. She deserves some fun this evening."

Cassie smiled. Julia would love that.

As Jim walked away, Tristan turned Cassie to face him. "I know it's been a rocky evening so far. I'll take you home now if you wish."

"Sir, I think I'd like to revise my hard limits. I'd like to stay and do a scene with you."

"Don't let Master Jim's words push you to do something you aren't ready for yet."

"I wouldn't, Sir. I want this. My reason for staying away from the club was my own embarrassment, even when you and everyone else tried to tell me there was no reason for it. I'm sorry. Being here again reminds me of how much I've missed it."

He pulled her into his arms. "I'd love to do a scene with you. Earlier, when I first saw you in that outfit I imagined doing a scene with my naughty secretary in the office alcove."

She smiled. "We could do that."

"And Jim did make a very good point. If you had fully submitted to me earlier and given me your complete trust, this wouldn't have been as painful for either of us. Perhaps you do need a punishment."

He was right. Cassie stepped back and knelt in front of him. "Whatever you wish, Sir. I'm yours to command."

"Very well. Much of our distress this evening was caused because you were worried people thought poorly of you, even after you were told otherwise."

"Yes, Sir. I'm sorry, Sir."

"I know. So stand and come with me to the alcoves."

She rose and followed him, her hands folded and her head down. They stopped at the entrance to the alcoves.

"If you were given your choice of rooms to use tonight, which would you chose, Cassandra?"

Without missing a beat she said, "The harem room, Sir."

He arched a brow at her. "Are you serious?"

"Yes, Sir. The harem room. And as a good slave, I hope you would use me in any way you wish." She hoped her meaning was clear. The instant she had knelt at his feet, she knew it was what she wanted to give him.

"Cassandra, are you removing sexual intercourse in public from your hard limit list?"

"Yes Sir, I am. That was only on my hard limit list until we had made love in a private setting and we've done that many times. I firmly believe I am ready for this, Sir. My only desire is to serve you as you see fit."

"Well, then, when the time comes, the decision will be mine."

"Yes, Sir."

The harem room was free, so Tristan led her there.

"Kneel and remove my shoes and socks."

She did, rubbing his feet as she took off his socks.

"Now my jacket, tie and shirt."

She did, leaving him wearing only trousers. She carefully folded the garments she removed and laid them to the side.

"Good slave." He moved to the bed where he made himself comfortable. "Now, strip for me. Remove everything except that necklace. For now, you are my slave and that is your collar."

Cassie smiled seductively. "Yes, Master."

She stepped out of her shoes and removed her sweater. Then she pulled the matching sleeveless shell over her head. She reached behind her to unhook her bra. She held it in place until she had removed her arms from the straps, then she pulled it away and dropped it. She stood before him in only her necklace and skirt, allowing him to enjoy the view briefly before she turned away. She reached behind her and slowly unzipped her skirt.

He gave a low sexy growl and she smiled, pleased he was enjoying this. She hooked her thumbs in the waistband of her skirt, bent over and slid it over hips and down her ass, shimmying slightly as she did. She stepped out of the skirt then removed her thong in the same slow, sensual manner. When she stepped out if it, she spread her legs slightly and bent over to pick up her abandoned skirt, bra and thong, giving him a clear view of her ass and pussy.

"Well done, slave. Now, come kneel on the bed."

He moved a large, wedge-shaped bolster to the center of the bed. She knelt and he pushed on her back until she lay over the bolster, head on the bed, ass in the air. He buckled wide leather bands snugly around her wrists, and secured them both to a ring on the head of the bed. He pulled her body down until her arms were stretched taut, repositioning the bolster as he did, so it remained under her hips.

He moved off the bed briefly and returned with ropes. He wrapped one around her right thigh several times, effectively creating a cuff just above her knee. Then he did the same thing to the other leg.

He took the end of each rope and attached it to something on the bedframe on either side of the bed, spreading her legs wide. Finally, he attached leather restraints to her ankles and tied them to the foot of the bed. She was completely immobilized and spread open to him.

"Now slave, the time has come for your punishment."

Her pulse quickened. "Yes, Master."

He stepped away from the bed again. When he returned, she expected to feel the bite of a cane or a paddle. Instead, she felt a cool liquid being dribbled on her ass. He used his fingers to spread it around and into her tight hole. This wasn't punishment. She loved the way it felt. After using his fingers to stretch her a little, she felt him press something cool and firm against her opening. He worked the butt plug in and out a little at a time. When he finally reached the widest point, he held it there, moving it ever so slightly, letting her experience the slight pain of the full stretch.

"Can you take it, slave?"

"Yes, Master. Anything for you."

He moved it in and out a little more vigorously, finally allowing it to go all the way in.

She sighed with pleasure. "Thank you, Master."

He chuckled. "You have the most beautiful ass, slave. I love seeing it plugged. That you enjoy it gives me great pleasure."

She sighed again.

He left the bed and when he returned this time, he had a powerful vibrator in his hand. He slid it into a crevice in the bolster, intended for just that purpose. Then, positioning it against her clit, he turned it on low.

Everything felt wonderful and she relaxed into a place of pure sensation. He rubbed her backside for a few moments before the first blow came. It was not painful, it just added to all the other sensations. His spanking continued, growing in intensity. The blows began to sting, but the pain was melded with so many wonderful sensations she couldn't separate them. She simply wanted more. She heard herself moan and cry out occasionally, but nothing on earth could make her ask him to stop. He held her on the edge of orgasm the entire time and she was content to stay there. Content to wait for him to lead the way.

Then she felt him on his knees behind her. *When had he removed his pants?*

"Are you ready, little bird? Do you want me to fuck you? Here, in the club?"

Even from deep within the fog of sensual pleasure, she understood what he was doing. He was reminding her where they were and seeking her consent. "Mmmm. Yes, Master. Please."

He entered her, maddeningly slowly. She wanted to push back on him, but he held her hips. "Not yet, little bird. I'll tell you when you can come."

He continued to fuck her in what felt like slow-motion. Burying himself inch by inch and then slowly withdrawing.

It was delicious torture. She was so close to orgasm, and at the same time impossibly far away.

"Who do you trust, little bird?"

"You, Master."

"And who knows what you need?"

"You do, Master."

"And who loves you more than words can say?"

She gasped. "You do?"

"That's right. Now come for me, little bird."

Instantly, he increased his pace and her entire being convulsed as she fell over the edge into an abyss of light and heat and utter ecstasy. He continued his unrelenting rhythm until he too stiffened in climax as she rode the waves of her orgasm.

Completely spent, she closed her eyes and rested her head on the bed. At some point, he had turned off the vibrator and now was releasing her restraints, rubbing her ankles, wrists and thighs as he did. Once unbound, he gently pulled her off the bolster, tucked her into the curve of his body and covered them both with the satin bed sheet.

She sighed, relaxing against him, content to stay there forever.

"That was...spectacular...amazing...mind-blowing."

"I agree."

"That wasn't punishment."

He chuckled. "No. I had no intention of really punishing you. I betrayed your trust once. Regaining it is a process. By agreeing to come here at all, you gave more than I had the right to ask. I cannot fault you for holding back a little. Then for you to agree to do a scene with me, *this scene*, I am in awe."

She smiled. "You said you love me more than words can say."

He kissed her temple. "I do."

"But you don't need words. Every action, every touch tells me that. I love you too."

He kissed her again. "I know and I love hearing the words. But everything you do and most especially the gift of your trust and submission, tells me you love me."

She smiled and nestled a little closer.

~ * ~

Tristan would never have imagined the evening ending this way. It was perfect. She was perfect and he knew, without a doubt, this was the right time. He rolled back slightly, reaching for his trousers, which he'd abandoned on the floor by the bed. "So, my beautiful little bird, since it has been established that we love each other without reserve..." He pulled a small velvet box from his pants' pocket, flipping it open. Inside was an engagement ring. A flawless oval cut diamond set in a white gold scrollwork band adorned with smaller diamonds. "Cassandra Hastings, will you marry me?"

"Oh, Tristan, of course, I'll marry you." She kissed him tenderly.

He removed the ring from the box and slid it on her finger.

She sat up and moved her hand into the light. "It's stunning."

"I'm glad you like it. I have carried it in my pocket since the day I bought it, certain that the right time would present itself."

"You've been carrying it around for days?"

He arched a brow at her. "I told you the day you brought Emily to Danielle that I wanted to marry you."

"You've had it for weeks?" She asked, incredulous.

"Cassie, I've had it for months. It was in my pocket the night you left. I continued to carry it after that to remind me of what I had lost. Every morning I told myself it was time to return it to the jeweler, but I couldn't do it. That would have meant there was no chance of ever finding you again and I wasn't ready to give up hope."

Cassie's jaw dropped open and she appeared to be at a loss for words.

He pulled another long, slender box from his pocket. "I've had this for ages too. I had it specially made for you. I didn't carry it with me, because I intended to give it to you here at some point. It was locked in my office safe. I removed it earlier today."

He opened the box and inside was a custom made, white gold choker. It was composed of small, delicate, quatrefoil shaped segments chained together. The center front segment was a slightly larger rectangular shape bearing his monogram, TCC, Tristan Charles Cabot.

"A collar?"

"Yes."

He took it out of the box. "The front segment is actually a locket." He opened it to reveal a beautiful piece of carved lapis lazuli with gold pyrite inclusions.

"Sir, that's beautiful. But why is it inside the locket?"

He smiled. "It's a hidden gem."

"Oh, so it represents the club?"

"No, little bird. It represents you. Nothing and no one is more precious to me. Not this club, or the resort or anything else. I had this part designed especially for you. I picked the lapis for two reasons. 'Cassandra' means *shining upon man*, and you are certainly the light of my life. The pyrite inclusions look like stars in the night sky. I liked the symbolism."

"And the other reason?"

"Lapis can be carved, look closely at it."

She took it from him and leaned into the light again to take a closer look. "It's a bird."

He smiled and nodded. "That's right. My little bird. Cassandra, will you accept my collar? Not to be my slave or a full-time submissive partner. Just as a symbol of our relationship within this community. A sign to everyone that you are mine and I am yours. My life would be empty without you in it."

Tears welled in her eyes. "I...I...I need you too. Of course, I'll wear your collar...Master."

He removed the necklace she was wearing, took the choker from her and fastened it behind her neck. "Very often collars will have a lock and a key. This one doesn't. Our love for each other binds us together more securely than rings, collars or legal documents ever will."

She put her hand to her neck to feel the collar there. "It's perfect and I love it."

"Good. Shall we go out into the club and announce the news to our friends?"

"Absolutely," she said with a broad smile.

Tristan rose from the bed and began to dress. He had his trousers, socks and shoes on before he realized she was still sitting on the bed, looking at her ring. He smiled until he saw she was frowning.

"What's the matter Cassandra?"

"Nothing really. It's just when you said 'legal documents' it reminded me of prenuptial agreements."

"Cassandra, I'd never require you to sign a prenup."

"That's really wonderful of you, Master, but we have to have one. I'm really sorry. I wouldn't care. I have no intention of ever letting you go, and the money doesn't mean much to me anyway. Still, it's a requirement."

"What are you talking about? I've just said, we don't need a prenup. I mean, my lawyers will push for it, but it isn't necessary. I have no intention of letting you go either."

"I know, Sir, and that's what kills me. I have to ask *you* to sign one. It was a contingency in the will."

"Cassie, a prenup is intended to protect the assets one brings to a marriage. I know you inherited your grandmother's estate and are comfortably well off, but you told me you make sixty thousand a year."

She smiled. "You asked me what I made *as an editor* and I told you. I also said I had other money. You're right, I inherited grandma's estate but I also have other income. I don't usually talk about it if I don't have to. And I really hate that we have to have a prenup."

"Cassie, conservatively I'm worth over five hundred million. Unless you have significantly more than that, there's no reason for a prenup."

Her frown deepened. "Um...yeah...but, conservatively, I'm worth over two billion."

"*Billion*? Did you say *two billion*?"

She blushed. "Yes. Unless I get married without a prenup in place and then I'm only worth about three million."

He started chuckling, then the chuckle built to a belly laugh. "Well, I'll be damned. I hate it when people ask me this question, but *who are you*?"

"Have you ever heard of *Handyman Harv the Harried Housewife's Helper*?"

"Harvey Dawson? The infomercial king? Who hasn't? Wait, was he your *Uncle Harvey*?"

She nodded. "He made a fortune from the infomercials and invested it wisely. But he also registered over two hundred patents in his lifetime, from which his estate earns massive licensing fees."

"You manage a two billion dollar portfolio?"

She shook her head. "Of course not. I show authors how to craft a compelling story. I find plot holes and all the other mistakes they make. I don't know anything about my uncle's business matters. In fact, growing up, I knew he didn't lack for money but I didn't have a clue just how wealthy he was until he died. And at that time I had too much to do, taking care of my grandmother, to sort it all out. He left lawyers and financial experts in charge of everything anyway. It's in their hands."

Tristan frowned. "That might be a recipe for disaster if you don't oversee things."

She shrugged and gave him a saucy grin. "I know, but the word around town is that I'm marrying a millionaire. He can either keep an eye on it for me or just take care of me when I lose it all."

She got off of the bed and began to gather her clothes.

He wanted to laugh but instead adopted his sternest Dom voice. "Cassandra, that's a rather cheeky answer for a slave girl."

"I'm sorry, Sir." She clearly made an attempt to look contrite but failed miserably.

"And did I tell you to put on your street clothes?"

"You said we were going out into the club, Sir."

"Yes. But I said nothing about clothes for you."

Her eyes went wide. "But I'm not wearing anything at all."

He grinned at her. "You are wearing a beautiful collar, a stunning engagement ring, and a nice plump butt plug. That happens to be tonight's dress code for newly engaged and collared subs, as well as an appropriate punishment for cheeky slave girls."

She frowned. "Yes, Sir."

"If it makes you feel any better, I'll leave my jacket and tie behind too," he said as he tucked in his shirt.

"Yes, Sir. That makes me feel *much* better."

He laughed. "It's a good thing I find that smart mouth charming tonight." He offered her his arm. "Shall we go, little bird?"

"Yes, Sir."

They stepped through the sheer curtains into the club. Cassie blushed a deep red. He leaned down to her ear.

"Cassandra, you are absolutely exquisite and it gives me great joy to have you at my side like this."

She smiled at the praise. "Thank you, Master."

"If you are truly uncomfortable, we could add a little something."

She shook her head. "No Sir, if it pleases you, I don't need anything else."

"It pleases me, little bird. It pleases me immensely. But just let me know if it gets to be too much."

"Yes, Sir."

"Because, I was thinking, a pair of nipple clamps would really complete the outfit."

The most delightful giggle erupted from her. "Thank you, Sir. I'm sure I'll be just fine as I am."

About Ceci Giltenan

Ceci started her career as an oncology nurse at a leading research hospital, and eventually became a successful medical writer. In 1991, she married a young Irish carpenter whom she met when his brother married her dear friend. They raised their family in central New Jersey but now live with their dogs and birds in paradise, also known as southwest Florida. Although still working occasionally as a consultant in the pharmaceutical industry, Ceci spends most of her time now writing "happily ever afters."

She is best-known for her Scottish historical and time-travel romances, but has enjoyed dipping her toe in kinky waters.

Follow Ceci at:

Website: www.cecigiltenan.com
Facebook: https://www.facebook.com/cgiltenan
Twitter: https://twitter.com/CeciGiltenan

Other titles by Ceci Giltenan
The Fated Hearts Series
Highland Revenge

Highland Echoes

Highland Angels

The Duncurra Series
Highland Solution

Highland Courage

Highland Intrigue

Ceci Giltenan

Duncurra Legacy series
Highland Redemption
A Wee Highland Predicament

The Pocket Watch Chronicles
The Pocket Watch
The Midwife
Once Found
The Christmas Present
The Choice
The Gift

www.ingramcontent.com/pod-product-compliance
Lightning Source LLC
Chambersburg PA
CBHW031703170626
46808CB00005B/1583